ONE OF OUR WARSHIPS

John Winton

ONE OF OUR WARSHIPS

Published by Sapere Books.

24 Trafalgar Road, Ilkley, LS29 8HH

saperebooks.com

Copyright © The Estate of John Winton, 1975

The Estate of John Winton has asserted his right to be identified as the author of this work.
All rights reserved.

No part of this publication may be reproduced, stored in any retrieval system, or transmitted, in any form, or by any means, electronic, mechanical, photocopying, recording, or otherwise, without the prior written permission of the publishers.
This book is a work of fiction. Names, characters, businesses, organisations, places and events, other than those clearly in the public domain, are either the product of the author's imagination, or are used fictitiously.
Any resemblances to actual persons, living or dead, events or locales are purely coincidental.

ISBN: 978-0-85495-127-7

CHAPTER 1

I have to call it a tragedy. It was nothing less. All right, it had its funny side, I have to admit. It did have its funny moments, if you've got that sort of sense of humour. Anybody who took a cynical view of life would simply split his sides laughing at what happened to James. But he was a big enough person for it to be a tragedy. Most of us would agree that it was a tragedy, pure and simple. I know. I knew James better than most people. I was a friend of his for years. Still am, of course. I shouldn't have had to say that. Come to that, I knew Olivia very well, too. And I used to know her very much better at one time. Nobody likes to see a man rushing on his own fate and that, I can't help thinking, is what James did, to a certain extent. I don't know whether he ever admitted to himself that what he had done was wrong.

I was actually there on the jetty the day *Pandora* came back from the Far East. I was on the staff of C-in-C. Fleet Environmental Control Officer, I called myself. It was one of the series of brilliant jobs I had after I was passed over. I remember the day well. Devonport Dockyard on one of those rare, heavenly days in June. Even the Hamoaze looked so sparkling, almost tropical blue, you almost expected to see a shark's fin in it. The water was shining and sparkling. It was a pure blue sky. There was somebody burning a bonfire over on the Torpoint side, probably burning weeds or something. The smoke was spreading but it was the only stain on the sky. Otherwise pure blue.

They came alongside with all James' usual dash. Well, perhaps not quite the same. They were just a tiny bit slow with the first heaving line, if you wanted to be a perfectionist, as James was, of course. It had been a long passage, and they were perhaps a bit weary. She was a new frigate. She was new when James took her and she was now only two years old. So she was like a new pin. Well, maybe the paint-work and the general air ... But I don't know, that's just me being hypercritical. But it was funny in a way, because James was normally even more particular than me.

We all piled on board, the staff and the press and all the families. There were wives and mums and girlfriends, children young and old, milling about all over the place. Like a hundred thousand other ships coming home after some time abroad. It seemed like a happy occasion. Home is the sailor, home from sea, and all that. After all, they had done well. They'd had a cracking good commission, by all accounts. James always ran a pretty crisp little ship. It is hard to put a finger on the atmosphere in that wardroom. I am not even sure I did actually notice anything at the time and how much one has been influenced by all that happened afterwards. It was nothing you could put your finger on. They were all smiles. It wasn't anything wrong ... But, there was something. Of course, with all the families there it was a jolly reunion and that swamped everything else. Any oddities would have been completely submerged in the sort of tidal wave of family emotion. The only time anything came anywhere near surfacing was during an interview with the reporter from the local evening newspaper. Again, it was the normal set-up, the reporter, his photographer with him, and there was also a TV chappie and a camera team from the West Country TV. They were just covering the homecoming as local news. The reporter was obviously looking for some kind of angle to it, and he asked if there had been any particular incident in the commission that they all remembered. This was when Confrontation between Indonesia and Malaysia was still hot news, some years ago, now, you must remember. They had come right from the hot spot. At once, there was the faintest tension in the air. It may have been my imagination, but the First Lieutenant and the Gunnery Officer exchanged glances, and I saw the looks on their faces. The reporter seemed to notice it too, because he at once turned to them, but by then the moment, whatever it was, had gone. They'd covered up, you see. It seemed to me a little odd, but you had to remember they had been away for some time. There was bound to be awkwardness. It does happen that people who have served together away for a long time develop a peculiar kind of *rapport* with each other. They have a fund of shared stories, a pool of shared experience, and suddenly when they come back they realise with a shock that their mutual experience might look a little strange to outsiders. You can see them, suddenly looking at each other with new eyes, suddenly recasting all their memories.

I went up to the cuddy to make my number with James and welcome him home. Olivia wasn't there, but there was no particular significance to be attached to that. Did any of you ever meet James? You may have seen his picture, but none of you actually met him? Well that was another thing about him. He was rather splendid to look at. And as straight as a die. After all the nonsense that has been talked since, it's vital that you understand that there was absolutely nothing funny ha ha or funny peculiar about James. He was a really good fellow, a really good sort. I mean, one of the very nicest and best and most decent men I ever met. And it makes it all the more astonishing. James was the very last man you would expect such a disaster to happen to. His grandfather was an admiral, as you probably know. His father was a four-ring captain, with a tremendous war record in World War Two. We were cadets at Eaton Hall, towards the end of the war, when he had his tremendous destroyer action. They read it out, all the details, at Sunday divisions. People said afterwards he should have got a VC, not the measly bar to his DSO they did give him. So young James was bred in the purple as far as the Navy is concerned. And everybody thought he was going to be the best of the lot. In some ways, he *was* the best of the lot. But there you are, clogs to clogs in three generations. That's not quite appropriate, but it's something near it. He was top man in our term, Chief CC, the lot. He was top boy again in our subs' courses. People seem to have forgotten just what a very able man James was at his trade. He was a gunnery Jack, in his family's tradition. He did the Long G course at Whaley and came out top of that again. He was a very good golfer ... as I say, James seemed to go through life in a whirling cloud of success and red recommends and accelerated promotion dates, and maximum seniorities and everything and all the rest of it. He was the last chap you'd expect ... That's if you agree he did do anything wrong. Most people don't. People are going to argue about that for evermore. They're hard at it now, still. I'm not so concerned about what constitutes official hostilities, and what a captain should do on sighting a vessel he believes to be hostile, and what action to take when the suspect vessel fails to respond, and all that international maritime law rigmarole. I'm more interested in what happened to James and Olivia.

I went up to see him in the cuddy that day. I expected the cabin to be packed but funnily enough it was empty. Not a soul there, except James himself. I didn't have much official business to do, in fact to be strictly honest I didn't have any, but I always enjoyed seeing James. For him to be coming back from the Far East, it was an occasion, not to be missed. I couldn't let a chance like that go by.

He was looking very well. He always did, of course. Always was the golden boy. He was standing looking out of the scuttle, with a glass in his hand. I knew what he was feeling. There's a moment when you come in, and for a little spell nothing happens. One feels a sense of release after every trip to sea. Like letting the weight slip slightly from your shoulders. It's one of the most pleasant feelings in the world. There are many pleasures in commanding your own ship, and this is one. You're safely in and safely secured alongside. There are all sorts of problems ahead. People are going to come clamouring at you, people from on shore and from the dockyard, people wanting decisions, people telling you about their decisions, people telling you about the results of past decisions. But just for a moment that's all ahead of you. In the meantime you can stand, in a little interval, like a gap in time, with time to have a drink, empty your mind, and just wait and enjoy it. It's very satisfying, I can tell you. It seemed a pity to disturb him, because I knew just how he was feeling.

He looked round at me when I came in. I'd knocked first, of course. There was that picture of Olivia on his desk and another oil painting of her, by my brother, on the bulkhead. I've got an elder brother who is a portrait painter. A very good one, too. James looked at me and for a terrible second I thought he didn't recognise me. He looked absent-minded and preoccupied. Then he did recognise me and it was like great clouds sliding away from the sun. He beamed at me and God, the warmth of him. It was exactly like standing in warm sunlight after a cloud has passed over. You know those days on the beach when suddenly you feel very cold and the sand goes all dark. Then back comes the sun again. Every time he looked away from you, you wanted him to look back. He had tremendous personal charm, James. Olivia always said he could charm flies out of spiders' webs if he wanted to.

I can't remember what we talked about at this distance of time, but he seemed genuinely glad to see me. He asked me how I liked being on Joe Drury's staff. It was a mischievous question. I told him I'd much sooner be driving the saucy *Pandora*, like him. He said he'd had his time in her, and the job would soon be open. Perhaps I might get it. Although I knew and he knew there wasn't a brass-bound cat in hell's chance of that. I looked at James very closely, as I always did. He used to fascinate me. He was almost a *hobby* of mine. I found him almost impenetrable. I said he was a golden boy, and so he was. But he also had a deep sombre streak somewhere deep down in him. It was like looking over one of those lakes in the hills. Dead still, without a ripple, and dark, very dark, but you felt there were forces moving underneath, monsters maybe, moving mysteriously about and their presence reached the surface not as ripples or anything as physical as that but as changes of texture in the colours of the water, just as though the whole plane of the surface of what you could see was shifting and altering while you looked. I was struck by a funny thought. That James could suddenly act, and the act might be disastrous. There were two sides to him. There was an active half, and there was a core of inaction. In some extraordinary way he was a mixture of movement and stillness. I never served under James, although I would have been quite happy to do so, even though we were both in the same term. I remember when we were in the same gunroom together as midshipmen. Now I think of it, it was in another *Pandora*, a cruiser, on the West Indies and South Atlantic Station, as it was called then, if I remember rightly. James was coxswain of one of the fast motor boats. I was driving one of the motor cutters that day. We were off somewhere like St George, Grenada, or somewhere like that, on a routine flag-showing and general jollifications visit. The sort of rather pleasant and not too strenuous visit which used to go on in those days. There were crowds of bumboats, little native boats, all round the ship. They used to cluster round the gangways, selling things like pineapples and straw hats and local souvenirs. I was at the forward gangway, waiting to unload some sacks of spuds, actually, when I saw James coming off from shore in his speedy craft, heading straight for a gaggle of these bumboats. He stood on and on, still at full speed, until quite honestly I thought there was going to be an accident. He drove his motor boat right in amongst them, only throttling back at the last split second. He was a superb boat handler, and knew what he was doing. But I nearly had a heart attack. The sub of the gunroom who was officer of the watch on the quarter-deck that forenoon gave James a tremendous bottle afterwards. It was only a silly little incident, but James took it hard, insisting that there had never been any danger. The Sub was a bit weak, I think he was secretly afraid of James, and didn't take it any further. But I remember it very clearly. It was as though he wanted to harass those little black men in their little boats. And, of course, there was the first time he met Olivia...

Anyway, he suddenly said to me, "You always were a great wheeler and dealer, Freddie, how well in are you with Joe Drury and his staff generally?"

I sort of pulled a face. Every staff officer likes to think that he is fully in cahoots with his admiral. Fair, I said. Fair to middling. I had to raise my eyebrows at this. It seemed that for the first time since I had known him, James was about to ask something of me. He had never done that directly before. I had always given, without being asked, and been glad to do it. James was the most self-sufficient man I ever met. What I am, I am, and what I have is mine, and what I think is my business, you go your way and the best of luck to you, I go mine, was his motto, always.

Why, I said, do you want any help?

"Help?" He looked at me as though I was talking in Swahili or something. "It's not help, no…" Whatever it was he was going to say, if he was going to say anything, he never got the chance. There was a knock at the cabin door and someone, I forget who now, came in. It was business as usual again. I pushed off soon afterwards.

Forward, in the main aircraft cabin, a blonde stewardess in a blouse and regulation grey skirt was backing towards them, pulling a trolley after her up the central cabin aisle. It was time for supper. They regarded it with no feelings of anticipation; as with most meals on board aircraft, this one was unconnected with any human need, answering no hunger, fulfilling no social function. It was a routine amount of food, laid down by the airline regulations to be periodically consumed by passengers during flight.

The four of them sat at the very back of the aircraft, in a small enclosure of only four seats which, through a design idiosyncrasy, gave its occupants a sense of unusual privacy. Freddie himself sat beside the small round window, cut in the body of the aircraft where its frame was so thick that the porthole seemed to have been drilled out with a massive auger. Several times he stopped, to stare out of the window, as though searching for a sight of the Indian Ocean sliding invisibly thousands of feet below, and hoping to look deeper, through the black depths of that sea, in search of another solution.

The others barely knew him. They had all met and had been introduced in Singapore a week before. Freddie was one of the innumerable staff officers who always appeared after major fleet exercises. But Freddie, a stout argumentative little man, with his lieutenant commander's stripes on his shoulders and his bald head fringed almost monastically with a circle of bristling red hair, had been a minor actor in the discussions and debates which had followed the latest SEATO exercises. They had been the largest land, sea and air operations in the Far East for some years. Freddie had made one unexpected contribution to the discussions, when he said that a particular ship had been 'precious close to another *Pandora* incident'.

When the lights of Singapore city had swung under the tilting starboard wing and had disappeared in the lower monsoon clouds, the quartet unfastened their seat belts, and one of them asked Freddie what he knew of the *Pandora* affair. He had only meant to make a polite conversation. Freddie had begun reluctantly, but someone there had known James and the mention of that name seemed to release Freddie from his inhibitions.

Freddie's audience were respectful. They were already amazed that such an unremarkable man should display such astonishing insights, mixed with such naïvety and snobbery. Freddie was maddeningly discursive, and disconcertingly perceptive. It was difficult for any of them to think of him as personally involved in the events he was describing, but no sooner had they accustomed themselves to this role, than Freddie's narrative changed. He became the necessary scavenger, sweeping up after events, picking up the discarded details. Freddie was both victim and protagonist, receiving confidences, and pronouncing opinions. Where he had not been present he had heard, and where he had not heard he guessed.

I was talking, Freddie said, about the time James first met Olivia. It was at the Summer Ball at Greenwich, when we were both sub-lieutenants. It seems so long ago now, and dreamlike, the Painted Hall in all its glory, music, champagne, buffet supper with turkey and salmon, walking with your partner down to look at the Thames, the girls all in long dresses and gloves, I feel I am talking about something that happened in the Eighteenth Century. We were in mess undress, the full fig, white weskits, miniature medals. That was not long after the war. Everybody had medals then. Not like these days. The Summer Ball was an occasion to go to a girl's head, unless she was experienced, and ours, too. I took Olivia as my partner. James did not have a partner of his own. He said she had let him down at the last moment. But as he wouldn't say who she was, I didn't think he ever had a partner. He purposely didn't, so that he could cruise around on his own and prey on the rest of us. He was a shark in that way, James.

They were both so young. We were all young. This is middle age, crying into its beer, lamenting the past. *Ubi sunt*, as they say. But James and I were only twenty or so, I suppose, and Olivia couldn't have been more than eighteen. She was a deb that year and she had given up one very grand invitation to a ball that night, so that she could come to Greenwich with me. As a matter of fact, they were rather a grand family. Her father was Lord Moilinann. He was a member of the Jockey Club, and White's, all very grand. Olivia was slumming it a bit, coming out with me. I only knew them because my father was the parson in their local church. His living was in their family gift. So Olivia was very much the Hall, and I was very much the Village. It is extraordinary how strong that feeling was, even in those days.

I introduced them. He had been cruising around with his eye on her for some time. For a moment I felt very sick about it. I was terrified of bringing them together, because I must have guessed what it might lead to, but somehow I could not help myself. I had a weird conviction that keeping them apart would be worse than bringing them together.

I have never seen anything quite like their behaviour, that night. It was most odd. It would be over-simplifying to say that they took to each other. They did. But there was very much more to it than that. It was as though they both realised … As though they both knew at once that whether they married each other or whether they became lovers or what they did, or even if they never met again in their lives, they would still never be the same again. It would never be quite as simple for them again. For them the mere business of living had become immensely more complicated. Everything they did, they would do in the light, in the afterlight, of the fact that they had known each other. Friends is certainly not the word to describe them. And as for lovers … well, that's a long story.

I found out later that James knew who she was, and that appealed to him, too. He was a roaring snob, I will have to admit that. In one way, I was in at the start of something exciting. Whatever else, James and Olivia undoubtedly generated excitement. The trouble was, they had to keep on proving something to each other. They could not rest. They could not let it go. They had to keep on winning. They couldn't both keep on winning. Somebody had to dip out. I knew how James was feeling. Because I couldn't look at things the same way again after I had met Olivia either. She had the same effect on me as well. They both had a quality about them

... I don't suppose any of you ever met James' wife and I do not want to dwell unduly on the past, but Olivia at eighteen ... Well, she was, to me at least, she was quite something, I can tell you. You have to remember this was in the late Nineteen Forties. Still pretty well the age of austerity. Long before the permissive age, as they call it. Personally, I think Olivia has got better as the years have gone by. But that's just me talking, maybe. At that time, in what seems looking back to have been a very grey era just after the war, Olivia was like a bolt of sunshine, cold winter sunshine possibly, but quite unexpected and all the brighter for being out of season.

In a word, they were made for each other. You could say they hunted in pairs. There was some poor old and bold two-and-a-half there that evening, with his faded old bat of a wife. God knows what he was doing at Greenwich, or whose guest he was. He looked as if he'd been boom defence officer in some remote Arctic fishing village for the whole of the war. She looked as if she'd been there, too, keeping the local cathouse. If you think this description hard, it's what James said at the time. He could be cruel, but bloody amusing. Olivia was a beautiful girl, and this old codger must have said something to her. I don't know what, or how it started, but they both turned on the poor old sod. They had been drinking. Olivia wasn't used to the hard stuff and she was probably a bit sloshed. Anyway, they both turned on him, and saw him off together. I never saw anybody slink away with his tail quite so firmly between his legs as that. Mind you, Olivia was supposed to be my partner that night. To hear them talk, you would never have credited that that chap was a lieutenant commander, while James was only a sub-lieutenant.

They were mocking him, of course. They were both young and brilliant and the future looked incredibly bright for them.

They could look forward and there was nothing they would not be able to do. He was middle-aged, and past it. You could see that in his face. Yet his wife was fond of him. I don't think she would have done any different if you had given her her chance again. I was very embarrassed. Nobody should torment anybody else like that. We don't know our own futures. Time keeps its revenges for us.

Some interesting things happened ashore, that first night after *Pandora* got back. It certainly was not obvious at the time, and it was not even obvious later except to somebody who specially chased it up, like me, but what happened was that *Pandora* released on shore that evening a mob of matelots with chips of varying sizes on their shoulders. This may be difficult to describe, but you see, a happy commission in a happy ship leaves an afterglow behind it. You remember events in that ship through a rosy haze. Everything was terrific, even the failures. Everything was marvellous, even the disasters. I am sorry if I keep on talking to you as though you were not in the Navy yourselves. You must excuse the explanatory travelogue bit. It is just me putting my thoughts in order as I go along. As I said, a good commission ... I remember the old *Superb* ... the old *Superb*. God, even that name's a cliché, now.

But, as you know, the opposite is also true. A bad commission in an unhappy ship can leave a nasty aftertaste. You can almost smell the cinders and ashes. It is like passing a place where somebody has vomited violently. *Pandora's* story was all there, if anyone cared to piece it together, from the punishment returns, from one or two newspaper items in the next few days, from patrol reports, and just from general gossip and talk in the Port. Those *Pandoras* went ashore that night, some to their homes locally for the night, some further afield on foreign service leave, some just ashore for a couple of pints. But they were all looking for trouble. Something was biting those matelots. At that time we didn't know what it was. They didn't know themselves. There wasn't one of them could have put a finger on what was wrong. Ship's companies' moods are funny things. They don't respond always as you'd expect. Sometimes they go along fine and you believe you have them well sized up and then just as you are patting yourself on the back, wallop, it hits you. It was just as though James' ship's company all piled ashore that night with a raging fever inside them. A hundred and fifty blokes all fanning out into the countryside with a disease. Naturally, we only heard what came to the surface. We will never know how any of the families reacted, once their lord and master got home and the front door shut behind him. The one exploit, if that is the word, which made any sort of stir, was those two engineering mechanics from *Pandora* who smeared the statues in Trafalgar Square with boot polish. Those busts of Cunningham and Beatty, is it? I can never remember, although I suppose I ought to. I think Beatty's one of them. Anyway, that was the story that made the news. Imagine it. Returning ship from the Far East. Our gallant sailors. Fine body of men. Led by gallant officers, gallant officers and gentlemen. And here are two of those well-trained, well-led, well-paid hearts of oak defacing what almost amounts to a national naval shrine. It was put down to high spirits. Understandable on the first night back in the Smoke. Nobody stopped to wonder why the two sailors had boot polish on them at two o'clock in the morning. It couldn't have been a spur of the moment affair. They must have brought it beforehand and prepared it.

I myself got my first real inkling of what might be happening when I met *Pandora's* First Lieutenant ashore that night. He was not drunk. That type never do get drunk, or not so drunk they will give anything away. So he did not even have that excuse. It was quite plain that he despised me. He seemed to know I knew James from a long time back. And if anything he seemed to despise me even more for that. I'm trying to think of his name. Simon something or other. I ought to remember it. It doesn't matter now. He was a young climber from nowhere. A real pusher, on the make. So he despised me. I was not a high-flyer, as he obviously was. I was just a poor old clapped-out old passed-over old two-and-a-half, who looked as though he drank too much. I learned later that this likely lad had been sniffing round Olivia, too. I've thought about him a lot since and the conclusion I came to was that his trouble was that he was much too like James himself. You put two performers together, all smooth on the surface but all raging with ambition on the inside, and you're bound to get results, although they may not be quite the results you wanted or expected. James picked this lad himself. He was always an excellent judge of men, James. For myself, the Simons of this world are ... I wish the devil I could remember his surname ... There's only one thing to do with the Simons of this world and that is to recommend them as highly as you can as fast as you can and get them promoted the hell out of your hair as quick as you can. And then you hope to God you never come up against them later as your senior officer. Simon could have been an admiral. The ironic part is that he would quite cheerfully have done the dirty on James, given half a chance. So it was justice in a way, I suppose.

Talking to James' First Lieutenant that night was damned hard work. Hard work to make some sense of what he was driving at, I mean. It was one of those curious conversations where he was trying to hide something, and I was trying to find out what it was, without knowing that I was trying to find out anything, if you understand what I mean. Even then, I didn't succeed in finding out what it was that was bothering him. In other words, I didn't know, until he more or less told me, that there *was* anything to find out. It was his shiftiness that made me suspicious. It was his very evasiveness that led me on and made me think there was something there. He was pointing to the very thing he did not wish to discuss, actually as though he was subconsciously wanting to talk about it all the time. That was his downfall. And his contempt for me. That was a mistake on his part, too. I may not be the most brilliant naval officer since Lord Nelson, but I'm still not a complete bloody fool. I may not have achieved a third stripe, but that still doesn't make me a moron. I was in the Andrew long before that little scorpion even got to Dartmouth. He shouldn't have tried to teach *me* how to suck eggs. Even snakes' eggs. Damn his impertinent eyes.

He compounded his offence by taking up space and generally disturbing my peace and waylaying me in the privacy of me own little favourite boozer. I have a somewhat perverted taste for faded grandeur. The twilight days of anything fascinate me. I like drinking in a place knowing that it is probably just about to go. Having my glass one step ahead of demolition. *Après moi*, the bulldozers, you could say. I like, I relish those last moments before the final collapse. That may be why I stay in the Navy. Everything, even a woman, is little better for being a little battered. I've always preferred women with those tell-tale lines, those little sags in the skin. A young girl is fine, if you like a smooth shiny silky body to exercise yourself on. But I want to look at her, and know she's been hurt. Even Olivia, she did not have perfect looks by any manner of means. Her skin was a bit coarse, at the corners of the eyes, I always thought, but that as I said, was all to the good.

My favourite drinking place at that time was that aged hotel on the Hoe, the old Coliseum we used to call it. You must all know where I mean. Heaven knows what its real name was. All been pulled down now, of course. But in those days it was still going and it still had a charming air about it, a kind of apologetic Edwardian splendour. There was Rudolf, do you remember him, that waiter with his black tie and his maroon coloured waistcoat, to bring you your drinks. He used to carry that splendid ebony tray, with the pile of change on it. Rudolf's change was always shinier than anybody else's. I think he used to go to the bank every day and get new coins. There was actually a stage there at one end, with a piano and a set of drums and some music stands, all jumbled together in the corner. I seem to remember there were some palm trees in pots. I never heard anybody play there. Except once, now I think of it. Olivia stayed there for two nights once, and played Chopsticks on that piano, while she was waiting to see James off to somewhere. The floor was marble where the carpet ended, and you could always tell when Rudolf was on his way, because his shoes used to go clop clop clop on the stone, and then make a funny sort of shushing noise when he reached the carpet. And when he had your order, away he went, shush shush shush, and then clop clop clop.

The armchairs in the place were all very old and the springs were shaky, occasionally one would give a great twang as you sat down, and they were all upholstered in some red plushy material that looked as if it had been chosen by Queen Alexandra. There were those gilt electric lamp things sticking out in clusters all around the walls and a superb cut-glass chandelier in the middle of the room. The ceiling was very high and coffered with gilt animals and flowers and birds and a sort of ornamental work in a great long frieze running right round the room. The pictures were damned great studies of animals with frames, all gilt of course, about a foot wide. It was a marvellous place to sit and have a quiet gin. Better than any wardroom I've ever been in, I can tell you. I was sitting there, and Rudolf had just brought me my first glass, when suddenly there was a clop clop clopperty clop clop clop in a messy sort of way and in came this Simon fellow ... I wish I could remember his wretched silly name, it's on the tip of my tongue.

He asked me if I wanted a drink. I said I had one. He asked Rudolf for a pint of bitter. Rudolf said they didn't serve beer in the conservatory room. That's what they called it, I forgot. There was a place with flowers and plants and trailing creepers, all panes of glass, just outside through a doorway. So he then said he would have a whisky and soda. When you think about it, it must have been a disappointment not to be able to have a glass of beer after being in the Far East and drinking that tiger's piss stuff. But, after all, he could have gone somewhere else. What the hell he was doing ashore all by himself in the old Coliseum on his first night back from the Far East I couldn't imagine.

Fiddich. That was his name. Unusual name. It must have been talking about the whisky that reminded me. Simon Fiddich, that's it. He was a small, darkish fellow. Smooth. Like a lizard. He had some manners, I'll say that for him, and a certain reptilian charm.

"One more successful commission over," he said. I looked at him. Perhaps he was having a quiet private joke at my expense. What an odd way of expressing it! Just like saying, one more day gone, or one more stamp licked.

"I saw you on board today," he said. "I'm sorry I didn't have a chance to have much of a chat with you. You're Fleet Environmental Control Officer."

He made it sound like Fleet Rodent Control Officer.

"Was there anything in particular you'd come to check up on? he said. Was there anything we could have…"

No, I said to him. Well, only that your Captain is a very old friend of mine. He must have known the reason I came on board. Somehow he had succeeded in making me feel sheepish. I call to see me best friend who's been in the Far East for eighteen months and this character makes me feel guilty about it, as though I were somehow spying on them. But it did show that he knew who I was and that meant he must have taken the trouble to find out that I was on the Staff.

"Are you a closely-knit bunch, the Staff?" he asked, "all one big happy gossipy family?"

Again, what an odd thing to say! I'd never been asked such a question in my life. And there was an echo of James in it too. He saw my astonishment, and he must have thought I was not bright enough to know what he was talking about.

I wouldn't call it a closely-knit Staff at all, I said. Again, he was embarrassing me, making me choose the wrong words. Certainly not one big happy family in that sense, I said. I mean … Well, I am not the best person to ask, in any case.

He would know that. He would know that my job was never going to give me intimate access to the Admiral or even to the Chief of Staff. We would meet at regular staff meetings, of course, and I would go in to the Admiral if anything special ever cropped up in my part of ship, which it never had yet and in fact never did all the time I was there. But otherwise, as far as social contact was concerned, one would expect to go to the garden party in the summer and to be bidden to have dinner with Admiral and Missis at Mountwise, say, once or perhaps twice a year. But, on the other hand, it was not such a daft question as all that. It struck me he might know more about my personal circumstances than I thought he did. It so happened that I was the only bachelor on the staff at that time. As the only bachelor, and I like to think an eligible one, I was asked to a great many more social functions than I normally would have been. People used to say to me jokingly, Freddie, you're the only spare man in the whole of the West Country. But it turned out that I had misunderstood him. I was thinking in social terms. He was talking about his career.

Rudolf brought him his whisky.

"Cheers," he said. "And here's to a cracking good commission. For those that like that sort of thing. Have you ever had a cracking good commission, Freddie?"

It was not so much the omission of the word 'sir', that annoyed me, although he was only a potty little two-striper not much more than half my age, as the insulting tone of voice. Had I ever had a cracking good commission indeed! This character had a knack of making me boil with rage. He knew it, and he enjoyed it.

"Have you ever served with our …" he hesitated just long enough, "… James?"

I said I had not.

"You would like it," he said. "James is the best worst captain in the world. Or the worst best. Whichever way you prefer."

Now that I have had the time to think it over, and now that I can look back and see matters in the perspective of distance, I can understand what a deadly accurate description of James this was. But at that time, all I could see was that this fellow was toying with me.

I said, Your loyalty does you great credit.

He laughed so much he had to put his hand over the top of his glass to stop it spilling. "Don't come the old sea-daddy trick with me," he said. "James is a very fine officer. As I said, one of the worst best or best worst, whichever you like. How did you ever come to know him?"

He sounded as though he were astonished I knew James. I told him we were in the same term. And in the same gunroom for a time.

"There's glory for you," he said. He went on, talking in this silly elliptical way, for some time. I could make neither head nor tail of him. When Rudolf came back, I let him buy me a drink. He raised his glass. "Here's to the saucy *Pandora*," he said. "Do you know that little tune?"

Arethusa, I said. Not *Pandora*.

"I know, I know," he said. He hummed it and sang some of the words. "She is a frigate tight and brave, as ever stemmed the dashing wave. Her men are staunch to their favourite launch…"

He stopped. And he burst into tears. When I looked across at him, the tears were simply streaming down his cheeks, absolutely pouring down. He shook his head, but he could not stop crying. He sat in his armchair, his head down, absolutely collapsed. Unable to say another word.

I must say I was not particularly surprised. The expressions on his face, the way he had been talking, the way he kept jumping about, the very fact that he was there at all, all on his Jack Jones, the whole set-up was so very strange that there had to be something the matter with him. And it is not so very outlandish to see someone cry when a good commission is over. I dropped a quiet tear after the old *Superb* myself. Mind you, I have heard them cheer when a *bad* commission was over, too. That's by the way. Good or bad, you might get sloshed, you see your old captain on his way, and then you start again in a new ship. New appointment, new faces. New ships, new cap-tallies. The first turn of the screw mends all broken hearts. To me, that's the tremendous thing about the Navy. It is such a romantic way of life. It still is. And here was this steely character sobbing into hisdrink. I suppose he wasn't so bad, when all's said and done. He had just been touched where he had no defences. Something had finally reached him. Because, don't misunderstand all my sentimental talk about tears after a good commission. *That*, wasn't why this character was crying. This was something quite different. There was something creepy about this performance.

"I was loyal to James," he said, at last, after he had calmed down a bit.

I believed him. Why stress it? He obviously thought he had been loyal to James. So what? Who was saying otherwise? James always insisted on personal loyalty from his officers. Of course, insisting on it, and getting it, are two different things. Have any of you ever read the *Iliad*? I read it first at Dartmouth, funnily enough. I say funnily enough, because Dartmouth has such a philistine reputation, quite unjustly, if I may say so, that Homer is not the sort of writer people might expect you to read there. But I read it and thoroughly enjoyed it. I still do read bits of it, whenever I get the time and feel in the mood. There is one part that particularly impressed me. I am vague about the details but it comes about halfway through, when two of the warriors on the Trojan side ... *Sarpedon* was one of them ... they stop in the middle of the battle somewhere outside the walls of Troy and one of them says to the other, why do you think we always get the best place at meals, and the first cut off the joint, and why are our glasses always kept topped up with the best wine? Why do you think we own the best farming land? It's because we have our obligations as leaders. We have the perks, but we also have the responsibility. Our troops can look up to us and say, all right, they may get the best of everything but they're always up there in the forefront of the hottest battle. There's a price to be paid. So they look up to us, and respect us as leaders. If we were going to live for ever, I would say to you, stay at home and enjoy yourself. But as we might die at any moment, come on, he shouts. You're absolutely right, the other one says, and off they go into the battle. As I remember, they both get killed. It's a marvellous bit of the poem.

Now, my point is, I've always thought that passage a marvellously romantic description of how an officer should behave. That is what being an officer means. There are those two sides to the same face, one side privilege, and the other side duty. And when I looked at that pitiful, tear-stained, bloody miserable face in that armchair that night, I knew that somehow or other James and this fellow and maybe the other officers in that ship had in some way let the end go. Because it involved James, I made up my mind I would damned well find out what it was and how it had happened.

CHAPTER 2

The last words generated a faint but growing condemnation among his listeners. Freddie tended to forget that he was not talking to a lay audience. To these listeners, his words had added connotations, rising up through layers of significance from a profound depth of shared experience. They could discount his rhetoric from their own knowledge, but that same knowledge made them unusually sensitive to innuendo. Freddie's words seemed to echo, like the sounds of disapproval. He was aware of them, and reacted to the faces of his audience. Self-justification was not what he had expected.

Of course, he said, when I say I was going to find out, I do not mean anything as formal as an investigation of any kind, or anything at all like that. One does not suddenly turn round and start investigating one's best friends, especially on anything as vague as this. And it was vague, as you all know. There was almost nothing to go on, at first, nothing but a hunch, although I cannot believe that it would have stayed submerged for long. There were too many people involved. Feelings ran too strongly. The matter touched us too closely, made us think of what we were and what we served for. There was little or no press mention, that I can recall now, after those first excitements in Trafalgar Square. It was an internal affair, within the Service. Even then it was desperately difficult to follow. It ran like a current, you know, deep and quiet for a long time and then surprisingly came out in a ripple or a race, so that anybody who knew what to look for could see there was something happening. That's the point. You had to know what to look for. It was as though everybody in the Service had made up their minds what James should do, and it was only a question of time before James made up his mind to do it. Although, that can't be right, not really. It is so hard to go back now and see things as they were at the beginning, or what seemed like the beginning. There has been so much talk and debate, clouding it over in a great tangle of interpretation and prejudice. It is hard to believe now that anyone could ever have seen it in terms of hard black and hard white. James had a whole range of choices open to him, of course he did. No, the whole business had a shadowy quality about it, which vanished as you searched for it. To get hold of it all you had to start off with a whole range of beliefs, about honour, to use that old-fashioned word, about discipline and duty, all those obsolete words, and to use the oldest-fashioned word of the lot, about love. You had to have the right moral equipment, like having the right pair of binoculars, or you would never see anything at all. Even then it would drive you mad if you thought about it too much. You would end up wondering what is a naval officer, and other leading questions. Why do we have a Navy at all? What am I doing here, what are we all doing here, all dressed up in smart blue uniforms with bright gold buttons? That way madness lies.

The very next day I had a stroke of luck. Of course, when I say luck I do not mean that I was chasing the thing that hard and needed any luck. It just happened to crop up again. As it so often does. You have never heard of a name before, and then you hear it two or three times on the trot, in different circumstances. *Pandora* had not been part of my life before, but here she was, bobbing up again. I telephoned James the next day, with some vague idea of inviting him ashore that night, to have a meal and a couple of pints of beer with me. James and I quite often used to go on modest pub crawls around the West

Country pubs in the old days. After all, I hardly had a chance for a chat with him when he came in. I was told he was out of the ship for two days. I knew they had a house near Chichester. Olivia must have been living there, because I certainly had not seen her around the social scene of the Port. I took it that James had gone up to the Ministry of Defence in London and was probably staying at Chichester, overnight.

So, not being able to get hold of James, that evening I went to the Skinners' barbecue. Tom Skinner, the Royal Marine. He was at Bickleigh then, doing something or other. He and Daphne had bought a seventeenth century farmhouse, somewhere quite a way out of Plymouth, somewhere like Meavy. It had an old barn, and some stables, a bit of land, some ramshackle out-buildings, a pond, you know the sort of thing. It was a barbecue but they actually sent out invitation cards. Come to a 'Beat the Retreatnik', it said. We were all supposed to come dressed like hippies and drop-outs. Nobody did, unless you are one of those who think that naval officers in plain clothes always look like hippies anyway. 'Beat the Retreatnik' was a good example of Tom's somewhat ponderous wit. Tom was always a trifle trendy, loved to keep up with the latest thing, and at that time the great thing was barbecues, with charcoal in a burner, and a record-player with pop music, and bottles and bottles and bottles of supermarket plonk *vino* to drink.

That sort of do is all right if the weather's good. That night it was miserable. Simply horrible. Cold and rainy, very cold, with that very fine West Country rain which eventually gets right through to your bones if you stay out in it. It never stopped all night. We huddled in the barn, watching it. Actually, I rather enjoyed it. There was something deliciously gloomy about that farmyard. The rain coming down, and a genuine midden heap, with ranks and ranks of great green nettles. There was what looked like marrow plants trailing about, all green and growing all over the place. There was a rambler rose, too, growing over one of the stable doors. Nobody had pinned it or touched it for years and it was running amuck into a blazing great mass of flowers. Tom and Daphne never spent anything on their property. They spent their money on their guests. There was a contrast, sure enough. Inside, bright clothes and chatter. Outside, the wet and all those broken flagstones, and that dark green slimy coating over the earth that you get in old farmyards. It was like bright tinsel next to graveyard moss. It was in a terrible state, but I liked it. It made me feel all shivery and melancholy, in the rain, and the darkness coming on. There's something about wildness and wet. Let them be left ... something, something ... wildness and wet. Long live the wet, the weeds, and the wilderness yet. Some whimsical West Country brickie had amused himself building the barn, working some of his bricks into the shape of aces, ace of hearts, ace of clubs, ace of diamonds, ace of spades, all along the wall. There was a damned great ginger cat, sitting on a ledge and glaring at us. Somebody told me she'd just had kittens and they'd all been put down. So no wonder she was boot-faced. Daphne had gone to some trouble with the food, chicken and salad, and strawberries and cream. As it happened, that must have been one of the very last parties Daphne went to, and certainly the last she ever gave herself. She had cancer of the liver, and she went down very rapidly. They operated on her, and Tom told everybody that that was it, that was the end, Daphne was fine now. I had a Christmas card from them that year. But then she had to have another operation. At Easter, she was dead. I still see Tom occasionally and I never know what to say to him. I think he and Daphne had the happiest marriage going for them of anybody I ever met. He loved her and she loved him. They never had any children, they just had each other. She used to be in the Wrens. The story I heard about the second operation was that the surgeon took one look and then sewed her up again. There was nothing he could do. It is appalling the way this thing strikes. Haphazardly. It doesn't make any sense. It makes it all seem like a damned great game of mad Russian roulette.

Anyway, the point is that at one time Daphne had been a great friend of Olivia's, although I think they had tended to drift apart a little in recent years. Daphne told me that night she had just seen Olivia again at somebody's wedding a few weeks before, and they'd had a good old chat. In fact, Olivia was supposed to have come down to Plymouth to meet James, and they were both supposed to be coming to that barbecue. But Daphne had not heard any more, and they neither of them had turned up.

Daphne was wearing a woollen shawl over her shoulders, and sunglasses in spite of the rain. She was very pale, I remember. She was sickening, even then. She was trying to rush round and be a hostess and keep an eye on things and have a gossip with me and kept on making faces at the weather and saying isn't the rain terrible, all at the same time. I kept telling her to relax, not to worry, even though I was dying to hear, but Daphne always did things, everything, at full tilt. I only got the story in fits and starts.

I must say Tom and Daphne used to know a tremendous amount of people. Their parties attracted all manner of odds and sods, including everybody who was in any way on the make. Young officers on the way up to the stars, or so they thought, middle-aged officers trying to stop sliding downwards and backwards, and the neutrals like me who were just suspended in space, like those funny organisms you see in stagnant pools. Not very complimentary to myself, I admit, but I would not have had the life I have if I had not been able to see myself steadily and see myself whole. Naval society in the West was quite lively in those days, in a feverish sort of way. There was always the nasty rippling sound of marriages tearing apart, the devil's applause. Although I must say not quite the same roar of falling marital timber that one hears today, but still, enough to make life interesting. Himself was away, but Admiral's Missis was there, dancing boringly blamelessly with Flags. There were various Royal Marines standing about, looking bootneckish. Daphne also had some friends from a local art group. She used to do weekly pottery classes, and she used to produce the most extraordinary-looking ashtrays and funny squashed bowls and things. Tom used to say they made him think of fossilised cow-turds. So there was an arty-crafty, somewhat raffish and bizarre flavour, too. One girl had a bare midriff and an almost bare bosom. She had the most splendid pair of breasts, slung in a net blouse. As somebody said, like two white rugger balls in a surgical hammock. It made a nice picture, for those who like to think of those things, that party and that farmyard. Vegetables, marrows, breasts, fertility and reproduction on one side, darkness and decay, the ace of spades and dung on the other. Life dying and life renewing itself. If I were a philosophical man, I would begin to think, how many liaisons began at a party like that? How many fresh relationships begun, old ones altered, dead ones revived, long-standing ones killed off? There were so many people at that party, for some of them it must have been a shot in the arm, for others the last straw. It seems we are all in a state of constant flux, a social mix, shifting and changing about all the time, whirling around each other, striking glancing blows on each other and then cannoning off to hit somebody else. At least one adulterous liaison started at that party, to my certain knowledge. But after all, it would be a dull party if we all went home after it exactly the same people as when we came to it.

As I said, everybody was there, from the staff and the dockyard, from ships and shore establishments, all round the place.

You could always be sure that you would see the very person you wanted to see at Tom and Daphne's. You stood a good chance of seeing a number of people you wanted to avoid for the time being, too, but that's by the way. Young Simon Fiddich was there, giving me rather a sickly smile. It may be intentional or it may be accidental but most parties have a theme. The food was memorably bad, perhaps, or they would keep on playing one particular tune over and over again which stuck in your mind ever afterwards, or something. A tune or a face or a taste or a woman, it's almost a cliché, isn't it? The theme of that party was unquestionably *Pandora*. It wasn't just seeing young Fiddich's face. She was the latest arrival in the port and naturally she was the latest topic of conversation. People wanted to talk over her experiences, weigh up what had happened to her, speculate about whether this or that was a good thing or a bad thing. You know the sort of mulling over that goes on. There were not all that many ships corning in then, even in those days, although it's much worse now. The return of somebody from what was jolly nearly a war area, somewhere where people were at least getting killed and getting medals, was worth talking about.

So it was a party to go to, in spite of the foul weather. The wives did tend to club together and talk about prep schools and their latest parking fines, but it was still a chance to do some business, in a discreet sort of way. Not talking shop exactly, but the preparations for talking shop. If you were bothered about the ventilation system in *Pandora*, say, I can't imagine anybody being interested in the ventilation system in *Pandora*, but suppose you were, you wouldn't talk about it there and then. That would be blatant shop. But what you might do, you might catch sight of somebody whom you knew you would want to see about it, and you might well have a quiet word with him and just prepare the ground-work a bit. So that when you eventually called or rang him up he would know roughly what you were on about.

It was a great pity for James that he wasn't there. It would have been a very useful opportunity for him to indulge in a little press relations. You know the sort of calls a captain has to make when his ship comes back, semi-official calls, just dropping in and making his number with people who might be of use to the ship. A great many of the people whom James would certainly have been calling on were there that night, conveniently gathered together all in one place. A few words dropped in the right quarters that evening would have saved him a week of tramping round offices, and would have been a much better way of doing it, too. It was a missed trick, if you like, in a very minor way. It was a very small trick, but normally James would not have missed it. Only a perfectionist would have thought of using a party to pay calls in the most efficient and graceful way, but then, James was a perfectionist, or he used to be. What would not have been a fault in a hundred other ship's captains, because they simply weren't as good, was a most uncharacteristic lapse for somebody like James. It was not a question of not hitting a wrong note. James was better than that. He didn't merely not hit a wrong note. He hit all the right ones, too. He was that good.

When I wanted to dance, I found my partner had vanished. I took a nurse with me that evening, a plump girl called Joan, from Stonehouse. She was heavy in the hip, it was all that starchy food nurses are supposed to stuff themselves with, and a trifle heavy in the hand, too, conversation-wise. But nice, if you wanted a nice, comfortable, squeezy-shaped body to wrestle with. I wasn't alone in that. She was always being carted off the moment I took my eyes off her. There was always somebody hanging about her, clearly aching to lay his hot and clammy hands on her bare bottom. She liked a bit of pummelling about there. I believe she met somebody that night and married him. It must be my fate to have my partner filched from me whenever I go to a party. I begin to think, are the majority of naval officers quite incapable of finding a woman for themselves? Do they always have to wait until somebody else produces one at a party on board? If I told you the number of naval wives I know who first met their husbands when somebody else took them to a party on board, you wouldn't believe me.

Someone pinched Joan from me again, so I went to the bar and there I met the Command Schoolie, the Staff Instructor Officer, and it was from him, oddly enough, that I got the first facts about what had happened in *Pandora*. He said he had been talking that morning to the editor of the local paper who told him that one of his reporters had met one of the *Pandoras* in Union Street the night before. He bought him a drink, and asked him how things were. To his utter astonishment he got a right earful, all about firing on unarmed fishermen and war crimes and so on. It all sounded fantastic, and he did not think it was a story worth chasing up. The events were all some time ago, and the evidence was all circumstantial, hearsay really. I suppose that even newspaper reporters sometimes believe in letting sleeping dogs lie. There was no point in raking things up from the past. Little did they know. The Schoolie then looked craftily sideways at me. "Wasn't James Bellingham a chum of yours," he said.

Still is, I said, very much so.

"Just thought I would make sure," he said. "Well, you probably know more about it than I do."

Well, of course, I did not know anything about it. It was like one of those ghastly dreams where you are plunging about, knowing something is happening and knowing what it is but somehow just unable quite to put a word to it. It's there, but you cannot describe it and the harder you try the worse it gets. What amazed me was how quickly and how widely the thing had spread. It was twenty-four hours since I first thought there might be something up. In that time it had gone from one of *Pandora's* ship's company to a local reporter to his editor to the Staff Schoolie and back to me. That was quite apart from anyone else any of them had talked to during that time. It seemed that the story would take a new shape each time it came back to me. Each time it rebounded it was more threatening, more violent, more difficult to fight against. But I still did not know what they were talking about. I refused to show my ignorance, although I was so desperate I nearly blurted out, for God's sake stop prevaricating and tell me what happened. Instead I made some bland remark, suggesting that James was probably justified, that circumstances are not always crystal clear in an operational situation, that James' actions would certainly be upheld, if indeed there were ever any possibility that they might be held in question.

"You're probably right," said the Schoolie, "but I get the strong impression that your friend may have blotted his copybook. Very slightly. Just at the edges."

In what way? I said.

"I should have thought it was obvious," he said. "He opened fire on some native craft off Borneo, and it seems he shouldn't have done."

My first reaction was, is that all? It seemed such a trivial thing, after all that build-up and mystery. But then I knew that this had all the makings of a professional disaster for James. My mind leaped to it. This was the very worst thing that could have happened to James. Shooting at some defenceless native craft. It had all sorts of unpleasant associations, of memories of the past, connotations of rage and rashness, of cowardice and bullying. It aroused a whole range of emotions.

The words 'native craft' suddenly gave me an odd and inconsequential memory about James. He spent some of his early childhood in India. I believe he could even talk Hindustani fluently when he was a very small boy. He learned it from the servants. His father had one or even it may have been two liaison appointments or something with the Royal Indian Navy before the war. James may even have been born out there. I'm not sure. I remember he said there were quite a lot of extra papers to be filled in when he went to Dartmouth, all to do with the fact that he had been born outside the United Kingdom. There is this something in his background about people of colour. It may not be important but it is there. He had an Indian nurse, what they call an ayah, to look after him and dress him. He also had what he called a Gurkha bearer, a retired Gurkha soldier, who used to teach him how to salute and drill with a wooden rifle. In the days of the British Raj the English children were almost worshipped by the Indian household servants. It might affect them in later life. They might go through life with a feeling of superiority, particularly towards people of colour. All this flashed through my mind at the time. It shows the devilish power of rumour. Here was a rumour discreditable to my friend. It was only a rumour. It may not have been true, and in any case, I had barely heard the outline of it yet. I had not even got the story properly. And yet there I was, not only half-believing it, but already trying to find justifications in James' background to account for it. The truth was that it was only too believable. There was something in James that made it believable.

Presumably this native craft, or whatever it was, was armed, I said cautiously. I still had no idea of the facts. Everybody else seemed to know all about it, except me. I was the last to know. An unusual experience for me. They were probably gun-running, or smuggling, I said.

"That's not what I heard," said the Schoolie. "I heard that the boat was no bigger than a dinghy, it was a canoe actually, no bigger than the little boat they bring the dhobying off from shore in. And the three bods in it were only fishing. One of them was a woman, I heard."

Was anybody hurt? I asked. Anybody killed?

"Not unless they died of fright," he said. "*Pandora's* shooting was so bad, or the target was so minute, but they never hit it, although I gather they banged away at it with the two forrard turrets for about ten minutes."

Each new fact struck at my heart like a heavy physical blow. It was worse than I could ever have dreamed. It did not matter whether it was true or not, now. The mere fact that people were talking in this way was a professional catastrophe for James.

Somebody else joined us just then. It was a fellow who was on the training staff of the artificers' school at Torpoint. I have a vague idea he was related to Daphne. He had a small wart on the side of his nose, I remember. "You talking about James

Bellingham?" he said. The man disliked James, because he was envious of him. It was written all over his face, it came through in the tone of his voice. Whether or not he had ever met James I had no idea and I certainly was not going to ask, but he had heard of him and was jealous. There were a number of officers who were jealous of James, who would have been glad to see him come a cropper. He had always been above all that. But it might be that he might for the first time in his life have to take notice of these people.

Somebody else came up. "Don't mind my butting in," he said, "but did I hear the name James? Would you be talking about the wonder boy James Bellingham?" There was a disgusting glee in their faces. They were saying to themselves, how are the mighty fallen, and they were loving it. They were huddling together to pick at his reputation as though it were some sort of corpse lying out in the open. And yet, to be honest, I had to admit the attraction of what they were doing, and a very powerful attraction it was. It made me almost begin to wonder, am I James' friend or am I not? Since then, I have often wondered did he want friends? It is quite possible that it is presumptuous of us ever to say that we are somebody's friend. We are laying a burden on them that they may not want.

In my distress, I made a daft remark. What's happening about it? I asked.

They all looked blank. "What's happening? Nothing's happening. What did you expect to happen? Nobody will do anything except James Bellingham. He is the only one who can do anything now."

That, of course, was pure rubbish. There were bound to be many more involved than James. This was all at a time when the armed forces were not particularly popular in the country. They never are, in peacetime, of course, but just at this period there was an element of boredom, of utter uninterest, in the general feeling about the Services. People thought we were all quite irrelevant to the modern world. They used to make jokes like the one about the general being shown round a hospital who said, 'Just think, for ten of these we could have another Polaris missile.' Maybe we were a little paranoiac about publicity, suffering from a persecution complex, but there really did seem to be an anti-Services pressure group in the media, always ready to pounce upon some story that put any of us in an unfavourable or, better still, ridiculous light. How that newspaper editor could think that there was no story in what his man heard from that sailor off *Pandora* beats me, but we must just be grateful for small mercies.

When I saw James in his cabin I asked him whether he needed any help and he had acted as though help was inappropriate. And in a peculiar way, he was right. It did not fit the circumstances. I wanted to help, but there was no way. One felt one should defend him. But who was attacking? One could argue his point of view. But nobody was arguing the other side. It was only sparring at the air. There were no accusations. Gossip, yes, but accusations, no. Only a general vagueness floating threateningly about in the air. I felt more strongly than ever, where the hell is James? He ought to be here, hobbing and nobbing with everyone, making his number, letting himself be seen. He should have been circulating about so that they could all look at him, look at his face, listen to him, and say at once, these things are not possible. All I could hope for was that wherever he was he was employing himself more usefully than he could have done there. I hoped that he was successfully defending himself against more concrete charges. I hoped so, by God I hoped so.

Daphne kept drifting by, catching my eye and saying, "Must have a word with you, dying to have a word with you." She was obviously bursting with news, and she would come up and just open her mouth to start saying something when something else would happen. Must dash, she would say, and off she went. It was all most frustrating. I had no real chance to talk to her until much later, when everybody had had food and started dancing in earnest. My Joan, and the bare-bosomed girl had both vanished, no doubt they were both performing their party pieces in some hay-loft or other.

I always found Daphne very attractive indeed. She was quite one of my favourite Service wives. If there was anybody's body I wanted to get my hands on, it was hers. I never got half the chance, though. Tom might have been a Royal Marine bootneck, but he was no fool and he was well aware of what was in my mind. But Daphne was the most refreshing realist. She always believed that marriages might be made in heaven, but they were made to work here on earth, and specifically in bed. Whenever anything went wrong with any of her friends' marriages, she always suspected what she used to call 'bed trouble'. I had long since stopped being amazed by the number of times she turned out to be absolutely right.

Daphne was not a good dancer, neither am I, come to that, and she got much worse, much less energy towards the end. That night she was tired and I was more or less holding her up as we shuffled about. It looked terribly sexy, but in fact was very exhausting. She told me she got very tired in the evenings. It became a well-known thing, that when Daphne went to a party, she would have a quiet kip in an armchair halfway through the evening. When she woke up, she would be as bright as day for the rest of the party. Everybody knew about this. It was a symptom, another one. In the last few weeks before she went to hospital she got tired earlier, slept for longer, and was less bright when she woke up. One can only guess what was going through Tom's mind. He was watching his wife, whom he loved, beginning to die a little more every evening.

We began to jog gently round the floor. I say 'floor', it was paving stones in the barn, sprinkled with sawdust. I said to Daphne, you look as though you're going to explode if you don't let go whatever it is inside you.

She took a deep breath and said, "Yes, did you notice I disappeared for a few minutes?"

Without thinking I said, I thought you'd gone off to have your mid-evening catnap. She frowned horribly at that. It was not one of my most tactful remarks. "No," she said, "it was the telephone. It was Olivia Bellingham."

Goodness, I said, are they coming after all?

"She is," Daphne said. "He isn't. She's left him, she says."

We stopped dancing with a jolt. Daphne leaned back to look at me. The next two couples shuffled into us and bounced off. One of them was young Fiddich, I remember, elbowing to and fro.

"Olivia was telephoning from North Road Station. Tom's gone to fetch her,"Daphne said. "He's not too pleased about it. He's been drinking a lot and if the police should stop him he'll be had. I don't know why she should ring us. I mean, it's very flattering, in a way, to think that anybody in trouble thinks of us to ring, but I've hardly seen much of Olivia recently. She used to be a great chum of mine, but until the Darley's wedding the other day I hadn't seen her to talk to for years."

I could not see the expression on Daphne's face. I had to judge by her voice and her body movements. It was almost pitch black in that barn, there were only a few candles set in ledges in the walls, otherwise there was just the red light on the front of the record-player. It was cold and damp, and we were shuffling about on sawdust shavings. I could feel them getting clammily into my shoes. Daphne was excited, as we both were by such news. An era seemed to be ending. She was sad, too, and apprehensive. I suppose when a woman learns of the wreck of somebody else's marriage she can either be satisfied that she herself is safe. Like lying in bed and listening to a thunder storm somewhere else. At least it can't happen to us here, she says. Or she can feel just as insecure. If it can happen to them, what is to stop it happening to us? In Daphne's case, it didn't matter anyway. But we are all vulnerable, just as vulnerable to this kind of disaster as we are to gossip.

"As you would expect, it's a long story," Daphne said. "Olivia wasn't saying any more over the telephone. She said she'd tell me when she saw me. She said it had been building up for a long time and she couldn't stand it any longer and she had to get away and could she come and stay for a few days. Funny, she didn't breathe a word of any of this at the Darley's wedding."

Ah, but James wasn't home then, I pointed out.

"That might be it, something to do with it," Daphne said.

Once again, I examined my own reactions, and I was surprised by my lack of surprise. Once again I had an overwhelming sense of being caught up in events that had to happen. I know that it is another cliché, perhaps the whole story is a cliché, except to those who experienced it, but I had never before felt quite the same sensation that James and Olivia and all of us were being overtaken by the inevitable. Twenty-four hours earlier it would have seemed incredible to me that I would be looking upon James from a totally new standpoint, as I now was. Things could never be the same again. But now that it had happened, I could see that it had to happen, and it was impossible for me to imagine a state of affairs when it had never happened. I felt that the fabrics of James' existence in his professional and in his private life, were crumbling away.

Has Olivia got a boyfriend, I asked. Is it on her part, all this?

Daphne sounded really shocked. "Goodness, no," she said. "Olivia with a boyfriend? I wouldn't think that was very likely. She's well above all that sort of thing."

I was not nearly so sure of that as Daphne seemed to be. It seemed to me only too likely that Olivia, from what I could remember of her, would have a boyfriend, and if she didn't have one now, she damned soon would. It was James whom I imagined untouchable, above all that, as Daphne put it. I could not imagine him having a secret liaison with anybody. But Daphne violently disagreed with me on that.

"James?" she said. "He's one of the most attractive men I know. I would have said it was almost certain he had a woman of some kind somewhere."

It was possible, I thought, that Daphne was as entitled to her special opinion of James as I was to mine of Olivia. But already, the significant point was that there was already this huge divergence of opinion, about them both, even amongst us, who knew them both well and had the story hot and fresh, as it happened more or less. How much more baffling it would be, how much more opportunity there would be for malicious distortion for those who had it second-hand and much later. It made me despair of ever hearing the truth about anybody.

Daphne suddenly stiffened, and I knew she could see something. We turned round. There was Olivia standing in the doorway, rather dramatically silhouetted, with Tom behind her.

He looked as if he was panting, as though he had been running about, but like all bootnecks Tom was always impossibly fit.

I thrive on dramatic social moments. I love the jolt and shock of any kind of personal confrontation. The return of the prodigal son, a lovers' tiff which one shouldn't overhear, the family quarrel, the dropped brick, the calculated insult that makes somebody miserable for the evening, and all the complex reactions to all these situations, are meat and drink to me. I was determined not to be disappointed by Olivia's return, and Olivia did not disappoint me. She enjoyed this kind of moment as much as I did.

She ran forward to hug Daphne. It was an impulsive and unconsidered act, and was probably quite genuine. I could hear the music thumping out from inside the barn as they kissed each other, and somebody's idiotically high-pitched voice ringing out from the stable bar. She turned to me. "How are you, Freddie?," she said, sort of throatily. She had not changed. I opened my mouth to speak and could feel myself gaping uselessly. My knees were loosening, and I could feel myself going under again. It was marvellous. Marvellous moment.

CHAPTER 3

All the world's a stage, as they say, rather tritely, and I believe Olivia was unconsciously, or maybe even consciously, thoroughly enjoying the scene and the drama of it all. She would die rather than admit it, but secretly she adored being the centre of attention. All the hubbub and the excitement. Everybody craning their necks, wondering whether they should come up and say something or whether they should hang back tactfully, everybody looking and saying isn't that Olivia Bellingham, why's she here, what's happened, is James here, and where is he, and something must be wrong, and why is Freddie scratching his head and looking so concerned, and so on, and so on. To someone like Olivia, this was all meat and drink.

Actually, concerned was not quite the right word, not nearly a big enough word, for the way I was feeling then. I was not only concerned, I was thrilled. Seeing Olivia again was like feeling a breath of air stirring down a long corridor, so that all the dust of the past was put in movement again. To put it another way, it was like life and breath being pumped back into a great musical instrument, so that I could feel all its pipes and stops beginning to vibrate and tremble with anticipation all over again. Olivia touched me in so many ways. I had completely forgotten how evocative just her presence was, her figure, her voice, her shape, everything about her. To see her again brought back a great range of reminiscence like a panorama in fact, of secrets and amazements and wonders. They talk about old flames. This was not just an old flame, this was a bloody great fiery furnace, just about to start burning furiously all over again.

We stood around for a moment or so, nobody knowing quite what to say or how to start it off, and then Daphne suggested we go into the sitting room. She turned on the light, and there was a couple, snogging on the sofa. It was my Greasy Joan, and a rather gangly-looking bootneck subaltern. They sprang apart, and up, with a great jangling noise of sofa springs. Although I must say, neither of them had the grace to look much abashed about it, either. I ought to have been peeved, finding somebody pawing his hands all over my partner, but I could not really blame them. Certainly not the fellow. She was good for a cuddle, was Joan. Willing girls are always so much more sexy, I find. All that stuff about girls being more attractive if they're aloof and untouchable and want you to chase after them, that may have been all right for the troubadours, but for everybody else it's strictly for the medieval birds.

Daphne murmured something about "Oh Lord I'm sorry," but the two of them pushed off at a rate of knots, presumably to carry on with round two where they left off somewhere else less crowded.

The rest of the room was in as bad a condition as the sofa springs. There was actually a hole in the floor under the bookcase, where the floor-boards had actually rotted right through. They had a fire laid in the grate. Daphne put a match to it, but it smoked a lot and then went out. I expect the paper and the wood were damp. I wonder whatever happened to that farmhouse? Tom must have sold it, I suppose. It was in a shocking state, but it would be worth a bomb now, with some land, and the view it had. Although you'd have to spend thousands on it.

So we just sat on the sofa and the armchairs. I sat where Joan had been, the cushion was still warm from her delectable bottom. I can remember all this so brilliantly clearly because that was the effect Olivia always had on me. Just to see her seemed to raise all my powers of apprehension, making me just that much more sensitive and appreciative, feeling more alive, like having a layer of insulating skin peeled off.

I was feeling quietly paralysed with pleasure, so we sat and shivered for a bit. Daphne's party was in danger of dying on its feet. The rain had settled in relentlessly and people were starting to go. There's a limit to the amount of jollity one can generate in spite of the elements, and a lot of people had reached theirs. It's fine if you're seventeen or eighteen, you can laugh through a typhoon. But when you get on to our age, it becomes more difficult. People also had begun to sense that Daphne had another preoccupation now. She had better entertainment, anyway, for a bit. Some people who knew Olivia put their heads in through the doorway and waved. But it was funny that nobody was quite brave enough to come right in.

Daphne asked Olivia if she wanted anything to eat. Olivia said she hadn't had anything since lunchtime, and she was simply starving. Daphne stood up, to go and get her something, but then she sat down again. We could read it all, in the expressions passing over her face. We all knew what was going through her mind. She wanted to look after Olivia, but she didn't want to miss anything. She was terrified that Olivia would spill the beans in the most entrancing detail while she was out of the room. Tom saw what was happening and said he would get Olivia some salad. Tom really was the most sensationally incurious man I ever met. I never saw such an astonishingly impervious chap to gossip. He simply was not interested. A story that would have Daphne and me and Olivia too, come to that, riveted to the edges of our seats, would leave old Tom absolutely cold.

Of course, the very first thing burning to be asked was, what on earth was Olivia doing down there? I mean, it made no sort of sense at all. James was in London, or supposed to be. What was she doing away from home, away from James, in the West Country, of all places?

It turned out that James had arranged for Olivia to come down, had arranged for them both to come down. Olivia said they were going to stay with the Carpenters. At that, Daphne and I turned and looked at each other. The Carpenters had been at the party. They had, in fact, only just left. Tom must have passed Oliver Carpenter's car, or bloody nearly, in his gateway. Oliver was the Training Electrical at the Engineering College, and a bright lad, supposed to be. He was all right, in a bumptious sort of way, but Jane tended to give one a pain in the neck. Everything had to be just so, for her. She always tried to fix things, down to the last detail. As someone once said to me, when you stayed with the Carpenters, everything became, an evolution. Jane used to serve your breakfast as though she was putting you ashore from a landing craft with all your bag and hammock on the Normandy beaches.

"James was supposed to fix it all up with them, they've always been his friends, not mine," Olivia said.

"I don't think he could have done," said Daphne. "Because the Carpenters were here tonight. They've only just gone. You must have passed them. They didn't mention anything about you coming to stay."

Obviously, like the arrangement to come to Tom's barbecue, it had been left open, and in the event nobody had bothered to confirm or change it. It was all most unlike James. And most unlike Jane Carpenter, too, come to that. It was a blessing they had gone, otherwise Jane would have been all over us for explanations.

"I couldn't face having to be polite tonight to James' friends, especially those," said Olivia. "So can I stay here?"

"Of course," Daphne said warmly. "We took it for granted you would be."

I had not seen any suitcase with Olivia. She must have had one, which Tom must have brought in and put somewhere. Looking back now, I think that for that one night at least Olivia really did not know what she was doing or what she was going to do next. I really think she was letting events slide and take their course. I think James probably had made some arrangements for their visit but Olivia had worked herself up into such a state she either forgot or deliberately ignored what she was supposed to do and just took off, and came down to the West Country because she remembered vaguely that was where she had planned to go next, and when she got to the station she remembered Tom and Daphne and rang them up. They certainly were not James' friends, in fact, as I recall, James was one of the very few men I ever knew of who had ever managed to quarrel with Tom.

"But what about James?" Daphne asked. "Is he coming down here, or going to your house in Chichester, or what? What's he doing tonight?"

"I don't know," Olivia said defiantly. "And I don't give a damn either. I don't care where he is. He can look after himself."

We all had the same guilty thrill at hearing that. The idea of James of all people coming home to an empty house and cooking his own supper, a boiled egg or something, somehow it just wasn't on, it just wasn't James Bellingham. The picture of James coming home to a house where everything was not organised, not prepared, not in its place, it hardly seemed conceivable.

We have to remember that nobody owed James or Olivia any goodwill. They had certainly never put themselves out to be particularly kind or obliging to anybody, or polite or considerate. They had always gone their own way and expected everybody else to follow or put up with them, or do the other thing. They had at times been downright rude to me. All the same, there was a certain delicacy in that situation in Daphne's sitting room there that night. Even if perhaps James and Olivia themselves did not quite deserve it, their very predicament compelled a sort of respect. The events themselves demanded that we treat them tactfully. Eventually it was Daphne who took the plunge and finally said, "Well, what happens now? Are you going back, or what are you going to do?"

I briefly held my breath at this, knowing how Olivia might take it. I knew her. I knew you could get anything out of Olivia provided she didn't know what you were up to. I knew she would tell everything, provided she didn't realise she was telling anything. The moment she realised she was gossiping about her own private life she would shut up like a clam.

Olivia said, quite firmly, "I am not going back. The moment I saw him again I knew it was all over. It would never work. We've been married nine years. We've no children. Nothing. Nothing left. Nobody needs to be sympathetic to me because I haven't got any children. I'm used to that. I don't need sympathy for that. There's nothing there. Nothing left."

"Oh Olivia," Daphne protested, "don't say that. There is something there, always there is."

"It's true," Olivia said. "I hate it. I hate him."

Tom came in, with a plate of salad and chicken, and a glass of wine for Olivia. She was obviously very hungry indeed and began to eat as though she was ravenous. Tom stood by the chimney-piece and kicked at the remains of the fire. He too had been one of Olivia's boyfriends, way back. I wondered suddenly whether Daphne knew about that.

In between mouthfuls, Olivia insisted that her marriage was over. "I've finished with it," she kept saying.

It was almost comical to see and hear Olivia then. She really was a bit of a ham actress in the most shameless way. Her words were so much at odds with her appearance. Here was a radiantly healthy and very attractive woman in the prime of life, heartily filling herself with the most excellent, health-giving, nutritious, calorific food, protesting that her life, including her sex-life, was finished. That did not detract from the sincerity of what she was saying. She meant it, all right. But it just made the whole thing that much more bizarre to listen to.

"That commission out in the Far East, confrontation, or whatever it was called, it was a godsend," said Olivia. "It saved me from going mad, and our marriage from going on the rocks right there and then. Everything started to go wrong in James' last job, before he got sent to *Pandora*. He was a term officer at Dartmouth."

But surely, we all said at once, that must have been the most perfectly marvellous job.

"Too marvellous," Olivia said. "I started off like everybody else, by liking it, by absolutely loving it. I ended by hating every minute of it and longing to get away."

"You hated the Britannia College," said Daphne, obviously hardly able to believe her ears.

"Yes," Olivia said. "Everybody there too self-consciously aware of how good they were at their jobs. I mean, everybody knew they were specially selected, or they wouldn't be there. Too many up-and-coming Chiefs and no honest-to-goodness ordinary Indians. I am sure everywhere needs a few duds about the place, just to redress the balance. It's not good to have simply everybody all burning with a hard gem-like flame the whole time. But there didn't seem to be any duds at Dartmouth. They were all trying hard to outshine each other, all in the most subtle and clever and brilliant way. There seemed to be a formal, ritual way of talking about College matters, so that you never quite knew what people were really thinking. They used to talk about things like enthusiasm and training and commitment in a sort of ritualistic way, using catch-phrases, so that eventually I began to wonder whether anybody really knew what the words meant or whether it was just me who was slowly going round the bend. Perhaps the reason was that it was so difficult for any of them to judge how well they were really doing or whether in fact they were achieving anything."

This time it was my turn to feel disbelieving. I had never, ever, in all the years I had known her, heard Olivia talk with anything like this detachment and sharpness. Poor James, must have felt himself punched in the solar plexus to hear Olivia in this mood. To have your wife suddenly show that she had rumbled you, and rumbled all your fellow officers, too, well it must have been like a solid blow behind the ear-hole.

"Of course," said Olivia, "it was a heavenly place. But it is still a very monastic set-up at the College. There's a feeling of claustrophobia about it all. Everybody lives miles away from each other and miles away from the College, everybody in heavenly Devon farmhouses or converted heavenly Devon cottages. It was all beautiful, beautifully claustrophobic and sweet and frightfully heavenly, frightfully, frightfully."

Once again, Daphne and I looked at each other. Could this be Olivia Bellingham of all people talking of the social life in this way? She and James had always been the pacemakers wherever they had been. It had always been a case of keeping up, not with the Joneses, the Joneses were dead easy, but keeping up with the Bellinghams. Wherever they went throughout their married life, James either knew people in the Service or Olivia had some relative or other on the spot, so that whatever they wanted, a furnished house to rent, or a room to stay for the night, they always knew somebody who could help out. They were the living, breathing, jumping examples of the old rule that it doesn't matter what you know, it's who you know.

Olivia was still going on about James. "He was frightfully worked up about his career at Dartmouth," she said. "He was always terribly terribly conscious that it was a good job to have. I did my best to play my part, too, I used to have all the right people to dinner, and go to all the College functions that I was supposed to go to. The funny thing was that I used to enjoy that sort of thing. Until at last, I asked myself, why am I doing all this? What am I doing? What's it all leading up to? Does it matter if it isn't leading up to anything? The answer to that was, yes, it bloody well did matter. It's my life, the only life I've got, or ever likely to have. I don't believe in anything after we're dead. We only live on in our children, and we don't have any children. This, this, is my only chance to exist and its slipping away from me. Half of it has gone already. Chatting to Mrs Captain of the College, and going to coffee mornings, and College chapel, and the local committee of the King George's Fund for Sailors or whatever they call themselves. My younger sister is doing exactly the same thing.

She married a lawyer who wants to be a Member of Parliament He's terribly terribly active and socially-aware in local politics in Richmond, Surrey, where they live. He was a councillor or something, until the Liberals got in. We did some house-to-house canvassing for him once. I remember, it was the most tremendous fun. You've met Toby, haven't you Freddie," she said to me.

Yes indeed, I said. I had indeed. He was a climber. He married Victoria, Olivia's younger sister, for social gain. It was sheer, naked, unashamed, unabashed social climbing. It was almost awe-inspiring to see such terrifyingly unclothed ambition at work. He couldn't rest, poor chap. It must be like having a great team of scorpions chewing you up inside, night and day.

"The trouble about Dartmouth," Olivia said, "was that it did go on so. It was like a garden party that never came to an end. Just as you thought everybody was going, it all started up all over again. What was interesting the first year you were there became a bit of a drag the second year, and if you stayed any longer it became a purgatory. I am sure that for those involved, like James and his cronies, it was all very rewarding and interesting and career-motivated, as they say. But for me it was one great yawn from about eighteen months on. How some of the teaching staff stayed there for years and years I have no idea. Perhaps they had a different outlook on things. For instance, it was quite fun to watch James playing cricket for the Officers and Masters the first summer. But the second was a drag. During one of the matches James hurt one of the midshipmen. It was rather an unpleasant incident. The boy was fielding very close to the batsman, at one of those positions, silly mid-off or something. It certainly was a jolly silly position to be fielding. James thought so too, he kept turning to the boy and waving his bat at him, telling him to move further off. But the lad stayed where he was. Eventually, James hit a ball straight at him. It hit him on the head with a terrible crack which rang round and round the field. The lad dropped as though he'd been shot. He'd been completely knocked out. Of course, everybody rushed to look after him and see what was the matter. Except James. He still stood at his crease. It seemed very obvious and it didn't make a good impression at all. They helped the lad off the field and took him to the sickbay. He had concussion. James merely said that it was all his own fault, he shouldn't have stood so close after he'd been advised to move away. There is something terribly callous about James," Olivia said.

There was a snap of malice in Olivia's voice as she told the story. This one, I knew, would gain in the telling. It would get smoother, and more circumstantial with use, more damning, more humiliating. If their separation lengthened into divorce, this story would begin to come trippingly off Olivia's tongue, because I suspected she was one of those women who would never let go. She would pretend to be indifferent to her ex-husband, but in reality she would always be watching and waiting for fresh ammunition against him. She would always be greedy for any story discreditable to him. We were hearing this for the first time, I expect, but it would get better. In a few years time, James would have aimed the stroke deliberately and half-killed that boy. That is, unless Olivia got herself a lover or another husband, to keep her warm and occupied.

"I had a great uncle Henry," Olivia was saying, "he was my grandfather's third brother, and he was in the Navy. He never married. Naval officers shouldn't marry. It's not fair."

This was absurd and unjust and ungrateful of Olivia. Her marriage to James had, as it happened, given her a great deal. I knew, we all of us knew, that she and James had had several early years of married life in which they had been very happy. As I said earlier, they suited each other, down to the ground. The reason Olivia had started to go sour on James was most probably because there was something of herself that she had discovered and disliked in him. It was not James so much as herself she was disgusted with. James had given her a great deal. Society being what it still is, a man does still offer a woman much on marrying her. The new company, the new life, setting up a new home, the expectation of a family, sexual excitement, for most girls this is a prospect of pure joy, to begin with, at any rate, whatever happens later. And you can say what you like but a naval officer still has a residual glamour. He is still what they used to call a catch. A girl who marries a naval officer may go anywhere, meet anyone, never know what the future may bring. Some girls like that prospect. Olivia was certainly one of them.

But all the same, I began to have a glimmering of insight into what had been happening to Olivia. It was something unexpected and rather brave. She was trying to break away. She had been a naval wife, and a very good one too, in what you might call a professional sense. But now she was trying to break away. It was an attempt at rebirth and of course it was very painful, all that tearing away of the tissue of a shared life. Part of her had died, in an emotional sense. Another part was reborn. And she was doing it in a typically 'Olivian' way. Not by adultery, not by overdoses of drugs or by taking to the bottle, but simply by taking a train and going to stay unexpectedly with friends. It seemed such a small and unimportant action to take, but to Olivia it was vastly important because she was doing it without James. That's the really crucial point. Without James. She was acting by and for herself, and not behaving as James' naval wife. It was an immense step for her to take because for all her glamour and her attraction, Olivia had never really been an independent person. She was a brilliant reflector, but never a source of light. At least, that is how she appeared to me. It seems now that I may have been wrong about her. As time goes by, it seems that the only thing one knows about people is that one knows nothing about people.

"People," Olivia was saying, "are always talking about the loneliness of the captain. The loneliness of command, she said it roundly and plummily, she was able to imitate very well the rather pretentious phrase spoken by some pompous bore. The loneliness of command," she said. "Nobody ever thinks of the loneliness of the captain's wife. I literally didn't have any friends at all. When I was playing at being the captain's wife, I might as well have been on the moon as on the earth's surface. There was nobody there. The Engineer Officer's wife used to come round for coffee, but she was careful not to overstep the mark, I think the phrase is, and she had three young and rather smelly and dirty children. Sometimes I used to wish to God she would overstep the mark a bit and for God's sake act normal. James went away on one of those courses which teach them how to be captain of a frigate, and he got frightfully worked up about it. Come to think of it, James was almost always frightfully worked up about something, and almost always away. I do think it is a myth about naval officers being at home more these days. They may not go abroad to China for a three year commission as they used to, but the Navy doesn't seem to be able to let them alone, they're always being sent away on courses and visits and God knows what else. They're only away a few days or weeks at most, but they mount up and if you choose a day at random in the year nine times out of ten the husband will be away."

Olivia stopped in full flood and looked at us. "Do you still do your mad pottery, Daphne?" she asked.

This was a very disconcerting shift of attention, and it caught us all flat aback. Olivia was so good at occupying centre stage, so certain and quite rightly that everybody wanted to look at her that it took us all aback when she suddenly shifted subject like that. We should have been relieved, instead of which we were vaguely impatient and resentful as though we had been cheated of what was our right. Yet even this small slide showed me something fresh about Olivia. She was like a kingfisher, all flash and colour, blue flash and bright. It was as though there was too much of her showing above the surface, too transparent she was, too shallow, if that's the right word, to bear up for very long against someone like James. The wonder of it was that she had lasted as long as she had. How they must have hurt each other, by saying too much and revealing too much. People can be too articulate to make a good marriage. It was like Olivia, just like her, to use the word 'mad' about Daphne's pottery. In her own way Olivia was a very conventional person. Mad is the word she would have used for anybody suddenly going off and doing something like pottery. Or come to that, like suddenly going off to the West Country, without her husband.

Daphne said. "Pottery?" in a sort of dazed way. She was just as taken by surprise as any of us and for a little space did not seem to know what Olivia was talking about. "Oh that," she said. "Pottery. Yes, I still do it. Every Thursday night."

Nobody wanted to talk about Daphne's pottery classes at a time like that, least of all Daphne. In any case, we were sitting slap bang in the middle of the biggest and most important room in the house, which should have been the hub of the party. And there was the even bigger attraction of Olivia sitting there. I have to admit that James was a Service celebrity in a way that I never was, never had been, and never will be. Olivia was his wife and known to be his wife, and celebrity on her own account and together as a couple they attracted attention, there is no doubt about that. They had a circle of friends much wider and much more senior than most officers of James' rank would be likely to have. People knew them, or if they didn't actually know them, they knew of them. Their doings were gossip. So that sight of Olivia sitting on that sofa with me tended to stop Daphne's party in its tracks. Daphne seemed at long last to realise this. She couldn't abdicate all her responsibilities as a hostess indefinitely. She still had guests she ought to be looking after. Everybody was coming up to her and saying "Hello Olivia, lovely to see you," and saying to Daphne, "Lovely party, Daf," in the sort of voice which showed that it was anything but a lovely party. Daphne began to get furious, I could see it, especially when Barbara Manning, that's Bob Manning the Gunner's wife, and Daphne's chief social rival, came up and said something sweetly poisonous. Daphne was chiefly furious with Olivia, for knocking her party sideways. I suppose the truth was that they were friends but much more deeply they were rivals, as I expect all women are really.

Obeying some spasm of flight routine, the stewardesses were once more approaching them, along the passenger aisle. The plates and cutlery of the meal had been cleared away, and coffee was being served. Once again, Freddie broke off his narrative to look out of the black porthole window beside him. His story, which had seemed to its listeners to be spinning out like their journey through the upper air, as headlong and as continuous, came to an uncomfortable halt. What had begun as almost apologetic gossip to the casual acquaintances of a journey had now taken on the stature of a saga. It was now as necessary for his audience to hear the story as it was for Freddie to tell it. Freddie appeared to be considering his own conduct, pondering whether he should go on or stop now. His listeners knew, without consulting amongst themselves, that he must go on.

The act of story-telling had made Freddie believe himself a better story-teller, made him believe that he was choosing better words and delivering them more interestingly. Like an athlete, he felt warmed up, all his muscles and fibres ready and eager. His reminiscence had generated its own glow, which now reached out to the farthest limit of his memory, illuminating matters which had lain hidden in the shadows for years, summoning back facts he had himself thought he had forgotten and was infinitely surprised to find he still remembered. There was a deep pleasure in knowing that one was telling a story well, but its rewards went further for Freddie even than that. He was convinced that the story should be complete and he would gain a long release from the telling. He would be shriven of it at last, freed from his old guilts. He could peel it away from him like an old spotted skin.

The listeners were already learning to interpret Freddie's vernacular. He had his own idiosyncratic way of remembering. He was not an accurate recorder. He contradicted himself, he left out some information and misleadingly embellished more. His audience knew they were witnessing only a form of the truth. Nevertheless it was a truth. His memory was selective, but within its limits his recall was total. Two of the audience knew James Bellingham slightly, and all three had heard of the larger events Freddie was describing. Thus they had at least some other perspective, however rudimentary, from which to judge Freddie's peculiar viewpoint. James Bellingham's story was already a shadowy fabric of rumour and badly-reported or blatantly misreported fact; it was a part now of naval folklore. Freddie's account of it was like a beam of intensely blinding light, directed here and there inside that structure of rumour. Freddie himself was like a man carrying a very bright torch, clambering and roaming about inside the crumbled ruins of some vast chamber, flashing his light from side to side and up and down, eventually subjecting the whole edifice to a momentary and seemingly random illumination. But Freddie's methods were not wholly without artifice. He directed his light only where, and for as long as he wished. His audience were well aware of Freddie's authority as a historian. These events had happened, and this man had watched them happen. Men and women had confided in him, and where they had not confided he had investigated for himself. He had been the participant of what he had seen. He had been recorder and rewarder, companion and critic. They all had a sudden and almost despairing sense that Freddie's memory, or rather the way in which Freddie chose to exert his memory, was now their only way back into the past. The events he was describing now only existed in the form that he related them. His version was now the only and authorised one.

The stewardesses had withdrawn, leaving Freddie and the listeners to their whiskies and their coffee. Still Freddie was silent, seemingly lost in his thoughts. The others were also silent, afraid to break the thread of his narrative. If they spoke amongst themselves, or introduced another topic to Freddie, he might never return to the main purpose. His story, they had decided, affected them all. James Bellingham's experience had as great a bearing on their own careers as it had had on James' own. His lesson was universally applicable. They had already learnt much, even at a basic level, from Freddie's strictures on James' uncharacteristically missed tricks. Freddie's story was worth listening to, even for such commentaries as those. But there was more, far more. James' predicament touched their own vocations. As Freddie had said, it raised fundamental questions to test every naval officer's convictions about his profession. They were all therefore relieved, in their various ways, when Freddie began again.

I could see there was going to be a slight hiatus in things just then, said Freddie, so I broke it up by asking Olivia if she would like to dance. Olivia, I should say, was the most fabulous dancer. Even as a young girl she had this talent. Her body moved like silk. You had the feeling of a real Rolls-Royce experience when you danced with Olivia. When we got to the floor it was almost empty. There was only Greasy Joan dancing with her Marine. She gave me an aggrieved look, which hurt me a little. After all, I hadn't done anything, had I? It was she who had rushed off with somebody else. And there was young Simon Fiddich, dancing with somebody else's wife, obviously.

"Do you remember us, Freddie?" Olivia said to me.

I didn't know which particular thing she wanted me to remember, but of course I knew exactly what she meant. She was talking about us, the two of us, when we were young. I had known Olivia all my life, just about. In that sense, James Bellingham was very much an outsider. He was very much a latecomer on the scene. I remembered the very first time I ever danced, danced properly, that is, and not in the nursery dancing classes, with Olivia. It must have been just after the war, at a Young Farmers' Dance down in the village at the British Legion Hall. Actually, hop would be a better word for it than dance. It was Christmas time, you know the sort of thing, Christmas decorations in the rafters, sandwiches, beer or cider or lemonade, a raffle for a bottle of sherry, and Victor Silvester records on a gramophone. Whenever I hear, even now, whenever I hear that sort of music, all those soupy strings with the two pianos thumping out the strict tempo, I think of that period in my life. I went in uniform, I was a midshipman then. My mother persuaded me to go in uniform, although like all NOs I always hate appearing anywhere in public in uniform. As a matter of fact, it did me a bit of good because Olivia loved uniforms. She was always a sucker for a uniform. Her elder brother took her to the hop. He'd been called up, and he was also in his uniform, a subaltern in the Coldstream Guards. Even in those days Rory was rather grand. He'd even been to Palestine or somewhere and he even had a medal up on his tunic. It was the General Service Medal or perhaps he was old enough for the Victory Medal, I can't remember now. Anyway, it was more than I could show, on my virgin doeskin. Rory always knew he was something special. He knew he wasn't cut out to be one of nature's hewers of wood and drawers of water. Not Rory. You had to admire him, someone who knew about himself and put on all the side in the world about it. He was one of nature's winners. But it was nicely done. You couldn't but admire Rory. Olivia was wearing a very old-fashioned-looking dress, it was quite out of this world, all frills and furbelows, she looked like something out of *Through the Looking Glass*. Her family were surprisingly unaware in that sort of thing. You'd think someone would know what sort of dress a young girl would wear to a dance at that time. However, I suppose it's a wonder they ever allowed her to go to a village hop at all. Olivia soon latched on to me. It may have been the uniform, it may have been the time was ripe, I don't know. As

I have said, she was the most sensationally sexy object, in spite of that dress or maybe even because of it. I was a virgin, too, and just the feel of her body against me was the most exciting feeling I'd ever had. I don't mind admitting, I soon began to get the most frightful aching pains in my balls, just holding her, and looking at her. She was eager for experience. I suggested going outside, for a breath of fresh air, to use the classic phrase. She jumped at it. Mind you, it was December, bitterly cold outside and drizzling with rain, and she just had that dress on. But Olivia wanted to know how much power she had. She had never really looked at me before, not properly, sexually, as a male animal. All of a sudden she changed, and suddenly she looked at me, a look as sharp as a jab with a spike. I knew she was looking at me for the first time. She wanted to experiment, the other girls had all talked. Now, she was thinking, here's Freddie, he's male, he's one of them, I'll start with him. I could almost hear her thinking it. I can try it out with Freddie, like a new game. Only, with somebody like Olivia, it soon stopped being a game, even though she was only just rising sixteen years old. Once Olivia started to experiment, things began to slip out of control. She allowed me to kiss her where I liked. I opened the front of her astonishing dress. I remember it had three large smooth buttons and a sort of hook and eye thing at the top. I can even remember that. It was the most curious feeling, of a young girl's very warm, astonishingly warm, flesh with drops of cold water on it. You could actually taste them. As I have said, she really was the most astoundingly sexually exciting experience I had ever come across, then or since. There is no doubt in my mind that if I had gone on I could have had her, to use a crude phrase, there and then, that evening, standing up, amongst dripping rhododendrons at the back of a village hall on a freezing cold rainy December evening. I had more control than she had. I always did. But even when I say that, I am not sure now. She was more than a sexual object, I do not want to give that impression. She was learning about her own future, so in a backhanded kind of way perhaps she had more control than I had. To put it in a rather pompous way, I think she knew then that her life, her career if you like, was going to be her life with men.

This was the background to my thoughts then, as Olivia and I circled rather carefully round Daphne's damp and cold barn floor. One thing I do remember about us, I said to her, you're purely as sexy as ever.

That was a fair enough thing to say to any woman for openers, but with Olivia it was fact and true, and she knew it was true.

"I would have been very disappointed if you hadn't said that," she said.

How could I say anything less, I said. You are, just as sexy. So what happens now with James and you? I said.

"Goodness how sudden," she said. "I have no idea at all, truly. It depends on a lot of things."

Shall you get a divorce, I said. In that light it was difficult for me to judge how she took the question. She just said, "I expect so. Why, does it mean anything to you?"

I was absolutely shocked. Of course it does, I said. I've known you and James, known you both, for a very long time. It matters a great deal to me what happens to you both.

"Why," she said, "do you want to marry me?"

Me? I admit I was amazed, utterly thrown off my guard.

"Well, that's a very flattering reaction," she said. "I must say you don't seem too keen. You needn't act so flabbergasted. One minute you're building a girl's morale up, the next you're making out she's past it."

Not at all, I protested. I was just a little taken aback, that's all.

I had been flabbergasted, but that did not last long. There's many a true word said in jest, and the more I thought of it the better idea it seemed. Why not marry Olivia myself, indeed why ever not?

CHAPTER 4

I must admit that it was an exciting prospect. Like everything else to do with Olivia, as far as I was concerned, it seemed to expand the possibilities of the future. It was the most intoxicating feeling she always gave me, that suddenly everything was magically changing for the better. But that was still in the future. In the meantime there was I, dancing around this barn-floor with Olivia, and still desperately curious about James. And oddly enough it was then that I got the first real information. It was second-hand, but at least not third fourth or *nth* hand, as it had been before. But I had to stretch for it, as with everything else with Olivia.

I said to her, did anything happen out there?

Not unreasonably, she had not a clue what I was talking about and asked me what I meant, did anything happen?

Anything wrong, anything out of the ordinary, I said, anything you heard about afterwards. My God, I felt I was being so clumsily crude, but I was desperate to know. Eventually I had to come right to it. Did James mention anything to you in his letters, I asked her.

She stared at me. "Freddie, what are you getting at?" she said.

Nothing, nothing, I said, nothing. I was just wondering if anything unusual had happened in *Pandora's* commission out in the Far East?

"Oh well," she said, "well, even if anything had, it would be no use asking me. That's all James' life, not mine. I play no part in that," she said, rather sadly, "never have had. As far as I know they commissioned, they worked up at Portland and then they went out to the Far East and then they all lived happily ever afterwards. The only thing I can think of now, now I think of it," she said, "was not something James told me about, but something that vaguely happened about five or six months ago. I don't remember exactly how long ago now," she said.

About the beginning of this year, I said.

"I suppose so," she said. "James' helicopter pilot came home, to do a course, or maybe he was leaving the Navy, I can't remember now. I remember James once telling me his helicopter pilot was a short service commission chap. One of those people who only sign on for a set period, you know?"

Of course I knew. What did he tell you, this man, I said.

"He called on me one afternoon and I gave him tea," she said.

The last thing I wanted was for Olivia to know how curious I was, so I did not say anything. I just had a tingling feeling that I was on the brink of finding out something. But then she looked like stopping and forgetting all about it for evermore, so I just had to prompt her.

Was that *Pandora's* chopper pilot, you mean, called on you? I said.

"Yes," she said. "A fellow called Hickey. He was a very nice boy. He had very crooked teeth and rather a bad complexion. But he was a nice lad, very polite and rather sexy, I should imagine. It was very nice of him to call. James certainly hadn't asked him to."

Yes, but what did he *say* I asked.

Now I had gone too far. "Why do you want to know so much," she said. She withdrew from me, and held her head and her body back and away from me. I had an irresistible memory of Olivia as a girl. We were both lying on the lawn outside her house, when we were both home for the summer holidays. She had an apple, and another one that she was supposed to give me, but she wouldn't. She held it at arm's length and rolled over, so that I could not reach. It happened that she was not wearing any knickers, and I can still remember being struck by a peculiar shock of feeling when I saw her body. I was thirteen, I suppose, and she was eleven or twelve. That incident was typical of Olivia. A tempting promise tempered with deprivation.

I had to try and restore the situation. I said that I was interested for the same reason as always. Because I had known them both so long and was always interested in what happened to James.

She snorted a bit at that. "He's not worth it," she said. "From what I recall of it, this story was not the sort that James would particularly want talked about. That's the impression I got."

Oh yes, I said, noncommittally and neutrally as I could.

"Yes," she said, "I got the strong feeling that the chopper pilot even disapproved of it. Damned cheek," Olivia said, somewhat illogically, "a fellow like that actually disapproving of James. Bloody cheeky."

It probably was, I said. What was it that he so disapproved of?

"It was some order James had given," she said.

I could feel this thrill in every part of me. Here, at last, I was going to get some real information. Something like a direct account, and not just party gossip. Eventually, bit by bit, I got it out of her as we danced around. Olivia was a terrible storyteller. No idea at all. If I hadn't been so keen I would have given it up as a bad job long before the end. Every bit of interest in James detracted from any interest in her, that was what Olivia thought, *ergo*, in her eyes interest in James was to be discouraged. She chopped and changed, lost the thread of what she was saying, waved suddenly to other people dancing by us, broke off in the middle of a word to shout to somebody she knew, went off at a tangent so that I had to keep hauling her back to the main point, as far as possible without letting her know what I was doing.

But briefly, I got something like the story. I have been keeping up the suspense a bit myself, for the sake of the story but it is a well-known tale now. Everybody has their own authentic version of it. But at that time, it was still news. I felt like a detective on a strong trail at last. It seems that *Pandora* was on one of these patrols between Borneo and Singapore, to intercept Indonesian junks, sampans and other small shipping which might be carrying ammunition or agents to Malaysia. This was Confrontation days, you understand. In the middle of one patrol they were called to do a special job along the coast of Borneo. There was a small town up a river, where the Resident and about six other Europeans had been captured by the rebels and were being held as hostages. The plan was for two landing craft full of Royal Marine commandos to go up river and surprise the rebels and free the prisoners. *Pandora* escorted the landing craft from Brunei Town, provided the landing craft crews, and generally watched over them and shepherded the whole party to and from the scene of action. She drew too much actually to go up the river, but she could wait off the entrance, ready to provide covering fire if need be.

Well, all went as merrily as a wedding bell. They arrived off the entrance at dead of night, off went the Marines in their landing craft, and landed in this town absolutely spot on, at first light. The rebels had sentries posted and opened up quite a heavy fire as the bootnecks landed. I should say that Olivia didn't tell me all this in so much detail. I am amplifying it with all that we heard much later.

Still under quite heavy fire, the Jollies stormed the police station, the hospital, and the local jailhouse which was next door, and where they had been informed the hostages were being kept. They found them all still alive and released them, took them back to the landing craft. Apparently it was just as well they got there that night. Two of the hostages were going to be executed in the morning, and two more the next morning. There were three women, too, with the party. They all embarked in the landing craft and set off down river. By this time *Pandora's* helicopter was airborne and it hovered over the river, spotting for *Pandoras* main armament which was providing counter-battery fire. Everybody came down river successfully. They even managed to take some prisoners and bring them, too. It was all rather splendid, cloak and dagger, an adventure story like one of those Victorian epics you used to read in the *Boys Own Paper*... *'Carruthers, the best opening bat in the flotilla, gallantly leads his men to complete success against the dastardly natives...'*

So far, so good, but when they reached the estuary, and the parties re-embarked and they all set out to sea, they saw a small sampan with three bods sitting in it, fishing. One of the three was subsequently thought to have been a woman. Somebody said afterwards that the sampan was not much bigger than a fourteen foot RNSA sailing dinghy, if that. It had been a long and anxious night. James had had no sleep all night. There had been casualties. Two of the Royal Marines had actually been killed and four others badly wounded. A third Marine, as it happened, died before lunchtime. So it is easy for people who were not there and not in that situation to be all cool, calm and collected about it and say what should and should not have been done. James was there, under stress, and had to make up his mind there and then.

To cut a long story short, James did not like the look of this sampan. He ordered his main armament to open fire on it. It seems it did not respond properly to the challenge and James wanted it clobbered, obviously under the principle of better safe than sorry. The guns' crews were amazed. So was everybody else. The Captain of Royal Marines, when he heard what was happening, went up to the bridge to give James the benefit of his advice. He had been out on the coast for eighteen months and was an expert on local conditions and local knowledge. James threw him off the bridge and the guns duly opened fire, in director control.

Well, they banged away in a desultory sort of manner for a minute or two, without achieving very much. The three bods in the sampan looked amazed but unhurt. *Pandora* was making the water all around them a bit choppy. They were getting wet, these three, but not hurt. Then James ordered them to go into local control and almost the very next round from 'A' turret hit the little mast of this thing. The sampan disintegrated into a shower of splinters. They never found any of the three bods. They were blown into the water and although *Pandora* closed them to pick up survivors, they never found anybody. They were only a maximum of five or six cables away, at any time, about half a mile or so at the most. Bloody nearly point-blank range.

After that, what somebody later described as a profound silence settled over *Pandora*. The chopper pilot, this Hickey fellow, had been overhead and seen the whole thing. When he landed on, he too went storming up to the bridge to tell James that he had seen that this craft was obviously only a native fishing boat and he had told the gunnery control so over his radio net, and they had acknowledged it. So why was *Pandora* opening fire on a non-target? James threw him off the bridge, too. That solved the problem of why young Hickey was home in UK. He was not going on a course. He was not going outside. James had sent him home. What his motives for going to see Olivia were, I couldn't think.

As she told me this, or as much of it as she knew, Olivia became much more interested in it as she became aware of its possibilities, as she realised at long last that there might be things in it discreditable to James. She asked me whether I thought it would harm James. I did not know quite what to say. I mean, it was already pretty damned clear it was not going to do him any good, that was for sure. But what the end result was likely to be, I could not say. And besides, something had just jogged my memory. I knew now that I had heard most of this story before. I had actually read it in the newspapers, early that year. I had not known that *Pandora* was involved in it. That had certainly not been mentioned in the Press. I began to wonder why. That alone showed there really was something behind all this business. You see, the Captain of Royal Marines got a gong. He got an MBE in the Birthday Honours, I had read his name in the list only a few days earlier. One would have expected the commanding officer of the frigate also to get something. OK, he might not rate a gong, but he should have got something, at least a mention, if not in despatches then at least in the newspapers. The more I thought about it, the more I thought how strange it was that neither I nor apparently anybody else had ever stopped to wonder what naval ship had been involved. Why wasn't she mentioned? They gave the names of the marines and the name of the minesweeper which went up the river the next day, and they even mentioned that the landing craft were ex-USN left over from the Second

World War. Why didn't they mention *Pandora*? Curiouser and ever curiouser. Again, it was evidence, circumstantial but direct evidence, that something rather shifty had been going on. It was like the dog in Sherlock Holmes that never barked. This was the frigate captain who was never named.

I am not going to tell you what happened later that evening because it is nobody's business but Olivia's and mine. I have never been one to kiss and tell, neither has Olivia, ever since we were children, although I must confess that I have come perilously close to it in the last few hours, it seems to me. However, enough to say that my plans for the weekend took a bit of a tumble. I kept a cottage over on the Cornish side and I was going to take Olivia there on Saturday afternoon and spend the weekend there. I was going to call for her at Tom and Daphne's before lunch, and I was looking forward very much to it. I normally went into the office in plain clothes on a Saturday morning, to look at the mail if there was any, and to check the signal log just to see if there was anything that required my attention. Nothing ever did, but this particular morning, by Sod's Law, I got a message that the Chief of Staff wanted me to go to sea. On Saturday morning, mind you. Not the usual day for staff trips to sea. And he meant it, too. He wanted me to go right away to check up on the messdeck ventilation of some frigate that was having trouble with hers. She was just commissioning and was going to go off to the Med. Happily I had a spare uniform hanging on a peg behind my office door and a shirt in a drawer, so after a quick and tender telephone call to Olivia, I was off. We did our trials, and on the way back, blow me down if we didn't get a Submiss signal. Some ruddy French submarine gone a-missing in the Bay of Biscay. So there I was, a whole weekend at sea, blowing a full gale, no rough-weather clothing, no shaving gear, not even a toothbrush. We didn't get in until lunchtime Monday. But that's all another story.

The Chief of Staff said he wanted a word with me before I left, and Dear God, before I properly knew what was happening I was up to my neck in James Bellingham again.

At that time the Chief of Staff was Fiery Ferdo. You probably all know the name. He's retired now, doubtless to the abundant relief of his many admirers. But in those days he was still in full flood and full flow. Like Ol' Man River, he just went rolling along.

Talking to Fiery in his office was always a highly nervous business, like fingering the sword of Damocles. At any minute he might come down chop and chop off your head. But as a rule I got on very well with Fiery, the reason for that probably being that my little part of ship never gave him any of what he called Nausea. Nausea with a decidedly capital N. By Nausea Fiery meant trouble, unpleasantness, tension, extra work, people coming down unexpectedly and unwelcomely from the Ministry of Defence, general distress, alarm and despondency. Fiery did not like Nausea. Whenever he spotted Nausea, or thought he spotted Nausea or there was even a suspicion that there might be what he thought was going to be Nausea, he went at it like a bull at a gate and battered it down and anybody who happened to be standing in the way or anywhere near simply got battered down flat at the same time. It was not wise to get anywhere between Fiery and what he thought was Nausea. He was a dear man, Fiery, actually, I was very fond of him. But this particular Saturday, after he had told me what the position was and why he wanted me to go to sea that day, he sort of hesitated. I could see he still had something on his mind. But I was not deceived. Fiery was often at his most dangerous when he appeared to be hesitating. He had a way of sometimes going balls out so delicately you didn't notice until it hit you. A mixture of Agag and Attila the Hun, that was Fiery.

"Look," he said, looking as coy as a virgin proposing marriage, "you're a great friend of Jimmy Bellingham's, aren't you?" Dear God, I thought, here we go again, is there no rest from it? It was typical of Fiery that he should call James Jimmy, as though he were deliberately trying to keep the conversation at an informal level, although nobody, nobody at all, ever called James Jimmy, and using the word Jimmy in fact only made the whole atmosphere that much more menacing, in some creepy unexplainable kind of way. I thought how odd it was that so many people had mentioned my friendship with James to me recently. In all the years I had known him, nobody had ever commented on our friendship before. I had not thought that anybody had even noticed it. Yet here they all were, queuing up to remind me that I was James' friend. Did they expect to find me betraying him in some way, I wondered? Now it occurred to me, there was an element of the Apostle Peter about it all. People constantly coming up and saying, "you're one of his. You know him, you're one of his friends, aren't you?"

Fiery was beetling his dark satanic eyebrows up and down at me. "Father was at a cocktail party with the Lord Mayor last night," he said, "and he was button-holed at one stage by Jonty Grigson who, in case you don't know," said Fiery, "is chairman of the local group of newspapers. He was going on about *Pandora*, as if he knew something about it Father didn't know, about that business at the beginning of the year which we had all thought was a very creditable piece of work, and then thought no more about it. It appears not to be quite the simple affair we thought. Anyway," Fiery said, "it is just possible it might not be." In other words, Fiery was saying, '*I fancy I detect the possible presence of Nausea, and I want to nip it in the bud, sharpish.*'

"Father isn't particularly concerned about it," Fiery said to me, "but he did think enough about it to mention it to me."

Fiery told me that the Admiral had discussed all that morning's business with him, gone over all the comings and goings and latest gossip, and then, almost as an after-thought, as Fiery was leaving the room, he had sprung *Pandora* on him. He asked him, very quietly, without making any fuss, just to look into this *Pandora* business. That was more than enough for Fiery. The casualness of the way the Admiral mentioned it spurred him on.

I thought, this, of course, is the beginning of the classical way in which James Bellingham affected everybody. For everybody, it always began as a little cloud out of the sea, like a man's hand. Nothing to worry about, really. Just thought I'd ask. No, I don't want to make too much of it. I knew the script well by then. It came on so gradually. The Admiral was a perfect case. He had thought everything was straightforward. Now, there was just a suspicion it might not be. He had heard something. Nothing much, nothing more than the faintest catspaw whisper across the surface of his awareness. But enough to pick away at his peace of mind. This kind of suspicion, the kind that was going round then about James, was the very worst for a professional naval officer. The least rumour of such a thing would warn anybody who knew anything about the Navy that it was bad, bad, bad, and had to be investigated. A doctor does a routine medical check on a patient, not suspecting anything in particular, when he notices the slightest change of colour or temperature, a tiny mole, say, where it shouldn't be, and because he is the man he is, because he is a doctor, he knows there might be something terribly wrong and he has to investigate. To use another analogy, to hear about James was to start a tiny wheel spinning, which eventually releases another, slightly bigger wheel which in turn relays a third, and so on, until you found yourself and everybody else in a damned great howling spinning roaring maelstrom.

But meanwhile Fiery was still darting his glances at me. It looked as if for the very first time in our acquaintance I was about to give him some Nausea. I could see his mind working. How could he head this off? And if he couldn't and it was already pretty obvious he couldn't, then how could he stop it going too far, how could he lessen its effects upon Father's peace of mind? He had a very able brain, old Fiery. Sometimes one thought that an intellect of that calibre was wasted in the Navy. He should have been employed in something rather more intelligently creative than saving Father from Nausea. Someone was telling me that he is now vegetating in his retirement somewhere in the country. Stoke Poges, or somewhere-ever. He too was contaminated by the affair, I believe. It was a damnable thing. It soiled everyone who came into contact with it in any way. Blackened them, at a touch, like pitch. They say that discredited French generals were always sent to Limoges. Perhaps our admirals go to Stoke Poges.

I knew that Fiery could be a most dangerous character if his hostility was once aroused. Once let him get an idea into that head of his and it would be the devil's own job to dislodge it. Let him once get the notion that James had brought the Service into disrepute, let him once think that James had done something slightly discreditable enough to get the Navy some slightly unfavourable mention in the Press, then he would be after James tooth and nail and claw his backbone open. He was a dirty fighter, Fiery.

"I am going to be absolutely blunt with you," he said, which was actually a hysterically funny cliché, because Fiery had never been anything but a bloody great blunt bludgeoning instrument in all his life. "If these reports are anything like true," said Fiery, "then it looks like cowardice at one end, or sadism at the other. Take your pick."

This was, of course, the most arrogant exaggeration I ever heard, designed to get me going.

"Well," Fiery said, "you're a friend of his, what about it?"

I felt like saying, what about what, but with Fiery in that mood it would have been the signal for him to go straight up through the deckhead like a rocket. In any case, I was suddenly tired of being messed about and quizzed and badgered and generally treated like a toad under the harrow over something that was basically nothing to do with me. If they wanted to know all these things, why the bloody hell didn't they ask James himself? Surely he was the most obvious person. That was in a way typical of James' life. He was never there when the brickbats were flying around. All the same, I made up my mind I was going to stick up for him and stop all this malicious chiyacking. As they say, I was going to stand up and be counted. All these shadows and innuendos and insinuations and rumours had better bloody well stop. That is what I thought.

I restrained my feelings as well as I could and told Fiery that it was totally absurd and a wicked libel to suggest that James was either a coward or a sadist. He was human, and liable to make a mistake, capable of making a mistake, just as we all were.

But my denial did not have quite the armour-plated solidity needed to stand up against Fiery. He could see he had reached me and he at once said, "by making a mistake, do you mean he could open fire on an unarmed, innocent native sampan, and not know what he was doing?"

This, again, was an absolutely monstrous question and I said that was not what I meant at all. I was quite sure that James would have identified his target properly.

That gave Fiery his opening. "You mean," he said triumphantly, "that he did know it was an unarmed innocent native sampan when he opened fire on it?" Fiery could detect Nausea now, all right, he could see it loud and clear, and the conversation was rapidly going beyond the point where I had any real contact with it. It was a completely unreal situation. Fiery was making the most absurdly outrageous accusations, as calmly as though he were talking about *Pandora's* paintwork or her defect list. I was beginning to get the eerie feeling that I was just a link in a circumstantial chain, which was going to work itself out to a conclusion whatever I did or did not do now. If I had not gone into the office that morning, I would not have met Fiery. If Fiery had not talked to me that morning, he would have had to wait until Monday, when he might have forgotten all about it and in any case everything would have looked completely different. If only … if only, if only, if only. As is so often the case, one can look back and think, if only, but then one sees that there really was nothing else he could have done. We were all being hurried, hurried, hurried onwards to play our little parts, each of us supporting the action for long enough to keep it going for the next, and then passing it on, like a line of firefighters passing buckets. Only, in my case it seemed that my bucket had petrol in it.

Because there is no doubt in my mind now that I made a complete hash of that interview with Fiery. I should have been far more firm with him, hard though it may have been. I should have trampled upon his suggestions, danced up and down on them, stamped them to shreds and kicked them out of doors, so that any question that James had behaved unworthily simply could not have survived. Fiery would have been convinced. I think he sincerely wanted to be convinced. He was only testing me. Or, I should have tried to persuade him that James really was guilty of some misdemeanour. Because, perversely, Fiery would have resisted that. He would have argued against it, and argued himself out of it. I should have been either exaggeratedly for, or exaggeratedly against James. What I should not have done was what I actually did, be in between, half and half, trying to be fair. You couldn't be fair with someone like Fiery on your neck. He had no time for people who tried to be fair. Being fair with him was like trying to be fair to a sabre-toothed tiger. With that sort of animal you either killed it stone dead, or you got out as fast and as far as you could. What you did not do was to hang about trying to convince it of the fairness of your case. Although Fiery was a very imaginative and sensitive man, dealing with him always had an alarming simplicity. He had a jumpy mind. He had a rat-trap mentality. Either open or, bang, it was shut, and God help anything that was in those jaws when it shut. It seemed that I had unwittingly led James up to those jaws and held him there while they closed, and all my efforts to wriggle him free only made it worse.

The damnable thing was that if I had actually tried to paint James as a double-dyed villain of the deepest and blackest hue, Fiery would have scoffed at me and ended up by liking James and being on his side. He would have resisted me. By taking half-measures, I did my full worst. I would have done better for my friend if I had tried to do him down. Very soon, I had the horrifying certainty that I had created an opponent for James. I had unintentionally got him an enemy. I had conjured up danger where there had been none before. And this enemy was far more dangerous, far more powerful and when aroused far more vindictive than any he could have reasonably expected.

It was partly to do with Fiery's own personality. Fiery had this enormous, unshakable, almost panoramic love for the Navy. He loved it above everything and anything else and he would protect it, come what may. He had a very simple code. You were either for him or against him. There was a kind of 'noble savage' simplicity about him. The friends of his enemies were his enemies. The enemies of his enemies were his friends. Yet Fiery's own private life was, to put it charitably, somewhat shady. He was always able to preserve this strange kind of dichotomy between his private and his professional existences. In uniform, on duty, Fiery was the parfait naval knight, pricking across the plain of life as straight as a die. In private, well, his wife had left him because she couldn't stand him any longer. His three children were at boarding school and came home for part of every holidays, and a right trio of tearaways they were, too. In the meantime, Fiery lived on and off in the most shameless fashion with a woman whom I happened to know from personal acquaintance was no better than she should be. She was a Second Officer in the Wrens, until the fifth month of her second child, when she had to retire. Hang up her boots, as they say. The first child died, but she had the second, a daughter called Emma. They all lived in a semi-detached up at Mutley Plain somewhere. Fiery used to take the sprog for walks in its push-cart in Central Park most Sundays, when it was fine. Unbelievable. Unbelievable sight. Dora, that was unbelievably her name, sometimes used to go with him. When his children were at home, she always took them out. In her bright pink woollen trouser suit, her brassy greeny-blonde hair done in a great beehive and her enormous glass earrings like young chandeliers. Unbelievable. Quite incredible, the whole set-up. But, there we are. As far as I know, nobody commented or said anything, to Fiery or Dora. Or Emma, come to that.

Of course, this most devasting effect of what I had said on Fiery may have been partly James' own fault. It may have been something in his own personality. There may have been something unlikeable in him which came over at second-hand. There are, certainly, most unfortunate people who always appear at their worst in anecdotes. However honest and modest and charming they may be in real life, and however much the person telling the story genuinely likes them, the person listening still thinks, goodness, what a snobbish, heartless, conceited or tricky man he must be. The fact that the teller means no harm probably makes it even worse.

Fiery said to me, "I'll tell you my opinion of your friend, from what little I know of him. I don't like the sound of him, that's a fact. Normally I would welcome a kindred spirit, especially one so junior. He's a flyer. I'm a flyer. He's an ambitious man. I'm ambitious. He seems to be able to manipulate people. So can I. He has you leaping up and down in his hand, doesn't he? We are birds of a feather, your friend and I. But there is still something about him that puts me off. The only point I can make in mitigation is that it is good to know that the days of ambition are not dead after all. Not that I really thought they were. But it is good to see that the Navy is still a career a man thinks is worthwhile being ambitious about. It shows there must be something in it, still."

Sitting here now, reflecting upon it all after the passage of so much time, I can see that Fiery really was talking the most arrant rubbish. After all, there was no evidence whatsoever that what James had ever done, he had done through ambition. Quite the opposite, if anything. If the rumours were at all true, then James had behaved in just the way an ambitious man would never have behaved. It seems to me that like so many others were going to do, Fiery was already using James as a yardstick to measure his own case by. It was as though James' story had a meaning and a practical application for everybody.

But I was not as wise as that at the time. I took Fiery at his face value then, and a pretty fearsome face it was. We had, in fact, got to the stage where it really did not matter anymore what James had done or not done. When it came down to it, it did not matter whether James had ever done anything at all. All that mattered was what people thought he had done, and how they altered their lives as a result of what they thought had happened. James made things happen. But he himself was not important. If it hadn't been him it would have been somebody else. In Fiery's case, I can see it now, James had the effect of making him cautious. The one thing a man like Fiery could never afford to be was cautious. His whole career had been a tremendous sustained *bravura* performance of confidence and apparent carelessness of consequences. Fiery had risen because it seemed that he never took any notice of anything that might stop him rising. So people got the idea that his rise was inevitable. The moment he hesitated, he fell. The man on the high tight-rope who all of a sudden looks down and thinks, Christ I'm a hell of a long way up here. Fiery never went on after rear-admiral. Whether it had anything to do with this, I don't know. Your guess is as good as mine. But that was a highly revealing remark about James being too junior. Too junior to be a danger to him, he meant. Never before or since have I ever heard a naval officer express himself in that way. Fiery had had several layers of self-protection scraped off.

James sometimes had that effect on people. I never heard what happened to Dora, either.

It was all most unfortunate. If only I had not come into the office that morning. I had a sudden thought of what I would do next, if I were in Fiery's place. He must have been a thought-reader, or perhaps there really is some mysterious way in which thoughts cross the gulf between us. But just as though I had spoken the words out loud, Fiery said "what's his Number One's name? Do you know him?"

I said I did and told him, thinking that this was a very ominous turn of events indeed.

Fiery had already picked up his telephone and asked for *Pandora's* wardroom.

By this time I was desperate to fend him off and so I blurted out, Surely, sir it wouldn't be ... I had to stop and search for the right word, I could not find it, with Fiery glaring expectantly at me. Surely, sir, I said, it would be unworthy to get at a man's First Lieutenant behind his back?

Fiery gave me a long, long look. But that shot went home all right. He put his receiver down and when it rang which it did almost at once he bellowed at it that he did not want a call after all.

I could do nothing right that morning. Having successfully warded Fiery away from James, he naturally looked around for another target. He was determined to have someone. And, of course, there was I, standing right in front of his Roman nose. It was the most peculiar, spine-tingling sensation, like watching a man-eating lion wake up, as I saw him slowly becoming aware of me in a new context. It was like watching helplessly while a great siege-gun barrel trains slowly round to point at you and you find yourself staring down its great black hole of a muzzle. It was that moment of recognition, which sometimes overtakes you, when you are talking to somebody and you suspect that there might be more to them than you thought.

"Just where do you come into all this, Freddie?" Fiery asked me. "You say you know nothing, and yet you seem to know a lot. Just what is your part in this?"

So I said it again, I was getting very bored with saying it, that I was probably, almost certainly, James' oldest friend in the Service. We had known each other since the day we both went to the Admiralty Interview.

But Fiery was on the attack now. "I am not sure I like you," he said, "any more than I like your friend. Of the two, I think I almost prefer him."

It was a serious temperamental weakness in Fiery and may well have been the reason why he went no further, that he did sometimes tend to drop his professional detachment and give way to this kind of wild personal abuse. Sometimes it worked, of course. In this case, as far as I could see, all it did was to complicate the situation.

"Let us see," said Fiery. "Let us get this on a proper footing. Since you already seem to know a lot about it, I want you to find out more. I want you to find out what has been going on in *Pandora* and come and tell me."

I said, do you mean you want me to carry out an investigation?

He roared at that. "No," he said, "I definitely do not mean an investigation. That is the last thing I want, and when I want it I wouldn't get you to do it. Investigations, courts martial, post-mortems, they only obscure the facts. There are too many people involved in them, too many reputations, too many people with too much face to lose, they're all too public and they allow too much time for covering up before they start.

No, I don't want evidence that you can use in court. I want the truth."

I could have said, 'What is truth, said jesting Pilate,' and would not stay for an answer. All the same, I knew what Fiery meant. The truth often cannot be expressed at all, not in the form of evidence at a court martial, anyway. I have been to three or four courts martial in my time and in every case it struck me that the nearest the proceedings got to any kind of human truth was in the speech of mitigation by the prisoner's friend. Fiery expected me to turn it down. I should have turned it down. I see that now. I saw it clearly enough then. Fiery could wrap it up anyway he liked but it was still a monstrous suggestion, that I should to all intents and purposes spy on my best friend. But Fiery was a difficult man to argue with, close to, eyeball to eyeball, as I was then. Besides, I have to admit that although it was a terrible thing to be asked to do, it gave me a secret guilty thrill. It was the sort of thing I am good at. I was already doing it off my own bat, anyway.

The first thing to do was what I had dissuaded Fiery from doing. Get hold of young Fiddich. I was sorry I had not taken advantage of his mood that first night in. He would have told me anything then, if I am any judge. He might not be so willing again. Anyway, when I got back from that wretched weekend at sea, I was on the lookout.

CHAPTER 5

Actually the first person concerned with *Pandora* I saw was not Fiddich but Hickey, the helicopter pilot. But I am coming to that in a minute. I got back from this wet, miserable, foul weekend at sea in a temper to match the weather. I must say, remembering it now, that summer must have been one of the worst in living memory. I don't care what the Meteorologists say about it, they never seem to have the same weather as the rest of us and they're always going on about a particularly fine August when everybody knows it rained cats and dogs almost every day. My memories of that particular summer are of days and days of grey skies, sweeping rain, going on board ships with everybody wearing oilskins and burberries, cancelled cricket matches, flooded fields, reading in the papers about railway embankments being washed away, and so on. That may be a subjective reaction of course, reflecting some of the events that were happening in our personal lives. One does tend to remember the weather in one's mind.

The ship did not come into the dockyard, but stayed out at a buoy in the Sound. She had only really come in to drop me and pick up some mail. The motor-boat taking me in broke down, of course, and by the time I did eventually get to Millbay Dock I was so late the staff car that had been waiting for me had pushed off, thinking I must have changed my plans. It was still raining hard, and when I did at last get to my cabin in the Barracks I was soaking wet, cold, tired, fed up, and in a fiendish temper. There was a message for me on a signal pad on my desk. It was from Olivia, asking me to ring her at Tom and Daphne's house.

Now this was a much more dramatic happening than it appears to be, because it was the very first time I could remember that Olivia had asked me to telephone her. I had rung her thousands of times, of course, in the past, but always on my own initiative, so to speak. I was welcome to ring her if I wanted, but only if I wanted. This was the first time she had taken such a lead and asked me to ring her. It is such a small thing but it was such an important sign of changing times. It was curious how Olivia was suddenly, and unprecedentedly, looking towards me and expecting me to take the lead. Somehow I had been mysteriously proposed, seconded and unanimously elected to look after Olivia.

But before that, I should explain that while I had been on that miserable weekend I had slipped on board and hit my head on a bulkhead. I had a damned great dark bruise on the side of my face, and a swelling which was very uncomfortable. It gave me a lop-sided and, Olivia said, a rather sinister look. She said she had spent the whole of that Sunday walking about on the moor. She said she hadn't been able to get away from cars and people near Yelverton so she got a bus up to Princeton, where it was bloody cold and windy and started to rain. There was no bus back, so she had to walk, until somebody gave her a lift. He turned out to be a friend of James' and she had the devil of a job to fend him off and stop him finding out too much with his wretched questions. He dropped her off, looking, so Olivia said, like one great big question-mark. She was annoyed with me for going off for the weekend and leaving her. That was a tremendously good sign, for me. I had thought about her a lot while I was tossing about and rolling to and fro in that damned frigate. It was curious, when you think about it. She had not known I was going to be there when she came down to the West Country. She had not even known that I was going to be at Tom and Daphne's party. But now it seemed that she was depending upon me, and waiting for me before deciding. This was a very new and intoxicating sensation. You must remember that I had what you might call a long back history of being second string and hanger-on where Olivia was concerned. She had always left me panting along far behind. Like the picnics at her home we used to go on, down by the river. She went on across the fields, while I carried the tea and her books and her hat and she never even looked back to see whether I had seen where she had gone. I don't know why I was always so subservient but I was. I just sort of grew up feeling that I had to let them take the lead. It was up to me to find out where they had gone and follow. But now, metaphorically speaking, she had stopped and was waiting for me to catch up and make up my mind. I couldn't help wishing she had stopped and waited more for me when we were children. Life might have been so very different for both of us.

It is strange, I can still feel vividly the force of the sunlight and the heat of those days by the river. That was a good summer, if you like. Rory used to come down sometimes. He taught me to swim. He was always a much better swimmer. He was brilliant, like a seal, a great brown sleek glistening seal. That may be why I never took a firmer line with Olivia, never pursued her. Never wooed her, that's the word I want. I was always afraid of Rory looking for me, judging me, laughing at me. I can remember one summer particularly. There were six or seven great baulks of timber lying in the park, down towards the river. They were the remains of the most giant oak trees, which had been cut down years before. The monstrous stumps had been grubbed up and left more or less where they were. They were superb toys. They were roughly shaped with a thick and a narrow end, and they stood about three or four feet off the deck. We used to pretend they were Spitfires or MTBs or tanks and used to play on them for hours. They are still there. I saw them the last time I drove through and it was so reassuring to see such tremendous landmarks from one's childhood.

There were some soldiers living in a camp in the park that year. They lived in Nissen huts. The huts are still there, too. The land agent and the Ministry of Defence are still locked in combat about who is responsible for pulling them down. There were Canadians amongst the soldiers, I remember, so I suppose that must have been the summer of the Dieppe Raid. One of the officers had rented one of the lodges and brought his wife and family up to stay. They had a child, a boy about Rory's age and size. He was called Matthew, I remember. We didn't like him, possibly because Olivia always used to pretend she liked him better than us. 'Us' being me, Rory and my younger brother Nick. And then there was Victoria, Olivia's younger sister.

One day we went down there and found Matthew playing by himself on the oak trees. Rory had a fight with him. It was a good match, although we thought Rory was winning. I was proud of Rory, and ashamed that it wasn't me fighting. My heart was banging away inside me. It must have been all over in a matter of minutes but to us it seemed to go on for ever, for hours, like the world. It was almost like one of those combats in the *Ilaid*, where there's time to describe each blow and where it landed and what injuries it caused and what the participants were thinking and what they said to each other. We thought, and we said, that Rory won. I am not so sure he was so certain about it. Neither of them won. It was a draw. They didn't shake hands or anything, nothing as sentimental as that, they were both the most tremendous realists, they got up and knocked the dirt off their knees and sleeves and then Matthew walked away. He didn't play on the oaks again, and Rory didn't fight him again, in fact, I think it was August by then, and the family left. I used to wonder what happened to Matthew.

When I had changed into a dry uniform I had to go back to the office to look at the signal log and see the mail and write up my profound thoughts about what had happened at sea during that weekend. It all took time. I saw Fiery coming down the corridor and I hurriedly nipped out of his way, hoping to God he didn't see me. The last thing I wanted was Fiery demanding progress reports.

So it was well on towards the evening when I got to the farm. I was a little taken aback to see Olivia apparently ready, with her coat on, sitting in the living room reading *The Field* and waiting for me. Her suitcase was packed and in the hallway. I damned nearly broke my neck on it as I went in. I must have looked at it, because Olivia at once said that she was coming to stay with me. I must have looked again because then she said, "I can't stay here, it isn't fair on Daphne." I asked where Daphne was. Olivia said she was upstairs resting. "She's been absolutely prostrate ever since her party. I don't think Daphne is nearly as fit as she makes out," she said.

That was true enough, and very perceptive of Olivia. She was the first to guess that there was anything wrong with Daphne. She called good-bye up the stairs and we heard a faint answer from Daphne. I am not sure, but I think, that was the last I ever heard from Daphne. Just a faint cry down a stairway. It makes you think.

At that time I had a cottage over on the Cornish side. Cottage was rather a grand name for what it was. It was the end one of a terrace of five small stone houses. I believe they used to be miners' houses at one time. They were on the main road just this side of Callington. They could not have been more inconvenient, the roar of main road traffic all day and most of the night, perched on the side of a steep hill, septic tank drainage, you had to park your car on the green grass verge opposite, cooking by Calor gas. But it did have a surprisingly big and pleasant garden at the back. They all did. I suppose they were built in the days when a miner expected to be able to grow all the vegetables for his family. Even in those days, there was a trend for weekend cottages. It wasn't as hectic as it is now but still, two more of that row were bought by somebody or other, I never met them or knew who they were, who came down at weekends. The terrace was called Sebastopol Buildings, so help me, that's what they were actually called. Sebastopol Buildings suited me in a strange way. It was somewhere to go if I wanted to sort out my thoughts, write a report or prepare a schedule of inspection, or anything which I wanted to do far from the madding crowd. It was where I took Olivia that evening.

"That's the good thing about you, Freddie," she said, as we went along. "You never give advice. You wouldn't believe how many people feel themselves free to give you advice. Everybody reckons they're an expert. Go back to him, they tell you. Leave him for good, they say. Get yourself a good lawyer and a hot lover, they say. They talk about Marriage Advice Bureau and marriage counsellors and Citizens' Advice Bureau and advisory boards and advisory panels, my God, the last thing we need any more of is advice. I am up to here with advice."

It seemed to me that Olivia was begging all sorts of questions by talking like that, not least, who was it who was giving her all this advice? According to her she had spent the whole of Sunday tramping about the moor all on her tod. There had hardly been time or the chance for shoals of people to give her advice. Most of the dialogue she was talking about must have gone on inside her own head. But still, and all the same, I knew what she meant, and I let it pass without comment, except just to make a mental note that she had apparently heard of marriage advice bureau. That could be an omen.

Then she said, "But what do you think I should do, Freddie?" I simply had to laugh out loud at that. It was vintage Olivia. One moment she was warmly praising me for not offering advice and the next she was asking me for my advice. Absolutely typical of her.

Not me, I said. Don't ask me. I'm an interested party, I said. The fact was that I was in a turmoil and I did not know how to answer her. My relationship with Olivia had so many layers and had been built up, if you like, over so many years. We had so many shared experiences, so much common ground. The memories merge after a time. It is hard to go back now and say, that is what I felt like then, that is what I decided to do then, because I am not sure now what I did feel and decide then. It is not like an archaeological dig, when you go down so far and when you reach a certain level you can say all this happened in the time of so-and-so. In our case, some of the most recent happenings lay the deepest in our natures. For a start, if I were to give Olivia advice, whose interests should I be considering? On the face of it, there was no percentage for me in encouraging her to go back to James or doing anything that would make it more likely she would go back to him. So not James' interests then, certainly not. But it could well be that where Olivia was concerned James' interests and mine coincided. With some wives it would have been quite enough to urge them to go back to their husbands to make quite sure they would not go back, at least for a long time. But with Olivia you never knew. She might take your advice, she might not. At the same time, Olivia did have a genuine need for help, and I recognised that. She was facing a future in which things might very well go very wrong for her.

There was nothing to eat in the house, and I hate cooking so I took her out that evening to the Abbey. It was just starting up then, and it was really good, the very best fresh West Country food. This was at the beginning of the boom in country restaurants, not just in the West Country but all over the UK it seemed. Most of them were rather precious and most of them still are. But this was a good one while it lasted. This was at the time when quite suddenly, over a period of what seemed like only a couple of years, everybody in the Navy all of a sudden owned a motor-car, even down to newly-joined ordinary seamen. Every ship alongside and every shore establishment all at once had a serious parking problem. First Lieutenants started to spend at least as much time wrestling with traffic problems as they did with problems on board.

I always found it difficult to think quite straight when I was with Olivia. She always infected me with her own highly individualistic way of looking at things. She always seemed to put me through an assault course of emotional gymnastics, like perpetually running up and down a register of notes, high to low and back again and up and down. I doted on her, and then I detested her, and hardly had I formed the thought that I did detest her than she would say something to make me roll over like a spaniel. And instead of rubbing then, she would poke me, hard. Yet I lusted after her, I plain lusted after her so much that I was sometimes in actual physical pain, and yet I had to restrain myself. I was a seething mass of contradictions, wanting to be her friend and yet knowing that friendship with a woman like that was like the kiss of death, much better to be her enemy, she would have to look at you, then. I would be furious that she was still taking me for granted, just like the old days, and the next minute I would know, from nothing more than her tone of voice, that she really was thinking of me and considering my feelings. Whether she knew what she was doing and tried to do it all the more, I have no idea. I believe it was quite unconscious, but whatever it was it kept me in a state of constant alarm and pleasure and chagrin and gratification.

Not to be mealy-mouthed about it, what I am trying to do I suppose is to describe the state of being in love. That's what it all boils down to. And I am trying to recreate it and redefine it many years afterwards and to an audience, if you will forgive me, of cool strangers. Not easily done.

When we got back, it was bitterly cold. In some of those Cornish houses, the damp strikes you right through to the bone. I lit a fire. Imagine it, a fire in June. We sat with mugs of coffee looking at it. Olivia didn't do a thing, never raised a finger. It was as though she had gone on strike as a housewife. She was not going to do a hand's turn while she was in this state of limbo, a sort of semi-matrimony, not knowing whether she was married or living in sin or what.

Not that she did any living in sin with me, not that night, there were two bedrooms in that little house and we slept in separate ones. I don't think I was capable of making love to Olivia that night and I think if I had tried she would have resisted me. I had talked so much and thought so much, and laughed and been annoyed so much that evening, and had my feelings hurt and then flattered and then hurt again so much, I was drained. A part of me was so keyed up and exhilarated I felt I could go on talking all night. But another half felt as though I had been up since very early that morning and was absolutely dog-tired. I went to sleep thinking about James and how strange it was that he should be so quiescent. It was ominous. I was afraid he was going to pop up like the Demon King at any time. *Pandora* had been back the best part of a week and he had been away almost all that time. It was very strange.

There was only one way to put this to a real test and that was to appear in public with Olivia and see what happened. It meant really walking right out into the open. It was the Command Sports Day that afternoon. What could be more public than that? It was a crazy situation really, most irregular. Here was Olivia, doing what can only be described as gallivanting about the place, living in various houses, sometimes with a man not her husband. It was all most peculiar, but I somehow accepted it.

I had to get up very early the next morning and go to sea yet again. I was preparing a new policy for the Command, based on Merchant Navy practice, where they always seem to be about five years ahead of us in living conditions, the modern merchantman anyway. The nearest we had to that was the latest fleet oilers and there was one coming in that afternoon. If I slapped it about I could spend the forenoon having a look round and get back when she sailed at noon. Olivia said she would come in later on the bus and meet me.

Father was always mildly keen on sports, you know, running and all that, and nearly always went himself, so the staff had a sort of tacit agreement amongst ourselves that some of us should be there at this sort of thing. Nothing as firm as a rota or anything, but a general sort of arrangement, and this year the lot had fallen on me to go to the Command Sports Day.

As a matter of fact, I had never been to one before and I quite enjoyed it. Looking down from the road above, the Brickfields looked like crocus-coloured dots on a green board. There were children running about and an ice-cream van and a Royal Marine band playing Gilbert and Sullivan or something. There were all manner of matelots doing all sorts of strenuous-looking things, hurling bits of metal about the place and propelling themselves horizontally or vertically through the air for improbable distances. It had been raining very hard most of the night and the tame springers on the staff must have thought seriously about cancelling it. There was still water lying about the place but happily the track was one of those all-weather, all singing all dancing ones. It had cleared up but there were low grey clouds rushing by overhead in a very freshish wind. The flags were flapping themselves to death. It looked as though it was going to rain again any time, and sure enough it did before the end of the afternoon.

It was quite pleasant to watch all that wasted energy, all that misdirected effort. Admittedly we are not so bad about these things as the pongos, but still I have sometimes thought we put too much emphasis on physical accomplishments. All these yacht races and mountaineering expeditions and canoeing over vast distances of impenetrable river and jungle and all that, they have always seemed to me to be merely exercises in self-advertisement and self-reassurance at the taxpayers' expense. I always say that if God had meant us to cross the Matto Grosso he would have built a motorway. But that may be sour grapes, I admit. I myself have never been the slightest good at any of these things. When I was a cadet I used to find such things as rope-climbing very nearly a physical impossibility. I was also what they used to call charmingly a backward swimmer, in spite of Rory's devoted tuition. I could play cricket, but that was all. And I could sail a boat, just about.

I am convinced that the emphasis laid on such things as sports days is the result of having Special Entry officers. I am sure that the average Dartmouth officer would be more than happy to leave such physical exertions behind him when he left Dartmouth. But the Special Entries all played for their first elevens and first fifteens and first eights and first sixes at their grammar schools and they merely carried on where they left off when they joined the Navy. The Navy must have seemed very like an extension of school for them. Sports days always remind me of what an essentially middle class service the Navy is. We even think everybody else is middle class. We call the Royal Family Brian and Brenda. After all, Nelson was a parson's son, just like me. Blake was a grammar school boy. Benbow's father was a leather tanner. Even in modern times, Cunningham was the son of the Professor of Anatomy at Trinity College Dublin. Max Horton's father was a stockbroker. You can't get much more middle-class than that. And if you wonder how I came to know so much about this, I once wrote an essay at Greenwich on the middle-class origins of the Navy's officers since Sir Walter Raleigh. Even he was a typically middle-class lad on the make. Needless to say, my essay did not win a gold medal. But I take that back. I may be being unfair. Maybe the essay wasn't good enough. But this Sports Day was just like any middle-class public school sports day. There was the Admiral, the headmaster, with his lady, and there were some of the staff. The housemasters, the captains of ships and shore establishments, were there, too, to cheer on their houses. And there, of course, were the boys, running about the place and disporting themselves.

My eye caused a lot of facetious comment, people asking me, didn't I like the shape of that doorpost as it was, and advising me next time that I should not be talking when I should have been listening. The first people we met were Bob Manning the Gunner and Barbara. At the time for some reason it was customary on the staff to call the Fleet Gunnery Officer by his surname and his specialisation, in a sort of Welsh way. Like Evans the Bread. Manning the Gunner. Manning the Guns it should have been, I suppose. Barbara was dressed up to the nineteens, she had given it the full Ascot in the Eighteen Nineties treatment, with a bloody great picture hat which kept on trying to take off in that wind, and she even had a parasol, of all the useless things that summer. As somebody once said, Barbara always dressed as though she was still trying to impress Queen Victoria. She was the most frightful snob, too, the most terrible name-dropper and social climber. But somehow it didn't matter with her. One didn't mind. She had a good heart. She was a great girl, Barbara, and I was very fond of her. She used to be a Wren before she was married. Her father was a dockyard matie in Pompey. They lived in a little terraced house behind the Keppels Head, somewhere near The Hard there. I know, because I once took her home, and met her old man. He was all over me. It was bloody tragic. He bloody nearly licked my boots. There was he, a foreman of slingers or something, and a big man in his own particular line, he could say unto one go and he goeth sort of touch, and just because I was an officer, though only a snotty-nosed sub, he was all over me. I should have been paying my respects to him. But there you are. I remember one New Year's Eve just after Bob and Barbara were married. They were living in a flat along the front at Southsea then. We all went to the Empire to see the nude show, about a dozen of us. Barbara was very incensed and said she was sure she could do better and when we got back to their flat, by God she did. She and another girl did the most fabulous strip-tease. She would have gone all the way if Bob hadn't managed to stop her. As I said, she was a great girl, Barbara.

It was at these Sports that I first clapped eyes on this Hickey pilot fellow. One of the oddest things about that whole *Pandora* affair, if I can call it that, was the weird way in which it used to produce new people in front of me and display them in a strangely intense light. This Hickey fellow was typical. From listening to him and watching him as he told his version I learned more about him than I would have done in ten years' normal acquaintance. Yet two days before these Sports I had never met him, never even heard of him, and I don't suppose I ever would. But now when I saw him I not only knew him, I knew quite a bit about him, too. And not only that. Because he was involved with James and *Pandora* and Olivia I was intensely interested in him.

I said before that Fiery had had several layers of protective skin stripped off. That was true of all of us, in our different ways. We were all that much more tender where this affair was concerned, more sensitive, more vulnerable. And although I did not realise it myself at the time, the same applied to Hickey, too. Of course he knew all about me, or rather as much about me as I knew about him, and for the same reason. He too was several layers shy. It took me ages to hoist this in, that everybody concerned was behaving abnormally. The atmosphere was always supercharged, with everybody acting unnaturally. We were all cavorting about in a strangely lurid light. It lasts today, the glow of it. Even now, if I meet somebody who was involved in that in those days, we exchange glances, and we know.

I was standing with Bob and Barbara Manning watching some race or other, I believe the staff actually had a team entered for those Sports so we had a bigger incentive that year, I was standing there just goofing when I noticed this young man with rather a red face which I saw was due to rather bad acne marks. He had a great tumble of fair hair and very white protruding teeth sticking out like a frill. He had a very smart blue blazer with a Fleet Air Arm squadron badge, all gold and black and scarlet, on the pocket and a stop-watch on a lanyard round his neck and a clip-board with papers on it. He was some sort of track official. Anyway, he was fussing around like a duck in a thunderstorm. It often happens at sports days, I've noticed, from Sunday School onwards. Give someone a little open-air authority and it goes to their heads. Bob Manning nudged me and nodded at Hickey and said, "Do you know who that is?" I looked at Hickey without the faintest clue who he could be. "That's James Bellingham's chopper pilot," Bob said. "Or ex-chopper pilot, I should say."

Now that, when you think about it, was another strange occurrence. Why, when you come to think about it, should the Fleet Gunnery Officer bother to point out to the Fleet Environmental Control Officer a young and almost totally obscure two-striper helicopter pilot? But he wasn't obscure, you see, he was James' pilot and that, whether he liked it or not, gave him a certain notoriety. He was notable for that, if nothing else. Bob Manning guessed I would be interested, and Bob was quite right. I was intensely interested, and very much wanted to meet him.

Barbara was looking intensely bored, and so was Olivia, when something happened that made both their days. This race was a fairly long one, three miles or something, it involved the runners running I don't know how many times round the track, it seemed about a dozen times. One of the runners had obviously left his proper running shorts behind and had so decided to run in his underpants instead. That would have been quite all right if he had had a normal pair, but whether he needed stronger elastic or whether he had an old pair which sagged like those Chilprufe ones one's mother used to buy at D. H. Evans at the beginning of the War, I don't know, but after a couple of laps this wretched fellow's John Thomas hung out in front of him and began to loll about from side to side. Barbara and Olivia soon noticed this, trust them, trust Barbara certainly, and they both went to the edge of the track to watch, absolutely fascinated, half gleeful, half embarrassed, every time this wretched man came round. Very soon nearly everybody noticed and they crowded the side of the track to cheer this poor bugger on. He was sweating and straining and his head was dipping from side to side and he couldn't understand why he was being cheered all the way round. He sort of half-waved and gave a tortured sickly sort of smile. The thing was that he was a very well-proportioned young lad but not a very good runner, so he fell further and further back in the race so he fell further and further out in front. And of course the further he fell back and the further he fell out the more he was cheered. I could sense the women tensing every time he came round. Eventually this Hickey man tried to tell him, tried to warn him, to draw his attention, making the whole thing much worse by hopping up and down beside the track, shouting and pointing. The runner took no notice and at last Barbara drew in her breath, inflated her massive chest until her breasts stood out a mile and bellowed, "Get off, you silly spoil-sport!" At which the whole crowd collapsed with laughter and Hickey dropped back as if he had been shot. I don't think I've ever laughed so much. Dear, oh dear oh dear, it was Barbara's voice, so indignant, that creased me. Actually, the runner took it all in very good part. After he had crossed the finishing line he noticed himself, tucked himself in and went off to a tremendous storm of clapping and cheering.

Hickey had noticed me, standing beside Barbara when she shouted at him. I found myself edging towards him. He went on with whatever he was supposed to be doing, officialling or whatever, but in that peculiar way one has he must have known I was approaching because at just the right moment, when I was near enough to hear him, he sensed that I was there, he turned round and said to me, "You're a great friend of Commander Bellingham's, sir, aren't you?"

Like a shot I said, yes, and did he want me to put in a good word for him? Now, I can't think why I said that. It was rude, unfair, unethical, downright disloyal, and disgraceful, all the disreputable things you can think of. He merely turned his lower lip down rather sulkily. He said it wouldn't do any good now.

I have to admit I found myself liking young Hickey. He was a likeable fellow. I liked him more each time I met him and I met him several times. What I am telling now he told me over a period of quite a little time. I won't burden you with all the ramifications and details of our acquaintance, just for the sake of this I am shortening it all and condensing what he told me over a period. I will just repeat in essence what he said had happened in *Pandora*. He even showed me a couple of letters he had written to his mother about it at the time, which he had written just because he wanted to set things down and get them clear while they were still fresh in his memory.

I have wondered since how Hickey knew so readily who I was. We'd never met before, to my knowledge, nor even seen each other before. He may have been cuter than I gave him credit for, and made it his business to find out who all the members of the admiral's staff were. Although it does seem very unlikely. Or perhaps he might have seen me or heard my name when I visited somewhere like Culdrose, which I did very occasionally.

Hickey turned out to be surprisingly articulate and intelligent. *Pandora* had been his first sea-going appointment and he adored it, until that incident. He had the greatest confidence in James, and the greatest affection for him. He relied on him absolutely. Whatever happened, Hickey believed that James would be able to sort it out. He had a vaguely provincial accent, Hickey did. For a long time I could not place it. It was not unpleasant, it just bothered me that I couldn't put a name or a region to it. Eventually I found that he came from Northampton. His father was an inspector of taxes, or something equally romantic.

It is very important to realise that Hickey admired James so tremendously. This is not some disgruntled matelot speaking. Hickey's account is all the more valuable because of it. He was ambitious, in his own way. I got the impression he hoped for a permanent commission, and he had hoped to get a good start towards it with James' recommend behind him. I suppose his was one of the minor tragedies, bound up in the major one. Hickey thought the Navy was a marvellous life. He was quite knocked over by it all, the social life, the new responsibilities, the life and atmosphere of a frigate wardroom, the strange places on the way to the Far East, the South African girls, beaches, barbecues, Cape brandy, the dramatic scenery, and then Singapore, the mysterious Orient, the whole Kipling scene. He lapped it all up. They were going on active service, too, not just peacetime flag-showing. Everything they did had a real purpose, they might get killed, they might distinguish themselves in some action, which all gave a tremendous appetite and zest to life. To someone like Hickey, a young man up from the provinces, a provincial hick if ever there was one, Her Majesty's Navy had an impact like a gigantic treble shot of adrenalin, neat, three times a day with his meals. Hickey was almost the perfect paradigm of the recruiter's dream. He actually saw an advertisement for aircrew in the paper, cut out the coupon and sent off for the bumph. When it came he read it, was thrilled and put his name down. He went through all the educational and medical and interview bits and pieces, thrilled to bits by it all. He told me that these first months of *Pandora's* commission were the happiest in his whole life.

Hickey worked up a very close relationship with James. Or he thought he had. A frigate captain and his chopper pilot have to be in fairly good tune with each other because after all, the chopper is a detachable part of the ship, like an extendable arm. A chopper pilot, a good one, should have a pretty firm grasp of what his captain is likely to want without having to be told in precise terms all the time. It was this supposedly close relationship with James that let Hickey down in the end. Someone like Hickey couldn't be expected to realise that you could only go so far on such presumption. Hickey presumed too far on his position and tried to tell James what he should and shouldn't do. James wouldn't stand for that, and he was quite right not to stand for it. But from that moment it all went wrong. I don't mean necessarily that Hickey won't now get a permanent commission. He might still do very well in and for the Navy. He might indeed. But something has gone for good and all. If happiness has any value then Hickey has had a tremendous loss. It will never be quite the same for him. What hurt him most, I think, was the feeling of having lost a hero. The lost leader syndrome, you could call it. Something mild and magnificent, in those words, had gone. Hickey was starstruck by the Navy and James personified it. He saw him as a sort of hero and father figure. I must confess that Hickey gave me a view of James I had never thought of before, it was altogether a new aspect. I had always, so to speak, looked across at James, from an equal position, of equality, socially and professionally, and the same age, too. Now I saw him through the eyes of a much younger, junior man, I was diving down and then taking a look up. It was quite a different perspective. You see people on a pedestal from down there. But it is down there, of course, that you get the best view of the feet of clay.

He was something of a poet in his own individual line, was Hickey. To hear him talk about flying a helicopter was quite an experience. A chopper is not the most elegant or the swiftest aerial charger, but he made it sound like riding Pegasus. To hear Hickey, driving a chopper was to go soaring up through the ways of the sun and the stars, up and up like Phaethon.

It was a shame, really it was. Hickey might have been quite something. He had an engaging personality, energy, tremendous energy, ambition, and an ability to learn, and most important, he really loved the Navy. He still does, but it is not the same. Ironically Hickey was probably a much better chap when it was all over, more mature, more mellow, much nicer. But something very vital and very important had been lost, sort of leached out of him by the acid of it. The Navy does not run on nice chaps and because of nice chaps and through nice chaps. It never did and never will, whatever anyone may tell you. The Navy works through men with that extra portion of zip about them. Nice is not the right word to describe them.

"This particular morning," Hickey said, "they took off just a few minutes before dawn." In those parts the dawn really did come up like thunder. One moment it was still quite dark and cool, rather quiet and pleasant. The next the sun came up like an explosion, like a great green flash up into the sky, Hickey said "you could feel the heat of it on your face at once, and the sea went an apple-green and opaque colour as though it was solid green jade with tiny ripples carved in it. The light was so bright in the cabin they had to wear sunglasses constantly, if you shut your eyes, you could still feel the light beating on your eyelids, and when they turned" Hickey said "the sunlight reflected and refracted on the glass in the most fantastic display of colours, splitting the beams into thousands of coloured sparkles, it was like sitting in the middle of a shattered rainbow, flashing and changing colour all the time. It was all rather beautiful," Hickey said he "never got used to it, it always made him blink and feel amazed."

"Anyway," Hickey said, he seemed quite carried away by his own narrative, "anyway enough of this travelogue stuff. It was a brilliant morning. They could see for miles and miles, right over the estuary and the scrub and the jungle across to the mountains inland. They looked like toy mountains. Actually they were reasonably high but on a morning like that they looked like a back-cloth on a toy-box, the background for a jigsaw puzzle or something. They could see some oil derricks clustered in a clump to starboard, to the south, with some rows and rows of pipes laid out in straight lines and some silver storage tanks, looking all neat and tidy like little snuff-boxes. All over the land beneath them they could see hundreds and hundreds of thin streams of smoke rising into the air, just as though someone had blown out dozens and dozens of little matches and left them to smoke on the ground. They were cooking fires or something. They followed the main river, there were two or three all joining in this common estuary, and they followed the biggest one upstream." Hickey said "it was a filthy brown mottled colour with bits floating down in it and what looked like currents, all knotted and twirling like muscles. The town they wanted was on the outside of a big sweeping bend. It looked, and I gather it was, a God-awful dump, a one-horse town if ever there was one, with just one street, leading down to a jetty on the river bank. There were a few white buildings, a couple of cars on the street, and a kind of matt-brown, a run-down-looking area behind with some ramshackle huts and old buildings. And that was all. It hardly seemed the place to make a fuss about. They couldn't see anything at first" so Hickey made a sweep up along the coast to the north, where he said "there was the most amazing sight of all, the trees which came down to the edge of the sea. They were like a thick dark blanket of thick dark furry stuff growing right up to the water. They couldn't go any further because the rest was literally mud-flats and tidal banks. The trees were cut off so sharply they made a clean line, as though they had been cut off with scissors. It was a peculiar optical illusion, you couldn't really judge how tall they were, but in fact those trees were ninety, perhaps a hundred, a hundred and twenty feet high. Inland the trees spread out, like a great green blanket," Hickey said, "but with humps in it, where there were small hillocks, and they were covered in trees, too. There was a long spit of land to the seaward and they could see that *Pandora* could have got closer to the action if she had gone round there to seaward and fired over the peninsula," with Hickey spotting for her. "She would have been safer and more accurate. As it was, she had to anchor in a quite narrow passage in the river with quite a strong current flowing. If anyone had looked at the chart, they could have seen the position. In a way," Hickey said "the Captain missed a trick there. Not often he did that," Hickey said.

I remember thinking, when I heard that, how odd, yet another missed trick by James. Odd that Hickey should have the same thoughts expressed in the same language as myself. Missed tricks. James' path recently was littered with them.

"It would have been much better," Hickey said, "if *Pandora* had been to seaward of this point of land because then she would not have seen this little sampan."

What about that, I asked Hickey, did you actually see it yourself?

"Oh my God, yes," he said. He could see it as he "started back towards the ship. They had done some spotting for counter-battery fire, as it was rather grandly called, actually it consisted of a few rounds of star-shell before dawn, before they got there, and about half a dozen rounds on a gun they had at a sort of post office place or a bank, it looked like." Hickey came back from this sweep to the north and the action had started. The landing party gave him the target, he identified it for the ship and everything was on its way. "It was all over in a matter of seconds, it seemed. The landing craft were on their way down-river, and it seemed all over bar the shouting." Hickey was on his way back to the ship when he saw what looked like "a shell-splash beside a small craft out in the estuary, it was very nearly out of the estuary altogether and in the open sea. There were two or three of them out there, but this one was the nearest to *Pandora* by about three-quarters of a mile. The others were much further out." Hickey listened on the gunnery net and to his amazement he said he could "hear ranges and bearings and target information being passed. They seemed to be talking about this little sampan and were firing at it." He said he could "hardly believe his eyes or ears." So he flew nearer to have a look, in case there was something he had missed about it. Perhaps it was towing a submarine or something! But he said he could see "absolutely nothing. Just three amazed-looking bods crouching in the bilges." They looked up and gestured at him in a kind of "indignant, or semi-indignant way as they came over." Hickey said he waved back. And then just as he was waving, "the little thing vanished in a tower of spray and splinters. Nothing left of it, except a few bits floating about like cork in a glass, a light mess on the water, perhaps some clothing. Otherwise, nothing left of it, not even three heads swimming for the shore." He told Guns over the speak-net who seemed very "curt and gruff." Anyway, he virtually told Hickey to shut up and land on again. He told Hickey he was well aware of what the target was and that was it. Hickey said "it must have been very disturbing for Guns to hear him talk like that just then. Guns was already upset by the choice of target" and then for Hickey to come chipping in screaming that it was only a native fishing craft, that must have been very upsetting. Guns told Hickey very curtly, "why had he flown over the target and fouled the range?"

I thought it remarkable, and touching, that Hickey should be so concerned about the Gunnery Officer's feeling. But Mickey was like that. People liked him, and he was one of those who came out of the *Pandora* affair with credit. One of the very few. Mickey Gibb, the Gunnery Officer, I mean.

Hickey was in no doubt about that sampan. He was sure then and he was sure now, he said, it was just a native fishing craft, nothing more or less.

But how could you be so certain, I asked him. There might have been something about it you didn't know.

He was a little taken aback at that. "There might have been, but there wasn't. And nothing has turned up since."

That was a good point and I had to give it to him. What happened when you got back on board, I said.

He said, he landed on and dashed straight up to the bridge. The Captain turned round and looked at him. They were all there, the whole bridge crew, standing in a group. Hickey saluted and said, "Sir, I am very much afraid that was only a fishing craft we were firing at. It was not a proper target."

I thought it strange that Hickey should recall the scene and the words on the bridge so precisely, what he said, what James did, where the others were standing, everybody's movements, it was clearly a fairly dramatic moment which must have impressed itself upon him.

"There was a silence," Hickey said, and what a silence. He could hear somebody "murmuring away in the background on the radio net with the shore." He began to be a little scared but he was so worked up he didn't care. He said "it was a criminal thing, a disgraceful thing to fire on that little boat." Hickey said he "must have been mad to go bursting up there to the bridge like that when it was obvious there was a hell of an atmosphere up there." He was told afterwards there had been some argy-bargy about it and James had simply over-ruled everybody. Things had only just calmed down a bit and there was Hickey, behaving like the proverbial bull in a china shop, blurting out what they were all still thinking. When Hickey started to say again that he thought it was only a fishing craft he suddenly exploded and blew him off the bridge. In front of everybody. Nobody had ever seen James so angry before. Hickey said "it really was a little frightening." He was quickly stopped because he honestly thought James was going to toss him overboard. There was such a highly-charged atmosphere on that bridge and Hickey arrived like a lightning conductor. The whole thing discharged itself in a great bolt to earth through Hickey.

I could see what Hickey meant, perhaps even more clearly than he could himself. That lightning bolt, as he put it, would charge every relationship he had with everybody on board. He would never stand the same towards James. Those who were loyal to James would look at him in another way now, so would those who disliked James or were envious of him. Hickey would be somebody new to them, too. Hickey had a sort of innocent, almost rustic, wisdom. To hear him talk about these things was to look at them in a totally new and fresh way, not like a professional naval officer but in a kind of wondering, nearly child-like way. The fact that Hickey was so innocent, so obviously free of any intrigue or personal animosity, must have goaded James all the more. He really was being accused out of the mouths of babes and suckling's. Hickey was a professional babe, in a nice sort of way.

"All this made us all churned up inside," Hickey said, "but two days later the General himself came on board, the General commanding all our troops in Borneo. Cor, he was a fire-eater and a half. He had a personality all right, like a drop-forge, crash he would come down on somebody as though a whole hillside had caved in on them. That was when Simon Fiddich began to play his tricks. I am not sure I like Simon Fiddich now," said Hickey. "He was very kind to me, but I don't trust him any more. He calculated too much. OK," Hickey said "I'm a newcomer, I don't know much about the Navy, I'm just a ruddy chopper pilot, just a dumb-headed chopper driver who regularly gets pissed ashore with his crew on Saturday nights. But there are some things you don't have to be a full-time naval officer to know about. There is such a thing as being too calculating, too clever. There are times when you should just forget about your career and just follow your nose and do as your conscience tells you. Simon was a wheeler-dealer. Always calculating the odds. He was rock determined that if there was going to be any nausea it wasn't going to affect him. Whatever happened and whoever else was going to get hurt, he was going to be fire-proof. And that's where he made his big mistake. He ploughed himself even deeper into the mire."

I remember what Hickey said particularly clearly because of his vivid mixture of metaphors. I am not saying I am repeating now exactly what he said, to the nearest word, but I am giving the general drift of it pretty accurately, as I remember it, as in fact I am doing all the conversations I am repeating now.

Hickey had seen Olivia standing with me and though he said good afternoon to her he did look somewhat abashed. I wondered why he had called on her, and what on earth they had talked about. Perhaps he had some notion of seducing her, in some way getting back at James. He said he wanted to meet the Captain's wife, to see what she was like. He had some mad thought that perhaps she could intercede for him, he said, or do something to help. But once he saw her, he knew she was not in his league.

It struck me that Hickey was being a mite too humble. From my own knowledge of Olivia I knew she was not as unapproachable as he seemed to think, in fact, given half a chance she might be only too approachable. However, I didn't want any competition from someone like Hickey. It was to my advantage to keep him in his state of self-imposed underestimation. I managed to imply by the expression on my face that yes, he had indeed been a bit presumptuous to call on Olivia and, no indeed, he didn't have a cat in hell's chance of getting anywhere with her.

But as I said, I got all this from Hickey over a period. At the time, on that day, I had very little chance to speak to him, because I suddenly looked over Olivia's shoulder at the gate entrance from Devonport and I said to her, don't look now, but here's your husband.

CHAPTER 6

James was striding along, down by the jumping pit. I could see his head and shoulders passing behind the crowd watching the jumping. Actually, he was easy to see because there weren't all that many people there. I may have given the wrong impression about that. These Sports were never very well supported. James was dressed just right. You could rely on him for that. A tweedish suit, and a dark green pork-pie hat. Exactly the proper rig for watching the Command Sports.

James looked the same as ever. I suppose I must have half expected him to look different, to reflect somehow in his appearance the great upheaval that had been taking place. But he was just the same. Fossilised into an out-of-date appearance. The rest of us had moved on through that weekend, but he seemed at rest, outside the main stream. He was the cause of it all, but he had stayed aloof.

Typically, James kept us hanging on one foot. As he seemed to be heading for us anyway, and as Olivia was not going to go to him, obviously, we waited where we were. But he stopped to chat with somebody, leaving us waiting. All my old affection for James, or most of it, came back as I watched him come towards us. After all, he was my friend still, and whatever he had done or not done, did not affect me personally. I mean, strictly speaking, he had not harmed me as a person.

James turned not a hair. He came up to us as coolly as though he had left us together for a few minutes while he had gone to get himself a programme or something. There was I, standing with his wife, having spent the night before with her, under the same roof. Not under the same blanket, but he did not know that. Olivia was a hard case, too. I do believe she actually liked the situation. Either the events of the past few days had been an elaborate joke, played by her, on me, or she was quite ready to take up with James again. Or, he had already slid so far out of her real life that she honestly did not give a damn. He did not kiss Olivia, or show any particular sign, as I said, just as though they had come that day together. He nodded to me, as if I had come up to chat with Olivia while he was away.

"Hello," he said, "hello Freddie. Not taking part?" By which I supposed he meant, was I running or jumping or something. Or perhaps he didn't mean anything.

"Freddie's got more sense, haven't you, Freddie?" Olivia said. That could have been a dig at James, who I knew used to be an athletic type. I heard when he was at Dartmouth he even took part in cross country runs and things with his cadets. Or it could equally have been a dig at me, because I was equally well-known as a non-athlete.

"All this," she said, waving her hand around at all the faces and the furious activity, "is far too much like hard work, isn't it, Freddie?" she said.

I could make a guess at what she was doing. She was playing the old trick of the girl in the schoolyard. The girl with two boys, both wanting her. Playing them off against each other. Though why Olivia should bother at a time like that amazed me.

Olivia was taking her line from James, of course. She didn't seem to care. The great blasé act. Where now was the Olivia who had said such sensational things at Daphne's party? Where was the desperate Olivia who had, at least according to her own account, paced up and down Dartmoor for a whole Sunday trying to sort her thoughts out? Where was the Olivia who had teased and tormented me for a whole evening at the Abbey and then stayed at Sebastopol Buildings with me? I don't know why I phrase it like this. Talking of Olivia always makes me rhetorical. Balanced sentences and rhetorical questions, and all that.

In a way, I suppose we both had to be grateful to James for playing it so icily coolly. We could not have afforded a scene of any sort then and there. We would not have known how to behave. He pitched in just right towards us. He had been away, there was no blinking round that, but only for a short while and for a short distance. He was, you see, beginning to assert his superiority again. He was manipulating things to suit his conception of them. I have no doubt at all that if James decided a scene would have suited his book better, we would have all been plunged into the middle of a furious row.

In his own style, James attracted as much attention as Olivia had done at Daphne's party. They had a maddening way of taking the centre of the stage, those two. Olivia walked off with James, hand in hand, if you please. I would not have believed it if I had not seen it myself. They promenaded along, in front of the main body of spectators. There was a form of grandstand, a contraption of staging and planks. The Admiral was standing on top of it, with a pair of binoculars, as though he was at a race meeting. James tipped his hat to Father, Father tipped his hat back to Olivia, and all went merry as a wedding bell.

I was looking very closely at James,, but when he met my eye he gave nothing away. Nothing at all. His face was absolutely bland. No sign that anything had affected him. I could see that if I was ever going to find out what went on in *Pandora* the hardest chap to find out from would be James himself. He looked impregnable, invulnerable. He had been vulnerable, for a short time in his cabin when *Pandora* first came back. By God, if I had known then what I knew later I would have made far more use of that time. But that little chink, that little gap had closed. A gap of another sort had opened up. I suddenly wondered whether I really knew him at all.

I could look at James' face that day, hear his voice, feel his presence. I am getting rhetorical again. I had this dead sensation, the very opposite of prickling feeling at the back of the neck, if you follow me, I had this feeling I don't know this chap. I don't know that voice, I don't know this man at all. And yet he was standing beside me the whole time and I knew perfectly well who he was.

James and Olivia were walking away, neither of them much concerned to see whether I was following or not. After all that work I had put in, all the things I had listened to, all the worrying and thinking and pondering on Olivia's behalf, it was a bit much. Only a short time before I had been, so I thought, the main influence in Olivia's life. It was a new responsibility and just as I was bracing up to assume it properly here was James back again.

James was very much more confident than when I had last seen him in the cuddy in *Pandora*. There was no doubt, I think, that *Pandora* had temporarily got him down. Even his tremendous self-confidence had been cracked a little. It was the closeness of all those faces, day after day, accusing him. But now he had had a chance to get away from her and from them, and this had encouraged him. He was very much more his old self. He might have been blazing mad inside, for all I knew, but on the outside he was as calm as an iceberg.

We passed Hickey, hurrying on his way to some officialling or other. He stopped for a moment in his stride and blushed. I did not know as much about him in *Pandora* then as I came to know later. All I knew then was that he had been James' chopper pilot and had left under something of a cloud. So although I expected him to react in some way when he saw James I remember I was surprised, slightly, to see him pause and then walk on, and blush bright red, even brighter red than he was anyway, and half-wave, half-salute, and shuffle on in an embarrassed sideways way.

Pandora actually had a team there at the Sports. It said a great deal for young Simon Fiddich's organising ability. They had been at sea for days and days, no chance to train or prepare, half their ship's company must have been on leave, and the other half must be duty watch, they had come back only a few days before from active service on the other side of the world, and yet here they were, running and jumping and generally gallivanting about with the best of them. I could see plenty of *Pandora's* officers. They seemed to have left only the sub on board as duty officer. It was a tremendous display of solidarity or defiance, or something. Was it solidarity against the world, or against their captain, or what? This was a factor I had tended to neglect, that very mysterious relationship between a captain and his ship, between the ship's officers and each other, between the officers and the ship's company.

Now I noticed it, I could see that all *Pandora's* team were wearing a special sort of T-shirt. I am surprised it was allowed but obviously special licence was permitted to a ship newly home, and I thought there might have been other reasons why the powers that be had decided to handle *Pandora* with kid gloves. They were the most absurd T-shirts, obviously from Hong Kong, a sort of sickly shocking pink, if you can imagine such a thing, a gooey electric pink you might call it, with a brownish tiger's head on the front and Tiger Tim written on the back, right across in huge Dayglo letters. They were not a very good team, they didn't seem to be winning anything, but at least they were taking part, in a terribly terribly British way. The bad boys of the Remove were redeeming themselves on the rugger pitch, sort of thing.

It was Olivia I was getting more and more annoyed with. After all she had said to me, here she was, walking along with James, not now quite hand in hand, not quite, but bloody nearly. Either it was an act, the whole thing, or she had been carried away by her own performance over the weekend and hadn't meant half the things she had told me, or maybe she really didn't give a damn for him. I didn't know which, but then something happened that gave me a clue. One of the *Pandoras* actually succeeded in getting into the medals.

It was the most unlikely thing. He did not win, but he was third. And it was in the javelin-throwing, of all things. It was one of their guns crew, I was told, a man called Prichard. Everybody was amazed, Prichard himself not least, I imagine. Because of all the events, so I was told, throwing the javelin is the one where you need to be most in practise, and of course, Prichard hadn't had the chance to practise at all. It demands, so they tell me, suppleness as well as strength, and the knack, the peculiar trick, of being able to throw the damned thing at all.

We nearly missed seeing it, as it happened. It was James who suddenly spotted the Tiger Tim vest running up and stopped to look, and so we all stopped. Up ran this lad Prichard, he was only a lad, and wound himself up in that extraordinary double-jointed sideways way they have and threw this javelin. It went up and up, it seemed to fly for miles, and all of us with it, before it dropped sharply and stuck itself in the grass. Prichard looked at it. Somebody clapped. But when James found out it was the last throw of the round, of the competition in fact, and it had put young Prichard in third place he went mad with delight. I've seldom seen him so delighted. He was like a rabbit with six tails, like a dog that's just dug up the biggest bone in town. He rushed up to Prichard and shook him by the hand so violently he must have nearly jerked Prichard's arm out of its socket. It was his throwing arm, too. Prichard looked terribly embarrassed by the whole thing, but still very pleased and bucked by it all, too. One or two of *Pandora's* sailors were saying 'Well done, Jan'. Prichard was a local lad apparently.

But Olivia never batted an eyelid the whole time. If she showed any emotion at all it was annoyance. She was not pleased that James was pleased. That gave me the clue. She didn't want him to have any pleasure. There was James leaping up and down like a two-year-old with a new toy engine, and there was Olivia looking at him as though he had made a mess on the rug. It revealed a somewhat unpleasant prospect for me, and a chilly feeling came over me when I saw it. If things went as I wished, would Olivia at some time in the future be as implacable with me? Would I catch her looking with those eyes at me, as she was looking at James now? That was not a very welcoming prospect. She wanted him to be hurt. I could not help thinking what marvellous actors they both were. I wondered how much more of their marriage was a brilliant performance. I mean, every marriage is a performance to a greater or lesser extent, but this one was way above average. This was in the international class. Anybody looking at them that day, anybody who didn't know, which meant pretty well everybody there except me, as I say, anybody watching would have thought, there is the Captain of *Pandora*, newly arrived from the Far East, and his wife, James and Olivia Bellingham, watching some of their sailors performing and putting up a pretty creditable performance at the Command Sports Day.

Bully for them. But underneath, things could not have been more wrong.

The same went for me, of course. After all, I was play-acting along as hard as any of them, and just as successfully. Anybody looking at me would have thought, there goes James' and Olivia's best friend, Freddie, bless his heart. Little did they know that I was lusting after her. I was the attendant lord in the play, swelling the progress and advising the prince and all that crap. Whereas, in fact, I was plotting how to stop the progress and put things into reverse, and if I had any advice for the prince, it would have been calculatedly bad advice. If there is one lesson that the *Pandora* business taught everybody, not just me, it was that things are seldom, if ever, what they seem.

It shows how conceited and self-centred one can be, given half a chance, but for a time that afternoon, as we walked along, the three of us, I was struck by the number of people we passed. Everybody was there. I had thought that the meeting was very poorly attended. I was quite wrong. There were loads of people there. I thought that the Command Sports Day was a very Third Division North fixture. Not a bit of it. Everybody had turned up to it and as we three promenaded along, I began to have the most eerie feeling that they had all come to see us, to see James and Olivia, rather. It was quite impossible, of course, but for a while it did seem that the word had got round that James was back and everybody had flocked to the ground to see what he was going to do. To see how he was taking it, would be a better way of putting it, maybe. I mean, when I come to think of it, it was very unusual to see somebody like Barbara Manning for instance at a sports day. My dear, that was certainly not her cup of tea.

I am appalled now to remember the baseness of my own motives in those days. I had only two objectives. One was

Olivia. The other was *Pandora*. In both cases I knew I was going to have to take on James by myself. And that was going to be hard slogging, I knew. I would have to take him on and beat him on his own ground.

James had been talking normally, I forget now what about, just ordinary gossip, and a bit of shop. Just what you would expect a very correct captain of a frigate to talk about at the Command Sports. Then, the atmosphere changed. He looked at his watch and said that he had to go back to the ship.

He whipped round on me. "I expect you will want to know what I'm going back for," he said.

Why ever should I? I said, knowing with a sinking feeling exactly what he meant.

"Why ever should you," he said, "because I hear you're doing some sort of investigation on us."

Not really, I said, wondering how he had come to hear so quickly.

"Not really," he said, imitating my voice in the most mocking way. "I know these not really investigations," he said. "They can do a hell of a lot of damage, in a not really sort of way. I am just waking up to an amazing fact of life, Freddie. I've just realised you can be dangerous to me. I never thought it possible. Dear, kind, lovable Freddie, whom we all know and love, because to know him is to love him."

That last bit was an even more subtle insult than any stranger listening to us could have guessed. When we were midshipmen together we had a bastard of a Commander and the gunroom used to say, the Commander, whom we all know and love, because to know him is to love him. So that had all sorts of connotations and memories and flavours. It reminded me that we had shared so much in the past, that I myself could never now be a Commander, that I was not alone in being able to coin insults. It brought the past back while at the same time reminding me how far away it was. It was an exquisitely pitched insult. Even I had to admire it.

I remember he looked at his watch again, in the most pointed manner and then directly at Olivia. "What about you?" he said, like a bull at a gate. "Are you coming with me or are you going with Freddie? You seem to be pretty thick with him again."

It was the way he said thick that hit me. I wondered how we had ever been friends. How can it be that you know somebody for years and years and suddenly find that you know nothing about him? Which is the real James, the friend of twenty years, or this last thirty seconds now of knife-play? I was quite wrong in thinking James had not changed. By God he had, and he had changed in a way which might make Olivia easier but would make *Pandora* immeasurably harder. It was perfectly obvious to me by then that the only person who really knew about *Pandora* was James himself and if I was ever going to find out, I was going to have to find out from him. That now was suddenly beginning to look impossible.

Olivia then astounded me by saying chirpily, "I'm going with Freddie of course."

Those two had always been able to outmanoeuvre me and dance rings around me. Here they were, doing it again. It was a devastating thing for Olivia to say. She simply had no idea of the implications of what she had said. She was just saying the first thing that came into her head and damn the consequences. Quite apart from any future legal repercussions of what she had just said, my life was not geared for the presence of any woman, not one woman permanently, or semi-permanently. In other words, now that what I had been gearing up to scheme for looked as though it was going to come about without any assistance from me, now that all my hopes looked as though they were going to be served up to me on a silver salver, I must admit that I had a pretty sharp attack of cold feet.

James did not show any emotion, but I guess she had hit him hard. It was not only what she said, but the airy flippant way she said it. She was not renouncing one great love for another. Not thinking the great world well lost for a great love. Not Antony and Cleopatra but changing your brand of margarine. Not dramatic, but domestic, if you follow me. It helps a man's self-esteem if he thinks he is an agent in a gigantic emotional upheaval involving three persons. Nobody likes to feel he is just last week's pair of shoes. It struck me that James had not been wise in going straight out for Olivia like that. She knew one or two worth three of that.

"All right," he said. "You must do what you think you must." I simply dared not meet his eye. But I felt the heat of it on my cheek. It gave me an inkling, a prickling feeling, of what I might be stumbling into. It was like moving a cover aside and looking down into a wickedly bright fire that you had never known was down there. Neither of them would have the least hesitation about using me against the other. Olivia was in fact probably doing just that. And yet, though I knew this, I could not stop myself. That's what lust does for you.

As though weariness had led to sudden discretion, Freddie broke off and craned his neck so that he could look out along the central aisle. The lights in the main cabin were dimming, as passengers settled themselves to sleep. Freddie laid his head back on the seat rest and closed his eyes. The others followed him, each man sitting capsuled in his own seat, listening to the sounds of the aircraft. Each could fancy he heard the quiet silken rustling of cold air rushing past the aircraft's smooth sides. Meanwhile each man struggled to resolve his own personal sense of disorientation. It was night and time for sleep, but none of them was ready for sleep, just as they had eaten a meal without being hungry. It was as though all their human needs and responses had been dislocated.

Heads lifted at a change of engine note, and a tilting of the deck. With disconcerting hesitations, the angles and attitudes of the aircraft were altering. The cabin changed its mental shape for the passengers, as they realised their aircraft was no longer flying steadily but preparing for landing. With fresh sounds, fresh vibrations, new pressures on eardrums and stomach diaphragms, the aircraft swung one wing up and slipped sideways, at once reminding every passenger strapped in of how fast he was being hurtled towards the earth. Lines and diagrams of lights slid under the wing, were blotted out momentarily, and appeared again, larger and brighter. While the passengers' bodies accepted the shock of landing, as though regaining a normal force of gravity, their minds were still amazed by the sheer unlikelihood of what was happening to them. Their physical frames were reassured to be once more back on earth, but a part of them was still shocked by its experience.

At rest, the great double doors opened, to let in the smells of dung and damp heat, the sounds of vehicles and voices, the sight of the terminal building lights, electric red and purple and blue, as violently coloured as Indian confectionery. After the first activity, there was a long lull. Nobody boarded the aircraft, and nobody left. The doors stayed open in the heat, while the passengers inside waited. There was an air of unfulfilled expectancy, as in a rural train standing stopped at a country station. In the dark beyond the door lay a great subcontinent, but it had no meaning for Freddie's listeners; their sense of unreality had been so heightened that the personalities of Freddie's narrative occupied all their thoughts. Freddie had described events which were dislocated in time and in space; there was the present, the 'now' of Freddie speaking, there was the immediate past, of his meeting with Olivia and James, and there was a remoter past, of *Pandora's* commission in the Far East. Freddie's listeners had to accustom themselves to the shifts in time, whilst themselves travelling from the theatre of one series of events to the scenes where the others had taken place. The sole link between them all was Freddie himself. When, eventually, the aircraft's double doors shut on the scene outside, Freddie's listeners were relieved, as though external irrelevancies had at last been excluded.

CHAPTER 7

New every morning is the light, our wakening and uprising prove, said Freddie. Or should it be, new every morning is the love, surely? I wonder what time it really is? Don't we have to keep putting our watches on, or is it back? I can never quite grasp it. I know we have to lose about eight gash hours before we get to UK. Odd how distracting a landing can be. It's thrown me all out. All I know is that I feel distinctly out of joint with myself.

It was still dark, although they had all woken from their light travel doze some time before. The stewardesses were bringing round breakfast trays with coffee and rolls and fruit juice, once again obeying some impulse of the aircraft's imposed internal routine rather than answering any bodily need of the passengers. It was time by the aircraft's clock for breakfast, and so breakfast was served. The passengers were getting up and taking it in turns to go to the toilet cubicle. One man was standing and stretching in the aisle, as though doing early morning callisthenics. There was a general air of domestic preparation for a new day. Dawn came through the aircraft windows, like a dawn at sea. The aircraft swam like a great fish above a grey sea floor of unbroken cloud. Above, the light was a deep violet shading to grey on the horizon. The others watched, mystified, Freddie leaning to and fro in his seat. There was a flaw, he had discovered, in the glass of the window nearest him. By leaning forward he could make a dark shape, like an intercepting fighter, appear apparently beyond the far wing-tip. When he leaned back, it vanished; forward, and it reappeared.

In daylight there was noticeably more noise in the aircraft main cabin. Sounds of rustling papers, crockery, people talking amongst themselves, though quiet, were enough to make Freddie pitch his voice higher, to carry to them all.

You, presumably, all still have prospects in the Service, Freddie said. Unlike me. Anybody with prospects, as they say, should be interested in James' story. It is not just idle gossip. There were all manner of people involved. I am thinking now of somebody else, and it all fits in very well with that day at the Sports with Olivia. She had said she wanted to go with me, rather than James. She was, of course, playing a game with me, just as they both always did. It was not important to her who I was just at that moment. All she wanted to do was to be able to say to James, I don't want you, I want this man. The fact that it was me, a not entirely impossible alternative, was just happy joss for Olivia. I don't flatter myself.

Just before we landed, I was remarking that that was what lust did for you. In fact, I never felt less lustful than when I began to walk back with Olivia to my motor-car, to set off again for Sebastopol Buildings, or somewhere, I was not sure where. It was all turning out to be very much more complicated than I had ever thought. I had made an enemy of James, or at the very least he was no longer my friend. I was involved in it all far, far more deeply than I ever wanted. It is one thing to be mildly interested in the comings and goings and general marital ups and downs of one's friends. It is quite another thing to suddenly find yourself one of the main protagonists. I was involved with Fiery, too, and that invariably meant trouble. He was no friendly, cosy sort of character to play about with. Worst of all, my name was beginning to spread about the Port in a way I did not want and did not like. I had been leading a comfortable existence down there. I was known by those who wanted to know me and whom I wanted to know. Life was pretty good. Now James and Olivia had dropped into everything. I might have given the impression that I was slightly jealous of their fame. Yes, I think fame is the very word I want. They were both famous. But I did not want to be famous. I had a dread of notoriety. I knew that the only way I could be who I was was by nobody knowing who I was. James and Olivia have this effect on me, even when I am just talking about them. They always made me start talking in paradoxical epigrams.

There never was a more reluctant swain than I was, at that moment. I can still remember vividly the sense of unreality I felt then. I was walking along with somebody's wife, James' wife, with not the faintest idea how I came to be so doing or what I was going to do next. My feelings seemed to have changed towards her completely. Or perhaps it is me who has changed. That landing has disrupted everything, shuffling up time and sense and recollection. I feel physically and mentally disorientated. There is a thought for all story-tellers, now. We not only remember what we think is the truth differently every time we tell it, we ourselves are changing while we are telling it. The story changes and so do we.

As I went along with Olivia, somebody said to me, you coming to the Plonk and Nosh Society tonight, Freddie? I had completely forgotten about it. In those days there was a sort of loose society, loose in the sense that there were no formal meetings or members or minutes or anything like that, just a few people on the staff and one or two others, with their wives, who every now and again got together to have some sort of party involving food and wine. Hence Plonk and Nosh, as somebody once called us. Anybody could come really, there was no membership as such. We used to go on trips occasionally. Once we went up the Tamar in a dockyard boat, and another time we went on a Dartmoor safari, to Yes Tor and High Willheys. Had our soup on Yes Tor and main nosh on High Willheys and came home via Okehampton. I remember we all gathered round a tarn somewhere up in the moorlands and threw stones into it. There we were, a crowd of townees, miles from anywhere, staring into that water as though we expected to see something moving about in it.

That night, I was reminded, the Plonk and Noshers were having another kind of safari, I don't know what the proper name for them is, where you all go to one house for soup, a second to have fish, third for your main course, somewhere else for your pudding and finish up somewhere else for coffee and sticky sweets. There used to be quite a fashion for these sort of parties at one time. They still do occasionally have them from time to time. Myself, I never really took to them because I found them so disrupting. A major part of any evening out is the atmosphere. No sooner had one got himself settled in one place and got a party atmosphere going than we had to up bag and hammock and away to somewhere else and start from cold again. It meant meeting three or four or five sets of hosts in an evening instead of one. The hosts themselves never knew quite whether to join in and let their share of the meal take its chance, when everybody arrived, or whether to hold back until everybody arrived at their place and then take it on from there, or just have people in to their bit of it and let the rest go hang, or what. I suppose it all depended on what your bit happened to be. I am talking about a disjointed episode of my life, when everything was rather fragmented, and it was kind of appropriate that we should go to a fragmented sort of party.

I remember that bachelor members like me, who wouldn't normally have the premises or the expertise to lay on a course of the meal, were expected to provide some of the vino instead. I bought six bottles of Pimm's Number One, and six bottles of Campari or something, put them in a box, and shoved them in the boot of my car. Olivia, of course, was game for everything or anything. The way she was feeling then I think if I'd said to her let's walk to Newcastle she would have said right away, right you're on.

So there we were, driving off again that evening, I seem to remember it was still drizzling, with Olivia in the front passenger seat and a crate of booze in the boot, all of us to have our meals on wheels. I wouldn't tell you everywhere we went and everything we did that evening even if I could remember. It was probably as disjointed an evening as I expected it would be. Only one of the places we went to was rather important now. It happened to be the last place on the menu, where we had our pudding, our cheese and coffee. The man I'm talking about is Mickey Gibb, who was *Pandora's* Gunnery Officer.

I can see, as I noticed when I mentioned him before, that of course you all know him. You all saw how well he did in *Pandora* in this last SEATO exercise. Ironic when you think about it, that he should be commanding *Pandora* now in the same part of the world.

Mickey Gibb was about the only one to come out of the old *Pandora*, that first *Pandora* I mean, with any credit. He did his job and there was nobody to cast any aspersions on him afterwards. He is an intellectual, a real intellectual. Very rare in the Service. There are many intelligent men in the Navy, lots of very fine brains, but that's not quite what I mean. There are very few who have the intellectual capacity and the application to sit down and really think hard, about the Navy, and where it's going, and what's going to become of us. Not many of those, but Mickey is certainly one of them. And he was, is, a very able chap, as well. But it was not enough to be an able chap in James' *Pandora*. After all, James himself was a very able chap and it didn't save him. James was able, but not indispensable, in that special naval sense that Mickey Gibb was, if only for the very good reason that the Navy very occasionally needs a bit of good old simple, crude, old-fashioned blood-letting. More as a relief, as a catharsis, than anything else. There's no lasting malice about it. You need the very best and most select, most bred in the purple blood you can get. If you are going to have a blood sacrifice, then it must be the top quality blood. James was set up to be a natural target. He was a natural born scapegoat. Mickey Gibb, now, Mickey was not that sort at all. He would never suffer the same fate as James. It just could not happen. Don't ask me why, because I have already done my best to explain and I won't get any nearer than I already have.

It was just the sort of thrash I had expected it to be, though with rather more people there than one would have thought, considering that we must have motored between twenty and twenty-five miles during the evening. Some were there at the start and seemed to drop out on the way. Others mysteriously turned up and joined us halfway through. Olivia came in for a lot of comment. I am not sure that many people even knew she was with me.

Mickey's marriage was apparently screaming with neuroses and hang-ups of various kinds. If ever there was a relationship that *Pandora* might have tested it was that one. I can't remember what sort of house they lived in now, but I certainly do remember their furniture. From the moment you stepped into their house you could see that here was a clash of cultures. Dawn was her name, very good-looking girl, but not the sort you would expect Mickey ever to meet and marry. I hope his family had the sense not to say anything. They were a naval family, not quite as distinguished as James', but fair enough. They had some nice furniture, some very nice pieces of old stuff, obviously from his old family home. But it was mixed with the most glaringly modern stripped pine stuff, and lit with the most bright of bright tungsten lights, with clashing patterns of electric red and shocking pink fabrics and purple stripes and green blotches. This was clearly Dawn's influence. You could see a nice old French escritoire, I think they are called, right next to a huge, shining, massive green chesterfield made out of some kind of glistening plastic. There was a beautiful carriage clock, with the most musical chime I ever heard, standing on the bleakest little table, with a smoked glass top and tubular steel legs. It all looked terrible at first, and yet I have to admit that when you had lived with it and moved around inside for a while it did begin in some peculiar way to work. In some peculiar eerie manner, the things began to blend.

Just as Mickey and Dawn blended, in some peculiar manner. I don't know where he met her. She was what you might call a political sort of woman. Committed is the word she and her friends might have used. No, I've just remembered where he met her, somebody told me that night. Mickey's father dabbled in politics for a while after his retirement, stood as a Conservative, of course, for somewhere. Dawn was working for the Labour candidate, and they met on election night, when the Labour man won. Rather romantic, in a left-handed sort of way. And I think the Navy had a peculiar left-handed glamour for her. She came all prepared and bristling with prejudices and opinions. She found to her amazement and slightly to her disappointment that many naval officers were excellent company. They had fun, they enjoyed life, they and their wives helped others and their wives when they needed a hand. They were so utterly non-political, most of them, so quite, quite, innocent of anything to do with politics, that I think Dawn found that she simply could not get annoyed with them or upset about them. They might have been imperialists, in her view, but they were charming with it, imperialist charmers. They were employed by a system which Dawn insisted she despised. So she said, but she obviously didn't despise the men who were paid to uphold that system. In fact, she found them rather gorgeous. She was, after all, going to bed regularly and as often as she could with an imperialist pig, and enjoying it. That was another of the things Mickey was good at, bed. In fact, he was so damned secure and invulnerable one used to wonder idly how one could strike at him, and hit him as James had been hit. But it was not feasible. So, poor Dawn was still indignant about the system, but rather adored the men. Poor girl, I suppose that put her in a difficult position, ideologically, whatever positions she might have assumed in bed. They are still together, against all the odds, and they've got three kids, now, somebody was telling me.

But at that particular time, Dawn was predictably horrified by *Pandora's* story. It seemed that it was the worst piece of iniquitous imperial oppression she had ever heard of, far worse than Amritsar, or Dresden or Sharpeville or any of the places they get excited about. To fire on a native sampan like that … well, Dawn thought it was *an atrocity*. "An obscenity," was the word she actually used. I believe it was the first time it ever dawned on her, if you'll pardon the pun, what being in the Navy really meant. Up to then, she had said she knew, and she disapproved of it, in general terms. But she had not really known what she was talking about. This was not general, it was very, very particular. It concerned her husband at a specific time and place, doing a specific series of actions. It was as though for the first time she came face to face with her husband's job.

All this came out on that Plonk and Nosh night, when Mickey was at his coolest. It had been a long, a fairly alcoholic, evening and for some reason, when everybody else had at last pushed off, there were six of us left. Mickey and Dawn, Olivia and I, and another couple, called Monty and Polly. Mickey and Dawn were already at home, Olivia and I had no homes to go to, but I don't know about the other two. Polly was a dish, one of the best-looking girls I have ever seen in all my life. She was rather like Dawn, they looked like each other, and they seemed to have the same ideas about things. They probably held up opposite ends of the same banner on protest marches. If that was so, then that would be a march I would not mind attending. Polly must have been the reason they were still there at that hour, because I cannot imagine Monty being invited on his own, not on his own merits. I cannot imagine him being invited anywhere, just for himself. He was one of the most nauseating men I have ever met. I never did discover what he did for a living. Some business in Plymouth. Perhaps insurance or something. He was not in the Navy but he gave the impression that he had been, during the last war, in the RNVR maybe. He looked the part. Large red face, bright blue blazer, bright brass buttons, gin and quarterdeck manner. He used the word 'job' as an all-purpose war-time description. 'Dunkirk job'. 'Dieppe job'. 'D-Day job'. Apparently he was captured in the Aegean, and became a prisoner of war, a 'Med job', and when he caused trouble as a POW he became a 'solitary confinement job'. And he never talked about the war, simply. He always referred to it as 'the conflict', or 'that last bit of bother' or 'the last spot of unpleasantness'. I got the strong impression that he had a whale of a time, and in fact has never ever enjoyed himself quite so much ever since. He leered a bit at Olivia in a desultory sort of way, and probably would have given her a good pawing over if he'd had the chance. Barbara Manning used to have a very good adjective for men like him. Yukky, she called them. How he came to marry Polly, I haven't the faintest idea.

Pandora had already been mentioned that evening, once, in the most embarrassing way for me. One of the wives, I forget who, knew that Olivia was James Bellingham's wife and having never met any of us before, she assumed that I was James. Even when she was told she got confused and still had a mental block about it, calling me James Bellingham. Mickey at once said, "Oh no, never, not Freddie." Which was true enough. I had about as much chance of commanding *Pandora* or indeed any of HM Ships as I had of being able to run to Newcastle. But it was the quick way Mickey said it. Oh no, not Freddie. The fact that it was said by Mickey, the most unmalicious of men, somehow made it more certain, more final, more true, more official. That was the official view of the Navy. Freddie could never be Captain of *Pandora*, or any ship, for that matter. Not now.

We were all sitting about in their living room, still growing accustomed to the shock of their amazing furniture. I suppose we really ought to have gone home, but they were very hospitable and nobody ever felt they had to go. It must have been cracking on for two o'clock in the morning by then. Not the time for abstruse metaphysical conversations. Not a time for talking about *Pandora*. But still, the subject came up, as though it were inevitable. I missed the actual exchange between Mickey and Dawn which seemed to start it all off, but from the way they were talking it soon became quite obvious they had both discussed it before. They were both taking up well known positions, using well known language in a ritual manner. They both had points to make, very good ones, but they had polished each other so smooth everything slid off them. Mickey was an unusual officer, as I said. He approached many Service matters in a questioning, sceptical manner, very uncommon. Most of us never bother to question except possibly in a vague and alcoholically hazy way after a mess dinner say. And Mickey had a very unusual wife. She was just as capable as he was of arguing a case on its merits. They were a formidable pair, I can tell you. I could tell that Olivia was a bit put down by it all.

Inevitably somebody said the emotive words 'war crime' and that started everything off, like a trigger. Monty bellowed, and bellowed is the word, "Nuremburg job", or something. "The only thing the Nazis thought they did wrong was to lose the war. So did the Japanese. The only really dishonourable offence they thought they had committed was to be captured alive."

A man like Monty aroused natural feelings against him. He only had to say something for you to want to disagree with it. But just because somebody like Monty says it, it does not necessarily mean that it is wrong. In this case. I thought he was right. The top Japanese Officials certainly thought like that.

I recall very clearly what Mickey said that night, because it seemed to me an admirable statement of the position. He said that "the whole war crime argument, that they batted to and fro at Nuremberg, was an interesting debating subject, but it had no meaning as far as *Pandora* was concerned. It simply didn't enter into it," he said. "It was irrelevant."

Dawn said, "but surely darling, you're not going to shelter behind that old threadbare defence, that if your superior officer orders you to do something, that clears you of all blame? In any case," she said, "that isn't a defence, that's been established. That's what the trials after the war were all about."

I don't think Dawn was aware that she was to all intents and purposes attacking the morality of what her husband did for a living. She was totally preoccupied with the ideological and moral argument.

Mickey seemed to think very hard for a long time. As I said, it had been a long and alcoholic evening. He said, "looking back now, I suppose I have to concede, if I was completely honest about it, I suppose one would have to admit that that little sampan was probably harmless."

"There you are then," said Dawn.

I said, but surely what is important is not what you think now, on reflection, but what you thought then? Or rather what James thought then?

Mickey said, "it doesn't matter what I thought then. It was an order."

"Here we go again," Dawn said. "If anybody ordered you to do it now, would you still do it?"

Mickey said, very carefully, "look you're still missing the point. In an HM Ship nobody orders anybody to do just anything. We were in the middle of an operation. They were shooting real bullets at us. We had been warned about some of these little boats lying offshore, looking perfectly harmless. Some of them were being used as a sort of spy-ship. Others were booby-trapped, hoping that we would put a boarding party on board and set off a bomb. John the Marine, our intelligence officer, knew all about them. He had been out on the coast for over eighteen months and he warned us. The Captain's order was bounded on all sides by all manner of considerations, tactical ones, disciplinary ones, technical ones, but never emotional ones. There are a number of definite clearly refined parameters of conduct inside which a Captain must come to his decisions. Most of them are accepted, based on usage and tradition. Others are governed by the situation as it arises and as it develops. So a Captain's order is a past tradition and a past philosophy of conduct which manifests itself in a physical and tactical situation. No Captain picks an order out of the air and just gives it, unrelated to anything. In this case the Captain was not ordering us to fire on any little sampan in any vague general circumstances. If you said to me, is it right to fire on unarmed small boats, I would say of course not, that can't be right. But if you then go on to say, but this was an unarmed perfectly harmless small boat and therefore it was wrong to fire on that, then I disagree with you. This was a particular incident in a particular set of circumstances. It was a matter of judgement. You might argue that the Captain was wrong in judgement. I am not even sure I would even concede that, but at least it could make up into a respectable argument which one would have to listen to. But you could never say he was wrong morally. Morals don't enter into it."

Dawn said, "that is exactly what we are saying. Morals do enter into it," she said. "It can never, ever be right to fire on a little boat. We are saying, and from what you've told us your Captain was militarily wrong, too, as well as morally wrong, to open fire. We are saying that however militarily right you may think you are, you can still be utterly and totally wrong morally."

Then they all seemed to be waiting for me to say something. I said I thought that if I had been there I would not have fired. But at once I sensed that Mickey took this as a betrayal, and I had lost some ground with him. I did not want to do that, so I hurriedly qualified it. I said, one's decision always depends upon one's knowledge. It is like, say, making up your mind that you are right and proper and fully justified in shooting somebody. You're all set when he says something that changes your mind. You have come to know a little more about it. But then he goes on to say something more which changes your mind again and makes you decide you ought to go ahead after all. You know even more now. So you metaphorically speaking go on raising and lowering your gun, depending upon how much more you get to know. In my present state, I said, I would have the gun lowered, but if I had been in James' shoes at that time I most probably would have done the same as he did. I would have had the gun up, just as he did.

I saw Mickey wince a bit at this. I suppose the choice of words had been a little emotive.

Monty had been snorting in a fatuous manner and trying to put in futile remarks every now and again. Nobody had been taking much notice of him, but suddenly he said, "What you are asking is, should we have a Navy?"

I thought that was the most banal and pedestrian and useless remark I had ever heard, but Mickey took it up at once. "That is why I cannot allow any of you any part of your point," he said. "I cannot give way an inch, because we are, as Monty has said, touching on the very basis of why we have a Navy. It is the permission that our state gives to use force in certain defined circumstances. That is why we still have armed forces at all. It is far more fundamental than the pure protection of the realm which, when you think about it, is a very simple concept. I am talking about something much more complex and subtle. It is the acknowledgement that force, violence if you like, has to have a recognised status in our community. I believe in that permission. That is why I could not allow any retreat at all in my argument. I think it is very sad that a feeling seems to be growing up somehow in the Port that my Captain somehow did something wrong. I dispute that absolutely. I think it is a most dangerous and iniquitous thing that anybody should listen to such talk even for a moment. It is not worth a moment's hearing. The people who are doing it are no friends of the Captain. They are all joining in a 'let's kick James Bellingham' movement. This is 'Be Horrible to *Pandora* Week,' and I think it is disgusting and inexcusable and downright dangerous. The people who are doing it don't seem to realise that they are putting their whole profession of arms in jeopardy."

Mickey had taken some time to shake off his feeling of inhibition that Olivia was there. She was his Captain's wife, he did not know her at all well, and naturally he was chary of being too forthright where his Captain was concerned. But as always with a man like Mickey, the intellectual argument intoxicated him. He could not resist debating even though Olivia was there. Mind you, he was still baffled by the fact that she and I were there together. He could not make that out at all.

Mickey had an obsessive need to find out what he called the truth, although he knew very well what a hopeless task he had given himself. "We are all talking, everybody's all talking," he said, "as though there were one version of the truth which was the whole truth and nothing but the truth. That is not so. I can see now how legends come about," he said. "It is the hardest thing in the world to stop legends forming. Things that seemed every day and casual and quite unimportant at the time somehow harden into the set mould of a legend. For example, all those soldiers who served in the Civil War, between Cromwell and the King. Did any of them realise that every move they made, every tactic and device, every gesture, would eventually be recreated, studied and debated in detail by military and local historians years later? Not just the major engagements, but where a commander stopped for the night, which way the messenger came, whether he turned right or left, who spoke to him or saw him, all this becomes legend in the end. And if there is any particularly brave action attached to the event it becomes legend quicker than usual. If somebody is awarded the Victoria Cross, it becomes impossible to find out what happened. The winner himself won't be able to tell you. He'll have told the story so often he won't know. It sounds silly but it's true. Our trouble is that we never know when it is going to be important to remember exactly what happened and who said what and how they looked and where they moved and what time of night or day or even what the weather was like."

"The other extreme," Mickey said, "which I always think slightly bogus is this thing called total recall. Some people say they can remember everything that ever happened to them. All I can say is, how inexpressibly boring. Nine times out of ten they write books, long and extremely boring books, totally recalling everything. Nobody wants to know. For all that anybody knows or cares he might just as well have had total amnesia. It is a great pity that these people with total recall are so seldom there when really important things are going on. It makes one wonder about history. Why do we always have to spend ages trying to reconstruct what it was like, out of a haze of conjecture and speculation? Why is there never anybody there at the time who can write it down as it really was? The answer is that it never really was."

"I can see the same thing happening in *Pandora*. I have an uncomfortable suspicion that that is going to be one of the occasions when it was important to remember what happened.

But nobody does. You only need to start reminiscing about anything and at once it crystallises into an untruth. If you are not absolutely scrupulously careful, and sometimes even if you are careful, you will find yourself remembering what everybody else remembers and not what you yourself really remember. It is a betrayal of ourselves, and it is contagious. We don't realise what we are doing. It happened in *Pandora* on the way home. There is a common story now, that everybody on board will swear happened, with his own personal embellishments, of course. They have talked about it and remembered it and discussed it and exchanged views about it, everybody adding a bit and changing a bit and polishing a bit, until all that is left now is a communal version, a received edition of the tale, a gospel according to the messdecks, and nothing you can do or say now will change it or even shake it. The only way you can change it now is to push it further from the truth. You can do that at any time. I think it remarkable, and suspicious, that if you ask any sailor from *Pandora* what happened that day, they'll all tell you much the same thing. I shouldn't have said remarkable, now I think of it. It is not remarkable at all. It is quite normal. They simply can't have all seen the same thing. It is unbelievable. Most of them never saw anything at all. They were below and out of sight. Even those who did see must have different memories. They must have. Show the same scene to twelve different people and they will all see twelve different scenes. Ask any policeman about eye-witness testimony. So our basic material that we have to work on is flawed to start with. We have no steady platform of fact to work from. We all see different things and remember different things and yet when we are asked we all say the same things. It doesn't seem logical."

We ask James, I said, because it is what he thinks happened that counts.

Mickey burst into laughter at that. Not very kindly laughter either, and for a surprising moment I felt a real surge of sympathy for James.

Or Simon Fiddich, I put in quickly, hoping for some reaction. What about him, I said.

"What about him," said Mickey.

He got out from under pretty smartly, I said.

Mickey just looked at me. "God," he said, "the speed that things get around. Simon was just being careful. Looking after Number One, literally in his case."

Nothing more than that, I said.

"Nothing more than that," Mickey said. "Simon was cuter than most of us. He saw there might possibly be consequences. He saw that very early on, although he's wrong."

What do you mean, I asked.

"There are no consequences" Mickey said. "The whole thing's been got up, and will go down again just as quickly."

I was not quite so sure of that myself, but anyway this seemed a good chance to find out something about Fiddich. I was going to prompt Mickey, but he was going to tell me anyway. "When the General commanding troops came on board," he said, "Simon did a bit of quick ... well, adjustment is probably the right description. He adjusted his version of events. Nobody knew quite why the General came on board. He had never been before and he never came again. But while he was there Simon took what he imagined was his chance to put in a good word for himself. The really interesting thing about it is that having done this, Simon then began to suffer the most terrible pangs of guilt. I imagine it was guilt. Could have been indigestion. They certainly lasted all the way home from the Far East. I used to find him rolling about on his cabin bunk, tears in his eyes. He would say, 'Mickey you believe me, don't you, I was faithful, you know that.' Just as though he was a dog or something. Nobody had ever suggested that he was not faithful. That's the trouble with old Simon," said Mickey, "he has absolutely no sense of proportion where anything concerning himself is concerned. To him he had committed the Great Betrayal, in capital letters, in lights on Broadway, in fact, a Cecil B. DeMille production in glorious Technicolor with a cast of thousands singing 'Ave Maria.' Whereas, in fact, it was a simple uncomplicated, rather squalid if you like, piece of common yard-arm squaring."

But surely, I said, it's all a matter of scale. It might be a big matter to him.

"Possibly," was all Mickey said.

I suddenly had a vivid glimpse of the stark, intellectual plane Mickey lived on. What a bleak view of life he seemed to take, where everything was reduced to its ordinary pitiful predictable human constituents, where everybody got their due, no more and no less. What a terrifying world it would be, where everybody always got exactly what was coming to them.

It also struck me that here was another thing about *Pandora*, It was belittling everybody, devaluing their responses. It made you no longer certain how you should react. One moment you felt you were being frivolous, the next you were overreacting. Mickey seemed to have said everything that could be said or needed to be said about Simon Fiddich, but still, I felt there might be something more in it. I might or might not bother to chase it up. I could decide that later. In the meanwhile, Mickey was a very smooth customer, and the only thing was to go bald-headed at him. So I said, I take it from everything you've been saying that in *Pandora's* case you are going to be the chap who writes it all down exactly as it was, without being influenced by what anybody else says? So go on, tell us exactly how it was.

He looked a little abashed, I was pleased to see. It was reassuring that one could arouse a ruffle in that formidable calm. Like James, Mickey had an outwardly calm surface, but every now and again you had a hint of powerful forces shifting about behind it. For one thrilling flash I thought I was on the verge of prising something out of him, when Dawn interrupted. I could have slapped her.

"Oh the hell with your boring old ship," she said, "I don't want to hear all that sad tale of woe all over again. We don't seem to have talked about much else ever since Mickey came home. You're all so damned stuffy about it," she said. "This is supposed to be a party, so help me," she said. She turned on me, as though it were all my fault. "I don't know who you are," she said to me, "but you come here like some sort of detective, with a long face looking like a bloody bloodhound, listening to what everybody has to say and watching all the expressions on their faces. Can't you put the handcuffs away for a bit," she said, "we're supposed to be relaxing, for God's sake."

I thought she was being very unfair. It certainly wasn't my fault. Worse still, she had completely disrupted the trend of the conversation and killed *Pandora* stone dead, just when I thought the corpse was about to come to life and prophesy.

Dawn said, let's play Bodies. Mickey roared with laughter, quite a different laughter this time and, again, I had one of these moments of revelation these people kept on giving me. I had a sudden vision of what their marriage meant to them. It was nothing to do with the difference between antique and modem furniture. The outward clash of styles was really tremendous evidence of another kind of harmony, deep down, at the crux of the thing. They suited each other. They could disagree about surface things, because they had much more at a deeper level going for them. They deserved each other. They were good opponents and partners. They hit it off with each other, in several senses. I think they were to be admired and envied.

Bodies turned out to be very like a game Rory used to organise and make us play when we were growing up and getting interested in sex. As you can understand by this time, Olivia's elder brother Rory was a somewhat diabolically powerful figure in our childhoods. Only then we used to call it Silkworms. So called, because one of Olivia's aunts kept silkworms and she told us that silkworms wriggled and turned to and fro in a figure-of-eight fashion for about two days while they were spinning their silk cocoons or something. Rory said it was because they were in a sexual frenzy, although I must say we never dared ask the aunt whether he was right. Silkworms was a form of heavy petting, except that it was look, mum, no hands. Two of us lay down face to face, with our hands behind our backs and we could do anything provided we didn't use our hands.

Mickey and Dawn's version turned out to be rather more adult, and they had both obviously played it many times before, because they both began to show a most alarming expertise. The arms and back of their huge green chesterfield collapsed, to form a wide bed, or sex surface, as Polly called it. She, too, seemed to know all about it. They brought up mirrors, and towels and lengths of string and very bright portable lights.

Monty, too, seemed to know what was involved and seemed to be looking forward to it, although when I heard what was required I wondered whether he was wise to be so confident.

He was a different age group, nearer me than any of the others. But no, he rubbed his hands together, looking as if he was anticipating it all.

Briefly, what it meant was that both partners did a striptease, to appropriate music provided, had their hands tied behind their backs, lay down on the chesterfield and after that it was no holds barred, so to speak. Although a tiny bit inside me was secretly looking forward to seeing how the others would perform, the rest and greater part of me was quite frankly terrified by the whole thing. To have to strip off, to have one's hands tied, to lie down with Olivia, in front of people I hardly knew, at that time of night, well, frankly, the whole prospect filled me with the utmost foreboding and dismay and embarrassment.

But it was extraordinary how quickly the atmosphere changed completely. We had been talking about *Pandora* and Service matters generally, and then, in the twinkling of an eye, in a moment, the atmosphere was strongly charged with sex. We were all sitting about looking as though we had cartoon balloons over our heads saying 'Bed?' and all eyeing the girls in an extremely aggressive manner. They were eyeing us back in an extremely questioning manner.

The reason for this highly charged atmosphere was, of course, the fact that the girls were all three of them so good-looking, outstandingly so for naval women. I have never been able to understand how or where naval officers got their reputations for sexual prowess, especially when you look at the wives most of them eventually marry. We all know, by and large, it is all a big confidence trick. We don't have a wife in every port, by any means. Go to any naval party, of any kind, and there is bound to be an overburden of surplus males about the place, the sort of males who look as if they are going to be sexually surplus all their lives. Go to any naval dinner party and there is almost certain to be too many men. There will be the married couple who are giving the party, the hosts, perhaps another couple or two, and then always at least one, two, three or even four spare men, bachelors, grass-widowers, from the same ship, or visiting firemen. It is very rare that they take the trouble to make the numbers even at a dinner party. It is the curse of social life in the Navy, always, all these bloody extra men around, just drinking and not contributing anything.

However, that was not our problem on this particular night. Dawn and Mickey were quite obviously experts at this sort of game. We drew lots to start by measuring the girls. Dawn had a tape all ready. The one with the largest bust measurement began. This all very childish, I expect you think, like schoolboys showing each other their private parts and being very pleased with themselves, but it was fun, and all so innocent really.

Dawn won, so they began. I must say they were magnificent. As a couple, they were on the top of a sexual curve, or perhaps even at the top of two sexual curves, where they intersected. They had been apart for some time, which gave them a sort of reunion lift, but they had been together again for long enough to get used to each other again, which gave them reassurance. So it was a combination of novelty and experience and I must say, it was sweet to see them. I admit there must be an element of voyeurism in all of us, but I cannot believe there is any harm in seeing two people so expert, so beautiful, and enjoying themselves so much.

It was, of course, Olivia's reactions and expressions which interested me most of all. After all, she was going to consent to strip off her clothes and compete, well, if not compete exactly, then certainly to allow herself to be contrasted with two younger women, both of whom were outstandingly good-looking in any company. As it turned out, Olivia bore up very well. She didn't compare at all badly. She was slightly baggy, I suppose, to be really harsh, and a little wrinkled. Hers was clearly not the body of a young woman, but she still looked to me wonderfully well. In tremendous form. It touched me so much to see that she was conscious of the passing of time and accepted it, I liked her all the more as she was. I would not have changed places with any of the others.

Now I am beginning to speak of things normally just a little too intimate for ordinary conversation, but it is worth saying how good it is to make love using only one's body once in a while. To be deprived of one sense always adds an extra aliveness to the others. Without hands, every bodily contact seemed to tingle, like fire running over your skin. Whoever invented that game knew something about sexual pleasure. There was an element of competition in it, and display and prudishness. It was pleasant and slightly shameful and exciting all at once. What did surprise me, was how absorbed we became in each other. Embarrassment after a time simply did not enter into it. I was for some time completely oblivious of spectators. I would not have believed it, had I not experienced it. I forgot about everybody else while I concentrated on Olivia.

For a time I could not make her relax. Lying there, eyeball to eyeball, so to speak, I could see what the trouble was. She was simply aching for reassurance. Terrified of somehow acting badly. The other two were playing, partly for fun, but also partly as an act of defiance. They were out to prove that sex was not a Woman's Sacred Duty, in Victorian capital letters, but could also be a parlour game. But Olivia was different. She was older and not so confident. Eventually I tickled her, with my big toe, actually, with the utmost delicacy, I may also say, and I murmured 'Silkworms' in her ear. Dawn said, "no whispering, you two," but it did the trick. Oddly enough, I don't think I could have made love to Olivia in any usual way, what the women's magazines call a seduction. She would not have allowed it. But this was a game, or it began as a game, a little exhibition, as though it did not count in the score. Or so I thought. I knew that I had given Olivia pleasure. I had made a tremendous advance with her, I could see that. I had reassured her and pleasured her and flattered her.

Then I rather spoilt the total effect by catching cramp. There was a sign of middle age for you. When I turned over to have my hands untied, I stretched out hard and at once got the most terrible cramp in my right calf muscle. It was pure agony. A day later I could still feel it. But once again, it all suited the occasion. It was fun, you see.

Monty and Polly were last, and I won't harrow you with a description of it. It was too painful for words. All that futile thrashing about. Monty had talked too much and drunk too much to be able to do more than just grunt like a stuck pig. It was all wasted effort on Monty's part and all frustration on Polly's. I suppose a scene like that might have a certain gloomy satisfaction for a misanthropic anthropologist, but for us it was all a hideous embarrassment. Monty behaved like a pig, too. Dawn and Polly began to tickle him. They were both starkers and Mickey or I would have been turned on in a big way. But Monty just bellowed with fury and demanded to be released. And that was that. Looking back, Monty and Polly on that chesterfield made a sight that absolutely summed up our decadence. There was an exquisite woman, shaped for love, and with the right amount of lechery in her. Any society which wanted to survive would have insisted on pairing her with the best man in the tribe. To put her with Monty as his wife was the most horrible waste and extravagance of nature.

I drove Olivia back to Sebastopol Buildings. It was a gloomy drive, one more gloom in a gloomy summer. We were both suffering from what you might call post-coital *tristesse*. I had stopped being so pleased with myself and remembered that my first experience with Olivia had only come about through a game. That night, we both slept the sleep of the just, in separate beds.

CHAPTER 8

That feeling of sadness was still there the next morning, said Freddie. It was a strange sadness which I had never experienced before. I was still very innocent then, in spite of my age. Still am, if the truth be known. I had an inkling at last of what life could have been like for me if I had somehow succeeded in marrying Olivia. We both regretted our antics in that stupid party game. We knew that neither of us were young any more. That is middle age. Coming down to breakfast one morning and being aware of it. It takes a woman's company to do it, too. Bachelors never know when they are middle-aged.

All the same, this sadness was worth having. It was new, even though it was so painful. It was an extension of my emotional range, even if it hurt. And shared experience with Olivia was worth it, to me. She could not take it away from me now. We were both a little sheepish, ashamed of ourselves. Sexual hangover, I imagine. Or strippers' remorse. Olivia was not proud of her experience, but at least she had shared it with me.

Sebastopol Buildings was in one of those miraculous districts that seemed to come early on everybody's rounds. I used to get milk and mail and newspapers at an astonishingly early hour. I just put out notes and it all arrived. Not many places you can say that about.

Breakfast with Olivia was a charmingly domestic scene. I could hardly believe it was me sitting here and her sitting there. She had a quilted dressing-gown over her nightdress and she had her hair done up in a sort of turban thing. We had toast and coffee and fruit juice. There was no jug for the juice, it was just out of the can, no jug for the milk, just out of the bottle, and butter off a plate still in its packet, no butter knife. Bread was sliced from a sliced loaf in one of those shiny wrappers.

Olivia had got up first and got it all ready. It was the first time she had ever done as much for me.

It was my first experience of the tensions of the marriage breakfast table. I enjoyed the novelty of it, even though I was disconcerted to see how nervous I was. There must be that middle-class English sense of guilt about sex. I was annoyed with Mickey and Dawn for having led us astray, for giving us the chance to lead ourselves astray, I should say. Olivia didn't meet my eye, as though we had both had too much to drink the night before and had made fools of ourselves. Which was not so far from the truth, I suppose.

But of course, breakfast after the night before was not such a novel experience for Olivia as it was for me. She had all the proper degree of early morning waspishness.

"I expect you're feeling pretty pleased with yourself," she said to me, "after all your adventures last night."

I said at once that yes, indeed, I was, I did feel extremely pleased with myself.

She said, "I've never seen such an exhibition."

I said, exhibition is right.

She said, "rubbish. We were all acting like a lot of children. I've never seen anybody act so childishly like that before. Do you want some toast," she said.

Olivia had much more experience of these early morning encounters than I had. It seemed that very rapid changes of subject were the tactics. Ask a man if he committed adultery the night before and whether he would like the marmalade, in successive questions. It was interesting, and rather reassuring, that Olivia still had such a strong streak of prudishness in her.

I said, yes I would very much like some toast and was all prepared to watch her wrestle with my toaster. It is one of those temperamental ones. If you don't get it just right, if you don't press it down with just the right pressure, it tries to take your hand off at the wrist.

"Well, you can put some bread in it yourself," said Olivia, very sharply indeed. "Is this all the fruit juice you've got," she said. "Just pineapple?"

I said, yes, pineapple was the only kind I really liked.

She poured me some, in a domestic sort of way, and then asked me what I was going to do that day. Somehow that completed the domestic scene. That was the final touch needed.

It was such a strange feeling to be discussing my daily programme with a woman. It made me eager and yet defensive. I was terribly pleased and flattered that somebody should actually be interested in what I proposed to do, and at the same time I was shy and rather chary of revealing too much about my doings. I had never been one to tell anybody about my comings and goings. So, once again, Olivia had this strange ambivalent effect upon me, warming me and warning me at the same time, if you like.

Actually it was going to be mainly an office day for me, which I anticipated I would have to spend somehow avoiding Fiery. He was sure to demand some sort of SITREP that day. Sometime in the forenoon I had to go down to the Damage Control School, I remember, to discuss ventilation fans again, of all things. There was some question, I remember, of the layout of the air conditioning systems. The Damage Control boys said the present arrangement left too many too large openings in the hull at action stations. It was in fact another instalment of the old, old battle between those who want to make ships habitable but vulnerable, and those who wanted them unsinkable but uninhabitable.

It was odd that Olivia and I should be sharing this domestic scene, without ever having been through all the layers of strangeness of a new marriage. I am speaking from hearsay now, of course, having never been married, but by all accounts a woman whoever she is, takes a good deal of getting to know. Yet here were Olivia and I acting like an old married couple at the breakfast table without all that intervening estrangement. We had skipped a whole span of shared experience and reminiscence. I was rather sorry we had, of course.

Olivia reminded me of my war wounds. She told me my eye was looking better that morning, and asked me how was my leg? I had more or less forgotten about both of them until she mentioned it. My eye was much better but my leg, now that she mentioned it, was still a trifle sore from the cramp.

Of much more importance to me that day was not what I was going to do but what Olivia was going to do. When I asked her she said she was going to go back, back to Chichester. We had not so much as mentioned James's name, not for a long time and nor did we then. But it was implicit. It was there in the air. It seemed that Olivia was not going to bother to look for him or even make any sort of enquiries about where he was or what he wanted to do. She was merely going to go back home and wait, and see what transpired. I wanted her to stay. I wanted that very badly. But I knew that if you once tried to dissuade Olivia it would make her all the more determined to do it. Logically then, I suppose I ought to have urged her to go all the more, on the principle that that would make her stay, but I simply couldn't make myself do that.

By then I could see that she herself did not really want to go either. "Do you know, Freddie," she said quite unexpectedly, "I have decided that I don't know you at all. You've always been there," she said, "you've always been around, whenever anybody needed you, for as long as I can remember, but I've never really looked at you before. I've always known you," she said, "but I know nothing about you."

That was precisely what I had always resented so much about her and James, but I did not say so.

"I don't think," she said, "I don't think I ever really looked at you properly until last night. There is more to Freddie than meets the eye," she said. "Perhaps we've all been misjudging you all these years."

I said, well you could hardly have had a better view of me than you had last night, at which she collapsed laughing. I found this sort of talk pleasing but annoying too. She was being condescending, in that maddening way they both had. Good gracious, she was saying, fancy that about Freddie. Like a tourist seeing a new view of something. The fact was that she had thoroughly enjoyed herself the night before. She could hide it but she could not deny it to herself. She might have been ashamed to think of it afterwards, but she thoroughly enjoyed it at the time.

As I have already said, there is a limit to the amount of detail I am prepared to go into in telling this. Briefly, this was one of those baffling changes of mood and feeling that always flummoxed me with Olivia. Suffice it to say that she went all broody on me, there and then at the breakfast table. I was dressed, I was in uniform, I was mentally and very nearly physically on my way, I was literally putting my table napkin in my ring, when she tried to seduce me. She succeeded, up to a point. Although I could never get it out of my mind that this was just one more demonstration of the contempt they held me in. They thought so little of me that they imagined I would be enticed to bed at ten to eight in the morning, after I had shaved, dressed, breakfasted and read the newspaper. I know it sounds amusing, but it was hurtful, too. What I had in mind with Olivia was a new start, a new way of life, a new way of enjoying things that would include her always. She would always be a part. But what was suggested here was an insult. The psychology was all wrong. She was one of them again. The night before she had been with me and one of us. Of course, it failed. It was the wrong time, the wrong place, as the song says, the wrong approach, the wrong method, the wrong everything. Had I tried to seduce her in the same way, had the roles been reversed, she would have said, quite rightly, Freddie, you want to brush up your technique. I left her in bed. I left her, I left us both, with much to ponder over about the future, while I drove into Plymouth. I still had no idea of what she was going to do. I decided I would try and find out.

It was a really lovely morning. One of the very few that summer. The sun was burning your eyes out, the birds were singing their heads off, and the traffic was already warming up to a real Bank Holiday roar. It had been raining slightly overnight and the road was still wet. Going into Plymouth, against the sun, the reflection was blinding. It was like a shining silver cover thrown across the road, so that you could not see what was underneath it.

All the way in I was thinking about James Bellingham. It was fairly obvious that he must be still living on board *Pandora* and he must know where Olivia was, but why was he doing nothing about it? It has often struck me about all those novels and plays, dealing with the problems of the lover faced with an aggressive and vengeful husband. All that hopping in and out of bed, and in and out of windows and hiding in cupboards and all that sort of thing. Nobody ever mentions the case of the adulterer and the passive, uninterested husband. One of the hardest things to bear is anti-climax.

Adulterer. Now that was a word, as I realised. What we had done the night before might have been excused, as not real adultery. But there was no going against what had happened that morning. It was one of the ways I felt I was being cheated. It was so joyless. At least sinning should be fun, surely.

As it so happened, I saw James that morning, going into the staff offices block as I drove by. I impulsively hooted my horn as I went past but he did not look round and though I parked as quickly as I could and dashed back he was gone and I could not see where he had gone to. Sitting in my own office I could not get rid of this creeping sense of uneasiness, almost guilt. I could not settle to anything. I did not know whether to bash some papers about or go down to the Damage Control School first, or whether to queue up and see Fiery now, or wait and let him send for me. I must have wasted a good half hour or so, just mooning about trying to make up my mind.

In fact, it was not long before Fiery telephoned me. He said he had one or two things to discuss with me over my visit to sea that last weekend, and could I drop in and see him if I had a moment. Now, as everyone who has ever served under Fiery knows, there was a scale of gradations in his phraseology. When convenient, really meant that, it meant sometime during the working day. But, if you had a moment, meant that very moment. It meant put your running shoes on and get down there right away.

I had an inkling that James had beaten me to it, and had already seen Fiery that morning. James, as I well knew, could charm birds off trees if he put his mind to it. As usual, Fiery beat about no bushes. "Just been having a chat with your friend James Bellingham," he said, once again putting a marked emphasis on the word friend. "We've been making a mountain out of a molehill, I fancy," said Fiery. "There's no need that I can see to chase this up any longer," he said.

Now this was really very indiscreet of Fiery. There was no call for him to be so direct. We were not, on the surface, chasing anything up, either of us. It would have been far more subtle, and far more like the usual Fiery, if he had frozen me off, by showing no interest whatever in anything I had to say about *Pandora*, in generally acting as though he had never asked me at all, so that eventually I would have taken the hint that my services were no longer required in this respect. To go bald-headed at it like this, was unwise and unnecessary, and unlike Fiery.

But I said I was very glad and relieved to hear it. I said I had thought all along that we had been behaving in a very slightly disreputable manner, that hounding a fellow officer, even in the mildest way, was hardly the thing, hardly a nice way to act. Fiery choked a bit on that. After all, since when had Fiery ever had anything to do with niceness? He said, "it was not the custom of the Service to hound anybody. We don't go in for witch hunts," he said in his most lofty manner. Now there was a very curious remark, if you like. You could call it hounding or witch-hunting or whatever you liked but Fiery knew as well as I did there certainly had been occasions when officers had been prevented from achieving their full stature in the Service. They had been hounded away and deprived of their proper expectations. It was made subtly impossible for them to progress further in the Service. This is not just passed-over paranoia on my part. I'm not saying this just because I was passed over myself and think I was robbed. Although, as a matter of fact, I did at the time. But you all know what I mean, without me saying any more.

Again, I had made a bad mistake in handling Fiery. By agreeing with him so readily I immediately made him suspicious. He really was the most suspicious man I ever dealt with and I really don't know what he expected of me, if everything I said was going to make him rush off and do the exact opposite. He seemed to examine everything I said to him as though he suspected it of being counterfeit coin, turning it over and looking at it, and biting into it with his teeth and ringing it on his thumb-nail and generally messing about with it.

All I had said was, yes, we should drop it, as he said. But he at once rounded on me and said, "do I take it you don't agree with me?"

I said to him, yes, certainly I agree with you, sir. I said there were certain small aspects of *Pandora's* commission which might conceivably be taken as slightly dubious by someone who was uncharitably disposed, but by and large, and taking one consideration with another, there was a great deal to be said for behaving as if it had never happened.

Now this, too, as I realised as soon as I had said it, and could have bitten my tongue off, was a very bad slip of the tongue. Fiery had a thing about people who refused to face facts, who behaved as he often said himself as if something had never happened. He was always very scornful about them. Ossifer-ostriches, he used to call them.

From there on in, the interview went from bad to worse.

Despairingly I began to see that this session with Fiery was taking precisely the same course as the last one I had had with him on that Saturday morning. As we went on, try as I might, everything I said to him only made things worse for James.

When I came into Fiery's office, he had been on the point of dismissing the whole thing. With luck we would never have heard another word about *Pandora*. But now, only minutes later, here he was breathing fire and brimstone and suspicion again.

One might well ask, what on earth had *Pandora* to do with Fiery in any case? She was only his responsibility in a very general way, as he was responsible for everything within the Command in a very general way. Whatever happened to her in the Far East was absolutely no skin off his nose at all. But, as I said, he used to get these sudden suspicious moods, suddenly used to get the idea that he was being threatened. It did him no good personally with Father, because I think that even the Admiral eventually began to wonder why Fiery was getting so steamed up about *Pandora*. As I said, Fiery had a jumpy mind and once he jumped at something that was that. It was like trying to get a mad bull terrier off your leg.

As a result of something I had said, it seemed that he began to jump at *Pandora* again. There was a strongly surrealist dreamlike quality about that interview with Fiery. *Pandora* was really nothing to do with either of us and yet it seemed that the sheer pressure of our two personalities coming to bear on each other was forcing us to carry on in a direction which we had both said we did not want to go. I did not want to go any further and yet everything I said to Fiery made him press me onwards. *Pandora* was nothing to do with Fiery and yet everything I said was making him more anxious to bear down on it. Yet he didn't actually tell me in so many words to go on. I was left to work that out for myself....

One thing seemed clear to me by then. Fiery had made a mistake. He had had no business to get himself involved in *Pandora*. He had lowered himself by showing such unseemly curiosity. It was true his motives were probably sound and good. He wanted to root out any nausea which affected the good name of the Service. But he should have left *Pandora* alone. By showing such an interest, he seemed in some peculiar way to be condoning it or at least compounding it. It is very difficult to explain this, but it reflected back on him. I myself think that *Pandora* was the reason, at least partly the reason, why Fiery never went any higher. There may be other reasons, of course, because naturally I don't know the full extent of his professional range in that job. But *Pandora* contributed in some fatal way, I'm sure of it. It was a slight aberration, a wobble if you like, in what had previously been a dead straight line.

I was still thinking about Fiery and still preoccupied by it all when I got back to my own office, and so I was quite taken flat aback by surprise to see James standing glowering at me beside my desk. He did not waste any time in civilities either. He said he did not know what I was up to, but he would thank me if I stopped. He told me I was prodding around *Pandora* and messing about with Olivia and I was to cut it out. He said he thought I was a friend of his and he wondered what game I was playing. He said there was no need for me to go snooping around the place, there was no trouble, there was nothing wrong, nobody was in any sort of difficulty, he was very sorry to disappoint me but everything was just fine and would I please get the hell out of his life? He said a good deal more, mostly repeating himself. And then he stumped out, having not given me much chance to contribute anything to my side of the conversation. I don't know what effect he thought such a visitation would have upon me, but the effect it did have was to encourage me. I got the feeling I was winning.

As you can well imagine, it was a very thoughtful Freddie who made his way down to the Damage Control School later that forenoon. It was no longer such a fine day. The wind had got up, the sun had gone in, there had been one shower of rain and it looked as if there would be another any minute. The Damage Control School looked an absolute shambles. There were puddles all over the place and they were digging up the road in what seemed like half a dozen places and there were heaps of bricks and timber and God knows what all over the place. The huts dated back to the war and perhaps earlier. It looked as if they really needed to start controlling a bit of their own damage. Of course, in a place where they are always setting fire to things and letting off smoke bombs and for ever spraying the scenery with water and fire-fighting foam, I suppose one must expect a certain degree of untidiness.

The idea that day was to test some of the effects of shutting down ventilation systems after a nuclear attack and examining how long it took to get rid of fall-out by washing down. That sort of thing. I was supposed to make an appreciation of the likely effect on habitability of a prolonged period of shut-down. They had a mock-up superstructure of a ship there, with compartments that could be flooded and pumped and filled with smoke and all that. It was quite fun in a way. Everybody likes to mess about with hoses and water and set fire to things and let off stink-bombs.

It is not important now what we did, but what was interesting was one of the sailors working the models in the demonstration hut. They had various models as examples there, to show for instance, how we should not have lost *Ark Royal* during the last war if we had kept our damage control wits about us, and that sort of thing. One of the sailors was Prichard, the javelin thrower from *Pandora*, and one of the guns' crew. He must have got a draft chit from *Pandora*. Why he wasn't on foreign service leave I can't think, but anyway there he was, and I recognised him at once. Later I managed to have a few words with him. I had to be extremely circumspect, because what I wanted to know was not something a leading seaman should know or discuss and certainly not with any officer. But I chatted him up about his last commission, congratulated him on his javelin-throwing, told him I knew his last Captain, and so on. He asked me if I was one of the officers who came on board the day they got alongside. I said yes, I was. He said he remembered my face.

I chatted to Prichard in very general terms, about what sort of a commission it was, was it generally a bind to serve in a situation such as Confrontation, and so on. Prichard said, "no, as a matter of fact it was quite fun." He quite enjoyed it all. There was rather a lot of sea-time but he didn't mind that personally. They went back to Singapore or Hong Kong occasionally. He liked Hong Kong, slightly cheaper and a much better climate. Singapore got you down after a bit. Not enough variation in temperature for people from the UK. I asked him about operations, they must have been pretty tough, I said? He said "no, not particularly, they were very enjoyable. You got the feeling you were doing something. Everything had much more point to it." He was a gunnery rating and for him firing the guns was the name of the game. That was what he was paid to do and that was what he liked doing most. I asked him, was there any particular operation he remembered? He said "no, he couldn't remember one in particular. They were all pretty much the same." I said I had read in the papers that *Pandora* had once had to go up river to save some people, some British people, who were in a spot of bother. The Royal Marines were there too, I said. He said "yes, he remembered that one." So I said, did they fire the guns that time. He looked a bit blank and said, "yes of course they had," they had "fired while the landing craft," he remembered that there had been landing craft, "while the craft were coming down river." He said they had "shot up a few sampans lying outside the river entrance." Ah, I said, what about that, did you sink a small sampan just off the harbour entrance? "Yes," he said, "it took them a long time to get on to it and the Gunnery Officer was getting narked about it, but once they nailed it they sank it." I said, was there any talk on the messdecks afterwards about that? He looked absolutely blank and asked me "what sort of talk." I said I didn't know, I just wondered whether they talked about it afterwards? Prichard said "yes" as far as he could remember "they talked about every operation, who wouldn't?" Exactly, I said, but what about this one? He said they "did several operations" and they "talked about them all." So, getting a bit desperate, because I could see he was getting a bit puzzled by all this, I asked him if anybody felt bad about it afterwards. It felt a stupid question when I asked and it seemed even more stupid when Prichard just looked at me as if I had gone out of my tiny mind. He said "why should anybody feel bad about it?" Unanswerable, of course. He said "the only thing" they felt bad about "was the time it took them to get on the target." He said, suddenly looking right at me, "was there anything to feel bad about?" I said of course not, I had just heard there had been a lot of talk on the messdecks afterwards. He looked amazed. "Not that I ever heard," he said.

So there we were. At least one highly intelligent, highly trained and skilled and very knowledgeable rating in *Pandora* had heard nothing of any subsequent discussions. It could have been that Prichard was extraordinarily insensitive or extraordinarily loyal. It was only the officers who were at all bothered, and making a fuss. All this talk of comparisons with Nuremburg and personal responsibility in time of war and the licensed place of violence in our society and the proper behaviour of officers under stress and all that, all that had gone clean over the heads of at least a proportion of *Pandora's* ship's company. I did not believe that Prichard was typical of them all, because there certainly had been incidents ashore on their first night back from the Far East. But they might have had quite innocent reasons or any rate, different reasons. Anyway, Prichard had unconsciously given me quite a fresh slant on it. It showed once again the folly of believing all that you hear, and only what you hear, in the wardroom. There is a whole lot going on beyond the wardroom pantry door and things seldom look quite the same when you see them from forward. Here was a sailor intimately involved in that incident. As one of the guns' crew he couldn't have been more closely involved. But did he worry? Not on your nelly. Did he fret? Not a chance. War crimes? Never heard of them. Personal guilt feelings? Not me chum, try the mess next door. I must say, it was quite refreshing, as well as enlightening, to talk to someone like Prichard.

I was itching to ask him more, but really I had spent too long already talking to him. He was already beginning to look at me as if he was beginning to wonder what the hell I was showing such an interest for. One can't go on indefinitely interrogating a member of somebody else's ship's company.

But I could not resist one more question. I asked Prichard if he was sorry to leave *Pandora*? He looked non-committal at first but he said "yes" he was, "very sorry to leave her." He said "she was one of the best ships" he had ever been on. I asked him how many ships he had served in. He was only a very young fellow. He looked embarrassed, a little, and said "one." So it was not all that much of a testimonial. However, there it was. He said he had "enjoyed the ship. Good skipper," he said, "good blokes on board, good time had by all." I must say life through Prichard's eyes was attractively uncomplicated. He took a simple, innocent view of life, idyllic almost. In a way I envied him.

Finally I asked Prichard if there were any others from *Pandora* who had got a draft chit with him. He said "no." So that was that.

The Damage Control School was on the Torpoint side and on my way back, I don't know why, but it occurred to me to make a detour and call round by Sebastopol Buildings and see how Olivia was getting on. You can see how disruptive all this was. This was the middle of a working day. I had a hell of a lot of things to do. But there I was, driving several miles out of my way to see Olivia.

Perhaps it was some premonition I had, but anyway I was not really surprised to find that she had gone. James must have called and collected her. I must have missed them by only a few minutes. I say I was not surprised, but I was still very dismayed to find her gone. I can't explain that peculiar feeling of absolute desolation that swept over me then. I understood why people committed suicide and did really desperate things, things which normally would be unthinkable for them. She had not only gone she had removed all traces of herself. She had washed up all the breakfast things and she had even washed out the dish cloth and hung it on the line in the garden. Upstairs she had stripped the bed and piled up everything neatly. I looked at the table and there was no sign of powder or tissues or a trace even of her perfume. Nothing at all. She had scoured that little house out. I went out into the garden. It was deserted and it seemed odd to be there in the middle of a working day. There were some irises and a cotoneaster bush, with lots of bees, and a great ragged bed of nasturtiums. Unprofitably gay. I doubt if I had ever been in the garden at that time of day midweek before. It seemed somehow hotter and quieter and even emptier than usual. I felt guilty at being there, midday. The people had arrived in the end house, the people I didn't know. I could hear shouts and a dog barking and I could see children running to and fro. It made my little strip of garden seem all the more deserted.

I drove back to the staff office buildings convinced that this was the end of it all. Olivia had gone. James had gone, with her, probably on leave. *Pandora* was paid off and whatever there was there to be learned from her would dispense with her people. Fiery was not interested, or said he wasn't. That should have been that. I had lost James' friendship, I had lost Olivia. That was the end of it.

So it might have been, had it not been for that wretched summer. I have said already how bloody awful the weather was that year. That day was typical. It began as I have said, beautifully, but it clouded. The wind got up and by evening there was a whole gale blowing. About midnight, something broke loose in the Hamoaze, I think it was a fuel lighter or something, came careering downstream and down wind and thumped *Pandora* good and proper. It actually holed her amidships, and it started a fire, with some flooding too. It was dark, it was blowing a hooligan, there was only a skeleton crew on board, reactions were a bit slow, somebody didn't call the dockyard brigade out soon enough and before they got the fire out it had managed to do quite a lot of damage.

But it is an ill wind and that fire was in a way a bit of luck for me. Strictly speaking, the whole business was a matter for the Queen's Harbourmaster, and the technical aspects were the concern of the damage control and firefighting experts on the staff, and only then much later, when all the reports had had time to filter their way upwards into the staff office. Strictly speaking, there was no reason for any member of the staff to go on board at all, and if you wanted to be uncharitable you could say I was snooping. But not really. There were aspects of the thing which did concern me and it was not at all unusual, in fact it was good and recognised practise, for people on the staff to go down and have a word informally with those involved. I was not snooping, not really.

The first person I saw was Mickey Gibb. He gave me what I can only call a knowing look, but he didn't really say anything, not about that anyway. The first thing he said to me was, "you didn't waste any time getting down here." That cut me, because the last thing I wanted to do was to get the reputation of being a bird of ill-omen, always hovering about when there was trouble. He also said something that chimed with a tiny suspicion that had been at the very back of my mind. The possibility of sabotage. But when I thought about it I decided it was impossible. The psychology was all wrong. Sailors damage a ship for a number of reasons. You get the nut cases and the fellows with grudges. Some silly sailor wants to stop the ship sailing because he wants to stay and see his girlfriend, or he doesn't like what the Master at Arms said to him, or some other silly reason, or maybe to draw attention to something that's happened during the commission. But in this case there was no point in it. It just didn't ring right.

Mickey said to me, "I suppose you want to see all the gory details now." I would indeed, although I was a bit put out by his choice of words. After all, I did have a much better professional reason for visiting *Pandora* than mere morbid curiosity. Though I have to admit that there is this something in all of us that wants to see the gory details, after a fire or an accident or anything like that.

I followed Mickey below and within a few steps I could see that this was a different ship. They had been home about a week, in fact it was a week to the very day, and already *Pandora* had gone right downhill. She was almost completely run down in that short time. They had all let the end go and no mistake. I could hardly credit that this was the same ship I had been in a few days before. She had been so smart and now she was so scruffy. It seemed amazing that paintwork could get so grubby in so short a time. Even our footsteps sounded differently on the deck. It was incredible that polished gangways and decks could get so scuffed and grimy almost overnight. I say it seems incredible, but there is one explanation for it, which I have often thought about since. The solution was that the ship had not gone down all that much or all that rapidly. She had never been as smart as I thought in the first place. I had been blinded by the fact that it was James' ship and she should have been absolutely on the top line and so I must have assumed that she was. It was a case of the eye seeing what the mind expected it to and not what it actually did. Admittedly, being in dockyard hands never improves a ship and some of the grubbiness was due to that. But most, as I say, was there already.

I kept behind Mickey, walking rather timidly and expectantly, looking around, half afraid I might turn a corner and run right into James, face to face. But we didn't see him, in fact we didn't see anybody. I never saw a ship so deserted. There wasn't even anybody at the scene of the fire. One might have expected somebody to be there, metaphorically raking through the ashes. But there wasn't a soul.

Pandora's fire was the old, old story of a train of small things, like a fuse being laid, combining together to cause quite a serious incident in the end. The lighters, they were lighters, I've just remembered, gave the ship's side a bump. They started some plating, let some water in, and displaced some electrical equipment off the bulkhead at the point of impact. It should have been safe on impact but for some reason it wasn't. There was a short, or something, a flash, which started a fire. There were paint and clothing and wire coverings there, where perhaps there shouldn't have been, it burned for some time, eventually through some more cables, more shorting, more flashes I suppose, slightly larger fire and so on, which caught some lockers and spare gear lying around. There was even an open can of diesel oil to complete matters. That burned very well. It was the classical case of the fire which at one time could have been put out by one man stamping it out with his foot eventually getting to the stage where it required half an hour's grim work by the brigade. The result of it all was an electrical store, a couple of messdecks and a stretch of passageway nearby quite badly burned and blackened and damaged. It did look a mess, with all that water and debris and general chaos lying all around.

It was fairly obvious to me how the fire might affect my department. Had a fire been allowed to start there during the commission, there would have been many more people about and although it was a little awkward to get to and some of the items of firefighting equipment were awkwardly placed, it is very doubtful if the fire would ever spread so far. Perhaps the naval architects calculated that there would be many more people about, and did not allow for a fire after paying off. But I doubt that very much. I could see that to make this part of the ship safer, so far as firefighting was concerned, it would also have to be made less comfortable. A little less room and accessibility for everyone. So it came back to that same old argument.

Anyway, I said to Mickey, and I meant it, I said I am very sorry this should have happened to you. Mickey at once gave another of his devilish chuckles and I still remember what he said because he cut me to the very core. It was like having one's backbone laid open at one slice. It still makes me wince to think of it. "Come off it, Freddie," he said, "don't waste your crocodile tears on us. You're not interested in the ship, you only want to get your hot and clammy hands on the Captain's wife." While I was still reeling from that, he said casually he would have to love me and leave me, because he had a lot to do that forenoon. He introduced his Chief OA who had approached from somewhere and said he would show me anything else I wanted to see.

The fellow's name was Noland, and he was a tall, dark and rather handsome man. Rather distinguished looking. Obviously a very responsible and respected rating. As chief ordnance artificer, or he's probably called some other title now, but anyway he was the top man in looking after the nuts and bolts of the gunnery department, one of Mickey's right hand men. He had a rather solemn manner and a voice like a padre reading the lesson, but he clearly knew what he was about in the gunnery world.

I began by saying to him, and nodding my head all around at the state of chassis everywhere, this seems to have done a hell of a lot of damage, I said. I meant it just as a conversation opener, but something in my voice must have suggested to Noland that I thought it all a pretty poor show, and that seemed to nettle him. He said, quick as a flash, "you have to make allowances, sir," he said, "we're paid off now in dockyard hands. It wouldn't have happened if we'd still been in proper commission. We were better than that, sir, I can tell you," he said.

That, when you come to think of it, was a very strange remark, and it illustrated a very strange attitude of mind. Of course they would do better when they were in full commission than when they were paid off. I should jolly well hope so. It would be a fine kettle of fish if they didn't. Yet, in a curious way, the remark also showed a very fierce residual loyalty to the commission. It was over and past and done with and yet Noland still felt strongly enough about it to defend it to somebody he had never met before. And in his determination to set what he thought was the record straight, he was not afraid of straying perilously close to being accused of being impertinent to an officer. Because his expression and tone of voice were extremely stroppy, I can tell you.

"You've been on board, sir," he said, "you know." I said yes I did know, while privately I was thinking to myself, how odd it was that so many noticed and remembered me in the short time I was on board that day.

Standing there in that blackened and scorched and ruined bit of James' ship, we had a most interesting discussion, Noland and I. Naturally we soon moved on from the fire, back into the past commission. Noland did not need much prompting although, like Prichard, I could not ask all the questions I wanted to, and for the same reason. But Noland seemed genuinely anxious to talk. It didn't seem to worry him that I was an officer and a stranger at that. As I did not come from the ship or from the flotilla but from the nebulous staff, whoever they might be, Noland evidently felt that he could be as indiscreet as someone you meet in a hotel bar where you've never been before and are never likely to go again, or in a railway compartment. Although I must say that in my experience one does tend to meet such people again, sooner or later.

Inevitably we got on to that incident, but only after Noland had badly misled me. I had asked him if there was anything in the commission, any event or incident, which had particularly impressed him, made him most pleased or sad. Noland said, by golly, he said, there certainly was. It was one of the times they had been operating inshore off the coast, he said. I thought ha ha, here we go again. But in fact it turned out to be a quite different incident, when *Pandora* had sent a boarding party aboard a junk and they were fired on by the junk's crew. The junk had arms, drugs, a crew of insurgents on board, the lot, it was a fair cop. But the petty officer with the boarding party, a special friend of Noland's, got shot in the stomach and in the spine and very badly hurt. He had to be taken off to hospital ashore, and eventually invalided out of the Service. Noland said that was a tragedy, and he used that word. His friend was really keen on the Service, all for it, Noland said. He said he went to see him in hospital in Singapore before they left for home. He could just about move one eyebrow, that was all, and Noland said it was the most heart-breaking experience. There was a young man, at the peak of life, unmarried, no ties, everything to give, no liabilities, and there he was with stomach and spinal injuries, useless to the Service and useless for anything at all, for many years to come. Curiously enough, that story reminded me of a friend of mine and James' when we were midshipmen. He was all for it, too, but he got accidentally shot when we were doing a small arms training course in Bermuda and invalided out. He's a bookseller now. But that's by the way.

Noland was a very thoughtful individual, a member of the Chief's mess, a very important body of men in any ship and especially so in a small ship like a frigate. While Prichard represented the ordinary matelot, the stuff of the messdecks, the rock-bottom, safe, marvellous base metal of any ship,

Noland was something a little more special. To run any ship properly you have to have people like Prichard going with you. That's the absolute minimum, because if you don't you will have every sort of trouble up to and including mutiny. But to get a really good commission, to get the sort of ship that lives in the memory and keeps you warm in your old age, the sort of ship that gets the extra stripe, the Chief Petty Officer's rate, the brass hat, for all concerned, then you have to win over the Nolands, too.

And that, strange to say, was exactly what James seemed to have done. Noland was all for him. Wouldn't hear a word against him. Could not speak too highly of him. So, I gathered, did all the senior rates. Noland went so far as to say that *Pandora* was one of the best, if not actually the best, commission he ever had. No need to ask him as I had asked Prichard, how many ships he had been in. Clearly this was a real testimonial, well worth having and hearing.

In Noland's opinion, when I finally got him talking about that incident, they knew it was wrong to fire and in his heart of hearts, Noland thought, the Captain knew it was wrong, too. But there it was. It just had to be. It was just one of those things, in Noland's view.

I asked Noland what the Chief's mess thought at the time. I had no business to ask any such thing, but it really didn't seem to matter much by then. Noland said he thought "some of them were disgusted, some of them didn't care a damn. But even those who were disgusted," and even then Noland went back on the word, thinking it too strong, and began to qualify it, "even those who were a bit put out by it," he said, "even they realised that there are times in everybody's job when you have to make a decision and then stick to it. It's what an officer is for," Noland said. "That's his job," he said. "Nobody thought any the less of the Captain for making up his mind and then sticking to it."

In its own way, Noland's point of view was as deliciously crystal clear and as reassuring, just as innocent if you like, as Prichard's was. You really couldn't argue with such certainty, with such serenity, I think is the word. James was very lucky in his ship's company, that was becoming quite clear. He may have had problems in the wardroom but his sailors were pure gold. Maybe they were lucky to have him, too. "The guns are there to be fired," Noland said, "I look after them and maintain them so that they can be fired and when the Captain says shoot we shoot. This was a proper target, the Captain decided to fire and the guns fired. It doesn't do any good," Noland said, to "waste time looking backwards and bellyaching about it." As I said, there was a kind of unanswerable, crushing certainty about Noland's point of view.

Noland sprang one last surprise. Almost as an after-thought, I said to him, did you by any chance see that little sampan yourself?

To my utter astonishment he said, "I wouldn't call it a sampan. More of a junk. Yes I certainly saw it myself," he said. "I had a very good view."

I said, but I thought it was only a tiny sampan, about the size of a dinghy, I was told it was about the size of the little widger that brought the dhobying out from shore?

"I don't know who told you that," he said. "It was the size of a whaler or a motor boat, at least," he said, "if not bigger."

I had another thought. How many people would you say were on board, I said.

He said he reckoned "there were half a dozen, perhaps a dozen. You could see their heads, some of them."

I said, but you must have very good eyesight to see them at that distance?

He said "not particularly, and in any case they were only about three-quarters of a mile away."

How interesting, I said, at last. So there we were. Prichard had confounded all my previously received theories about it, and Noland had contradicted all my previously received facts about it. As Mickey Gibb had said, there was more than one way of telling how the cat was killed.

CHAPTER 9

Freddie's party, as they had begun to think of themselves, had now been travelling in their aircraft for so long that their sense of its sheer physical oddness had worn off. Their cabin and their seats had become unfamiliarly real and as the passengers became accustomed to them, as their apprehensions of their surroundings became less obtrusive, so their memories, and their anticipations of the ground below, the world and their destinations became more credible. The nearer the aircraft came to their destination, so the more real that destination became. Freddie was not now talking to them of long ago and far away. He was talking of the recent past and the immediate future, in a world which was coming closer every second.

The stewardesses were bringing round trays of cups of coffee and for almost the first time on the flight their ministrations matched the needs of their passengers. Everybody genuinely wanted and was ready for coffee. It tasted for the first time like something that was real and recognisable from the outside world. Their cups were hardly empty when the aircraft's deck trembled and the cabin body began to shudder and plunge as though the aircraft were fighting through a stream of violent turbulence. At once the passengers' minds leaped back to the frailty of their positions, sitting in the sky. The old fears sprang back, of falling through the deck, of slipping out through the sides into space. The steady seat-belt and smoking warning lights, now on, promoted mental images, not of reassurance but of disintegration and disaster. The aircraft still fought and plunged and shuddered. The deck dropped through air with a lurch that left the passengers hanging in their straps. After one last twist and swoop, as though finally shrugging off its load, the aircraft suddenly soared up into calmness. The voice of the Captain assured them all that the disturbance was temporary. They had flown too close to the aircraft ahead, also lining up for a landing at the same airport. They would, his voice said, be landing in a few minutes.

Once more the aircraft tilted on its side and slipped sideways. It sank through layers of sky which once again took on colours, of grey and yellow streaks. Once more the passengers underwent the final apprehension, suspense and grateful shock of the landing. They looked at each other and mouthed soundless words of relief under the solid drumming of the tyres on the runway.

When the tidal doors opened the mid-morning heat flooded in. The airport was in a different continent, but it was the same. The odour of the dust was different, but the same. The airport sky was a different colour but had the same glaring intensity of light. The airport buildings were the same, low and grimy and seeming a long way away across the heated tarmac.

We can go ashore here, Freddie said. Middle Eastern time here. There's a wait of two hours, maybe more.

Gulping in the heat, bowing their heads under the sun, Freddie's party made their way across the apron, treading like waders. They wandered about the deserted galleries and empty concourses of the airport building for some time. The airport was a place of hot dry winds blowing paper along the passageways, loudspeaker announcements on which nobody seemed to act, knots of officials gathering in corners and dispersing again, displays of advertisements set out with such artful, deliberate skill that the eye simply passed over them without seeing. Through a window, they could see a line of large gleaming cars, silently waiting in the heat. The road behind them curved out of sight; it was like an image from childhood, gazing out of the school window at a hot, empty road, lying in the sun, waiting for someone to come along.

They all went back to their aircraft seats as though to familiar surroundings, in their favourite club. They sat down like a team. Lunch in the air, with paper napkins and red wine, was almost festive. The airport below was already an irrelevance. The listeners were now thoroughly accustomed to the pattern of Freddie's narrative sessions. They knew he had first to warm himself up with his memories, and then unload until he himself recoiled from his own indiscretions. Thus there were always successive stages, of diffidence, exposure, and then remorse. The listeners themselves were beginning to have intimations of tragedy. From their own experience they knew they looked forward to a gloomy prospect. Freddie, as the speaker at least was a survivor. That was certain. Everything else was still conjecture. But the listeners were becoming more and more aware of the tension between Freddie and his story. He was a figure of comedy, not tragedy. He was more convincing when he was describing comic events. He simply was not an appropriate recorder of tragedy. He had a diarist's proper concern for the sequence of events, but his listeners had to try and disassociate themselves from their own prejudices, at a time when Freddie and his story were appealing to them all the more strongly. They were coming to realise that, although Freddie might be the wrong teller, they themselves might also be the wrong listeners.

Nevertheless, Freddie took up his story again where he had left off, smoothly and accurately as though obeying some internal metabolic clock which led him effortlessly back to the break in his narrative. His listeners, too, followed him as easily. In a few hours he had artlessly created for them a complete world, in which they felt as at home as he did, in which they saw familiar faces and heard familiar voices, in which every gesture and action came from their own experience, in which indeed they could often recognise their own features.

That evening, said Freddie, I went to the old Coliseum for a drink, the first time for a week. In one way it seemed about a year since I was last there, in another it seemed only a few minutes past. There was Rudolf still, shuffling about as though he had the cares of the world on his shoulders. There was the same smell of old velvet and moth-eaten leather, and Angostura bitters about ten years old, what I always think of as a smell of aspidistras, if aspidistras have a smell. It was not quite the same though. Somebody had taken some of the plants out of the conservatory, I could see, and when I came to look there were not so many armchairs in that lounge. It was as though they were economising on atmosphere. I asked Rudolf and he said he had heard the hotel had been sold. It turned out that it had and that as far as I can remember now was one of the last times I ever had a drink in that favourite old bar of mine. Certainly a year later the hotel was gone, all of it, knocked down, demolitioned, whisked away. God knows what happened to Rudolf.

To complete that weird feeling that time had passed and had stood still at the same time, in came Simon Fiddich again. That was twice I had seen him there. Either he had come hoping to see me or because he too genuinely liked the old Coliseum, just as I did. Either way, it made me warm just the smallest bit towards him.

But this was a more wary young man. Much more on his guard that night. A week earlier I had been some seedy old two-and-a-half he happened to run across in a rundown bar.

He knew much more about me now. Now, there was a different, dare I say it, a more respectful look in his eye. Funnily enough, though I had had it in the back of my mind to have a word with this fellow some time, now that he was here, now that he was filling the whole frame so to speak, now that he was actually trying to buy me a drink, perversely I did not feel like talking to him.

He had no such doubts of any such sort. When I said respectful, I think he had realised I might conceivably be dangerous to him, but I do not mean he was any more respectful in his behaviour towards me personally.

"Found out all you want," he said to me, heaving up an armchair beside me, uninvited, I may say.

I suppose it was very childish of me to get in a huff, but I didn't reply. Just went on pretending to read my evening newspaper. That was one of young Fiddich's devilish abilities, this ability to make me feel I was an old gentleman of eighty, and a peppery one at that. But from importunity he soon went to impertinence. "Why don't you lay off," he said to me. "Why do you keep on at us? There's nothing to find out," he said, "no secret, no mystery, no reason to go snooping about the place. I don't know what you think happened to us or why you should be so interested," he said, "but there was nothing discreditable, and whatever happened, it was none of your business anyway. The Captain is a very fine fellow indeed," he said, "I have the greatest admiration and respect for him. He's done a lot for me and I don't want to see him worried or persecuted."

That made me give a quiet chuckle to myself. You didn't always feel you'd been so terribly loyal to your Captain, I said to him, on your own admission, the last time I saw you here, in this very room, sitting in this very chair, I said. There was something biting you then, and it wasn't a feeling of loyalty whatever it was.

That hit him. "That's all past now," he said, "and again," he said, "anyway it is all absolutely sweet bugger-all to do with you."

Fiddich was disconcertingly well-informed about my movements in the last week or so. He knew, apparently, that I had had a chat with Noland, and he seemed to know pretty well what we had talked about. That was not so very surprising, I suppose. But it turned out he also knew that I had been across the river to the Damage Control School and had met Prichard. That, when you think about it, was very strange. I still wonder how he came to know about that.

He also knew about Olivia and to my utter astonishment he knew where my house at Sebastopol Buildings was. More than that, he had even been there, that very morning. I was absolutely dumbfounded to find that it was Fiddich who had collected Olivia that morning. It shows I must be getting better as a story-teller, that I held that back before. But I can't properly describe now, not fully, how much that hurt, how insulting and contemptuous that was. James had not even come himself but had sent his First Lieutenant, his henchman, his faithful deputy dog. It was Fiddich who must have helped Olivia collect up her things. It was Fiddich with his damnably tidy mind who had cleaned up so thoroughly. I was furious that those two should have been rooting around in my house. Again, it showed the utter contempt they all had for me. The thought of Fiddich of all people going through and doing a sort of messdeck rounds through my little house, it was too much. I would not have dreamed of going into their house if the situation had somehow been reversed.

He was furious, too, towards me. It was unmistakable, a kind of edge, a really ferocious cutting edge in his tone of voice. It was not just personal dislike, though there certainly was that, too, but something extra and unexpected. After a time I realised it was something to do with Olivia. I detected an element of rivalry in him. I remembered that it had occurred to me once before that he was soft on Olivia. It was only just becoming clear to me at about that time what an effect Olivia had had on James' officers. It was one of the bitterest things I had to face, this knowledge that they were both so popular on board, both so successful, both respected, both loved, even. There was no way I could get into it. They were all impregnable.

Suddenly sitting there in that old Coliseum lounge, looking across at this unfriendly little character, I suddenly thought to myself, well now, surely I can learn something here? That there is the shape of success in this modem Navy. That's where it is. If you want to succeed, that is what it looks like. This fellow is going to be successful. I was looking across at him, across a great gulf of what you might call culture, and background, and the way we looked at life in general. The things he wanted out of life and the things he was prepared to put into life were not the things I wanted or was prepared to give. His Navy was not my Navy and his ambitions were never my ambitions, and never had been and never could have been. Talk about the generation gap. This was the Grand Canyon of a gap. This fellow was a different species. He came from a different planet. But still, I thought I could learn something from him because he was going to do all right. He was going to be promoted, whereas I was passed over. He looked and felt pleased with himself and things were going right for him, whereas I probably looked discouraged and seedy and more than a bit disgruntled and fed up with life. I was not married, he probably was. He had everything going for him, where things seemed to be slowing down for me. There could not be a greater contrast. So I thought, well I'll ask. What is it exactly that makes a modem naval success story? How come this little reptile was quite plainly going to make it whereas I never did? I'll try and find out what makes Fiddich tick.

Of course, I did not know then that he was not going to do quite as well as anybody might have expected and that was partly due to *Pandora*. At that time everything looked golden and all systems seemed go for young master Fiddich. For a certain kind of cussedness, because the whole thing was academic for me by then, I thought I would try and find out how it was done. It would be too late to help me but there might be a certain gloomy relish in knowing why not.

I remember I said earlier that Hickey the chopper pilot was something of a poet. So was Simon Fiddich in his own peculiar way. He had a vivid way of putting things. He was a poet of the administrative life, if you like, in the organising of men and ships. I learned a lot from him that evening, in fits and starts, in between insults and innuendoes. It is surprising how much somebody who dislikes you can reveal about himself without meaning to. The very business of recoiling from you and rejecting you adds a certain counter-energy of its own.

One thing I did find out without any question was that Fiddich was a cracking good First Lieutenant. No doubt about it. Admittedly he was always trying to blow his own trumpet, but even allowing for that I've been in the Service long enough now and served with enough blokes good and bad to know the real thing when I see it. It was what he didn't stress that showed, the things he rather left unsaid than what he did say that proved it. You could see that he possessed a whole range of assumptions and definitions and conclusions from experience, which he could only have got from a good ship, well run, and well thought out.

It was all the more praiseworthy because reading between the lines he must have got off to a somewhat shaky start. It was his first time as a Jimmy, he was naturally dead keen to do well. They were all new. He was new, and like a lot of new brooms the bristles were rather new and bristly and they rather stuck out and got up people's noses. I got the impression that there were one or two sticky episodes in the beginning. But the situation was saved each time by James who apparently behaved in the most exemplary manner. He supported his First Lieutenant to the hilt, while still keeping flexible on the issue concerned. He listened to his ship's company and made allowances for their point of view, but making it clear all along the line that discipline had to come first and foremost. The way Fiddich told it, James Bellingham gave a bloody faultless exhibition of how to get a new ship and a new wardroom and a new ship's company all off to a good start together.

The way Fiddich told it, *Pandora* had quite a commission. Of course they were lucky to have all the romance of the Far East and all that, and an independent ship most of the time so that they could take advantage of all that Rudyard Kipling scenario. Their operational life was like something out of the *Boy's Own Paper* in the Nineteenth Century. *Hurrah for the Life of a Sailor*, or *Jack the Pride of the Fleet*. Like one of those stories by Percy F. Westerman we used to get in our Christmas stockings when we were small. They seemed to do a bit of everything. Chased up gun-runners, and arrested pirates. They patrolled the coast during Confrontation, looking for subversive elements. Sometimes the sailors went ashore in a sort of Naval Brigade, again just like Victorian times, to help out the soldiers and the

Royal Marines. Once they stood by and took off the crew of an iron-ore steamer wrecked on the Anambas Islands. They just escaped a typhoon. As I said, it was an all-singing, all-dancing commission, something happening all the time. James and Fiddich seemed to have done a great deal on the *morale* side, too. Sailors love to read about themselves in the papers, so they made a point of having reporters on board whenever they could. They arranged film shows and banyan parties, and mail, of course. Mind you, on some of the banyan parties, half the party might be swimming while the other half had to patrol the beach up and down with guns to protect them. But nobody minded that. The sailors played football against the pongoes. James and Mickey went duck-shooting. They had plenty of gunnery and missile practice, plenty of helicopter flying. In some ways it was like one's mental picture of a pre-war commission. It made me quite wistful to hear about it all. It made all the more impression on me because of the manner in which it was told. Fiddich made it insultingly clear that I would never have a commission like that. Never again.

He told me about one particular incident, not the famous one, which really did read like something out of G. A. Henty. There was an election coming up in Singapore and a great deal of political tension. There was a tremendous increase in clandestine traffic. The whole area was seething with potential trouble. The commando carrier cut short her self refit in Hong Kong and came back to the coast. The Royal Marines were reinforced. A battalion of Gurkhas and two more companies of Jocks were specially flown in.

One day *Pandora* got the tip that one particular junk at one particular place on one particular night was going to be carrying a big shot in the underground politics of Indonesia. Big Red, he was called. I told you it sounded like a film script.

Anyway, one dark and mysterious night they lay in wait for this Big Red in his junk. The point is that although they were pretty sure they had the right one, it was virtually impossible to identify a junk at night from all the hundreds of others there were likely to be around. So they had to follow their target until dawn and then close it as rapidly as they could before the other side woke up to what was happening.

Of course, the moment that junk saw *Pandora* looming up astern, it turned north and cracked on the knots. Fiddich said they reckoned at the time that junk must have been fitted with some kind of MTB engine and it must have been specially tuned because they were both very soon doing twenty knots plus, and *Pandora* was hardly gaining an inch. Now, the normal law-abiding junk simply doesn't have anything like that turn of speed. If nothing else, a blinding burst like that showed guilt. James had to pile on the revs and, according to Fiddich, they had to work up to twenty-four knots before this junk finally began to come back to them. They fired one shot ahead of her, she having totally ignored all their flag and flashing signals to stop. The junk took no notice. They fired again, much closer this time. The junk merely drove straight forward through the spray of the shell splash. Fiddich said it was the most amazing feeling. Here was the medieval-looking junk, with sails made out of what looked like rotten palm leaves, fishing gear or something all lying in tangles on the deck, untidy-looking ropes and ends all over her, nobody on deck, but creaming along at nearly twenty-five knots, chucking up the most enormous bow wave. They fired a third shot, right over the wheel-house and it was as though they had shot the captain. The junk stopped at once as though it had been shot. Fiddich said it must have had the most fantastic astern power as well. It swung in a very tight circle under *Pandora's* stern. Its turning circle was very much less than *Pandora's* and by the time James had put his wheel over hard a gilbert and come round that junk was beetling off again, full bat, back the way she had come. They overhauled her again. More shots, another turn hard a gilbert, and again James had to stand off. He didn't want to sink the thing, or ram it. If this Big Red really was on board, the powers that be wanted to have a talk with him.

As time passed, they clicked that there was a pattern to the junk's manoeuvrings. It was trying to double back to the shore line where they had sailed from the previous evening. James latched on to this, and every time they doubled back he was there in *Pandora* to head them off. Fiddich said the junk's ship handling was really excellent. They jinked and jerked and sidestepped like a frantic snipe. But it did them no good and at last they seemed to realise this. It seemed they were just about to chuck it in when down came a squall. Rain so hard you could hardly breathe in it. It came down with a sound like a thousand kettle drums on the side, Fiddich said. They could only follow the junk on radar while the squall lasted. The junk of course lit out for home again, and they just had to track it. Fiddich said he thought that rain was never going to end. They seemed to be travelling along with it, and at about the same speed. I suppose that must have been a subjective reaction, but I know the feeling. It seemed an agonisingly long time before it cleared and they could start again. By this time the land was a lot closer and they realised that this junk one way or another had made up quite a lot of distance to safety. However, fortunately, the junk evidently decided that there was no future in this. It stopped and waited. *Pandora's* boarding party were ready. The motor boat was soon in the water and off they went, tin hats and Lanchester carbines and a nervous feeling in the pit of the stomach no doubt, with Mickey Gibb in charge. I myself have never been on a boarding party, but I can imagine the feeling. It comes nearest to what we all imagined as small boys serving in the Navy would be like. Somehow we always saw ourselves sitting in the stern-sheets of a boat, armed to the teeth, with a party of gallant bluejackets on our way to put things right for Queen and country. It's like being twice as alive as usual.

They needed to be on this occasion, because Big Red and all his chums were waiting. It was very unusual for a junk to put up any resistance to a boarding party, but clearly Big Red was a very important man and obviously worth the extra trouble and aggravation. No sooner had Mickey and his party got on board and moved towards the main hatch when the fireworks started. They opened fire from below, somebody firing up through the deck boards from the hold underneath. One of the boarding party, the petty officer who was Noland's great friend, was quite badly wounded at once. There was quite a lot of firing and shouting and tumult before it all went quiet and the men below came out, with their hands satisfactorily in the air. There were four of them and two more dead bodies down below.

One of the survivors was a very polite little Malay who spoke perfect English and had the most perfect manners. He turned out to be Big Red. John the Marine, the intelligence officer on board, was delighted with him. They found all manner of things in that junk that shouldn't have been there. Piles of small arms, and explosives and detonators, and currency, there was even a printing press, and boxes of coloured chalks and rolls of political posters. They couldn't read the Chinese signs, but they were obviously not very polite. There were also stacks and stacks of subversive literature, some in Chinese, some in Malay, some in English. Fiddich said they were all rather amazed to find amongst it copies of such things as *Ashore and Afloat*, you know, the newspaper for Aggie Weston's sailors' homes. The thoughts of Chairwoman Aggie. John the Marine had a field-day with all this and so did all the security boys in Singapore. Fiddich said they were gloating over it all for weeks afterwards. Hickey flew Big Red and the junk's crew inshore for interrogation. He also took the petty officer, whose name was Hastings, I've just remembered, into hospital. The Sub and a prize crew of four took the junk back to Brunei. Incidentally, they found that it had two Mercedes engines, great big supercharged brutes of things, and a specially coated fibreglass hull. It wasn't a junk at all but a high speed motor-boat got up to look like a junk. I believe the sails actually were made of palm leaves.

It seems that James was none too pleased about the way everything had gone off, according to Fiddich. There had been an element of the ludicrous about that chase, like a greyhound chasing a hen round and round a field and taking far too long about it. Mind you, that hen had turned out to be a lot nippier and a lot more shrewd than one would have expected a hen to be, but still James was peeved at the time it had taken. Quite apart from Hastings' injuries. That might have been avoided, although it is always easy to be wise after the event.

After he had finished telling it all, Fiddich looked at me and asked me, "is that what you wanted to know, that sort of thing?" I said yes, of course. He said, "well, I can't see anything discreditable to anybody about that. Things could have been improved," he said. "Everybody knew that, nobody better than the Captain."

I wanted to get away from this semi-success story for a bit and so I said, was the Captain always as peeved when things didn't go quite right? He looked a bit blank at this, and then he said "he was peeved only when he could see how things could be improved and in any case peeved was really the wrong word. It was just that he was always trying to cut out mistakes and make things run more smoothly." I said, was there any time, any of these operations, when you thought the Captain came a real cropper and made a mistake? This was virtually the same old question I asked everybody. He said flatly, "no, never." I said wasn't there a time when the General commanding all the land forces out there came on board afterwards? I expected him to react a bit to this but once again he looked blank but after he had thought a bit he said, "yes, there was," he remembered. "I am afraid," he said, "I'm afraid that was one time I rather let the boss down. I've always felt guilty about it." How come, I said, feeling that at last I was getting closer. "Well," he said, "it is difficult to explain. That General was a most awkward customer. We had just had rather a tense time of it. In those days there had been a spot of trouble with the Army. For some reason they felt that we were not giving them quite the close support they wanted. I suppose there must have been a few occasions when there was no ship to do something when the Army thought there should have been one. We were very tightly stretched, of course. Everybody was working pretty well flat out most of the time. But I suppose the pongoes did have a point, one must reluctantly concede it. The General was making a general tour of his parish, as he called it. He was a very big man physically, a very big physical character, with a very, very, loud voice. He ran his staff ragged. They looked the most thoroughly down at heel, down in the mouth, down-hearted shower of dismal pongoes it was ever our misfortune to have to entertain in the wardroom. The General started to browbeat us, while he was having a drink in the wardroom. I suppose I was not quite as firm as I should have been. He was searching for some kind of admission that the Navy were not doing their job a hundred per cent. I must have given it to him inadvertently. Probably out of sheer weariness. Anyway, we heard later that he had quoted something I had said, quite out of context, and either he or his staff had attributed it to somebody much more senior than I was. So they translated what was wardroom chat by me, when I was pretty tired, into something that had the weight of an official statement of policy by a senior naval officer. This got back to the ship eventually, of course, and it didn't reflect too well on the Captain or on me."

I said, so you felt that you had somehow betrayed the Captain? Let him down, rather. Betrayed is a bit strong.

He said "yes he did feel like that, and it had worried him ever since."

I asked him, was there any element of self-excusing, or yardarm squaring, in what he had said? He said he thought it was "quite possible to read it like that. It made him look as if he was criticising his own Captain and the Admiral and the entire direction of the Navy's effort off the coast, in an attempt to justify *Pandora's* point of view. That was not true at all."

All this was astonishingly candid of Fiddich. One really could not compete against honesty like that. I said, but what exactly did you say to the General that day? He said he "couldn't remember exactly," he had had "no idea that such importance would be attached to it? and neither did anyone else in the wardroom." He thought he might have said something on the lines that "yes, perhaps the Navy might possibly have missed a few tricks and yes, perhaps certain ships might be able to step up their efforts." Whichever way you look at it, Fiddich must have been extraordinarily indiscreet. No wonder people might have thought he was deliberately trying to do his Captain down. But I myself think it was nothing more than indiscretion. But I wanted to make quite sure of this, so I said, what you said to the General was meant in very broad terms, and not meant to refer to any particular incident?

He said, "yes that was it." To be absolutely sure, I said, it had nothing to do with the day when *Pandora* opened fire on a very small sampan, a day or two earlier? He said "no, not at all, although perhaps that was the sort of thing that could have been used as ammunition against the Navy, because it hadn't been too delicately handled." I asked him what he meant by that and he said that "the rescue part had gone extremely well considering everything, but firing on small shipping offshore afterwards was probably unnecessary. Although it did seem at the time that the intelligence evidence was pretty strong that one or more of those sampans were manned by Big Red's men."

So I asked Fiddich what he thought himself. He said "it was right tactically at the time, probably wrong morally on reflection." And that was that. He then gave me what you might call a very old-fashioned look and said, "I think the Captain was totally right in the circumstances," he said, and "if you somehow succeed in undermining the Captain's confidence you will have done the Navy no service, and you will always have something to answer for."

I thought to myself, what an extraordinary remark. I still do think it an extremely funny remark.

So there we were. I had found out a little more, in fact a great deal more, about what had happened in *Pandora*. Simon Fiddich's so-called great betrayal was at the same time rather more serious and rather less important than I had thought. What he had said had had an effect far beyond one incident. Yet it had had far less bearing upon that one incident.

I asked him one last thing. What did the Captain himself think about that incident when they had fired on the small sampan? Fiddich said "it wasn't all that small," now he came to think of it. I said, but what did the Captain himself think? Fiddich said "he never discussed it with him." I said, never? He said "no, not once."

But it had still been a most informative conversation. It was extraordinary how much I was learning from *Pandora's* ship's company. They really were a remarkable body, officers and men, and I learned more and more from talking to them, about themselves, about the Navy, about myself, too. It was a ship of wise fools. It struck me that quite a lot of them would remember *Pandora's* commission all their lives, as one of the golden ones. That turned out to be true. I have met some of them since, quite apart from people like Mickey Gibb whom one is always bumping into, and they all say how much they enjoyed that commission. So much for first impressions when they first arrived back.

But at the time I merely said to Fiddich, it seems to have been a very instructive period, your commission. "Oh yes indeed," he said to me, "it certainly was." Then I asked him what he personally had learned from it? He gave me a sort of sidelong glance. He had a thin, dark, suspicious face, like a ferret. Like an assistant prisoner at the court of the Borgias. An intriguer with a sudden flash of candour. "Loyalty," he said, as though butter wouldn't melt in his mouth. "I had a complete course," he said, "in how to command a frigate on detached service in the Far East."

I should mention it, I have not stressed it up to now, because it is impossible to recapture Fiddich's exact tone of voice, but all the time he was speaking to me he had this infuriating manner. He knew I was a passed-over two-and-a-half ringer. A failure, in Service terms. He had this irritating combination of condescension and mock deference, and underneath it all, a constant, broad, unshakable, all-embracing contempt for me.

We had been talking there for quite a long time. Rudolf was shuffling about, as though he wanted to close up the place. They never did anything quite as discourteous as shut the bar at the old Coliseum, Rudolf simply made you feel that it was a bit inconsiderate of you to go on drinking. But I could not help myself asking Fiddich about Olivia. It reveals how vulnerable I really was, in spite of all my questionings and buzzing's about the place. I could say what I liked and do what I liked, but it always came back to her in the end.

He said he had "taken her down to *Pandora*." The last he saw of her, she was "sitting in the Captain's cabin, pouring herself a large glass of sherry."

CHAPTER 10

With Olivia back in *Pandora* again, Freddie said, and presumably also back in James' ever-loving arms, it seemed to me that that must now, finally, be that. I was very unlikely to see James again on any reasonable terms of friendship and if Olivia had deliberately made her choice then, as I say, that seemed to be that. I felt I had lost something, but I also had a strange feeling of relief, as though I were well out of all that. But I must say the feeling of loss was much the stronger. That night I took a big bundle of papers out to Sebastopol Buildings. I made a large pan of scrambled eggs for myself, had a great hunk of cheese, got out a bottle of whisky and settled to do some work. I did more solid, constructive work that night than I had for some time, than I had since *Pandora* came home, in fact.

But *Pandora* was full of surprises. She kept on coming back to life again, just when you thought it was all over. The next day, let's see, the next day was Friday, and I had lunch in the staff mess with a fellow down from Rosyth dockyard, a fellow environmentalist, so to speak. He was very much younger than I was, only a two-striper, in fact. He was doing virtually the same job as I was, but on the way up. It showed how passed over I was. He was making the rounds, to see what was happening around the various bazaars. He was the expert on nuclear submarine habitability, with special responsibilities for the Polaris programme. That was at the time when the first Polaris patrols were just starting and we were still just beginning to evaluate the physiological effects on the ship's companies. After all, nobody on our side of the Atlantic had really properly appreciated just what a very strange existence it was, locked away for weeks at a time in a totally sealed-off environment. He told me that they were finding out some very curious things. For instance, the sailors' peripheral vision was one of the first abilities to suffer in a long patrol. They tended to develop a kind of tunnel vision so that they didn't register as quickly to anything happening to the side of their vision. After staring at bulkheads and gauges and each other's faces at close quarters for about two months they found they couldn't focus on things at a distance so quickly. So in any circumstances where they had to judge distances and on-coming objects and where they had other objects moving about at the side limits of their vision, they were bound to be at a disadvantage. Driving a motor-car was the obvious case. It seems there was some evidence that Polaris sailors were not really to be trusted behind a wheel for some time after they returned.

They were finding out all sorts of interesting things. For instance, the terrifying pollution effects of cigarette smoking. It put the most scarifying range of noxious substances into the submarine's atmosphere. Everything from arsenic on and out. The quantities were minute, of course, but over a long period they built up surprisingly. The crew were also very susceptible to bugs and flu when they got home. They'd got used to their own bugs, you see. I don't know if it ever came to anything but I do know that we put a tremendous amount of effort into designing Polaris submarines' interiors and decor and lay-out. We gave a lot of thought to habitability. I say I don't know if it ever came to anything, because I've never actually been inside a Polaris submarine. It's a terrible admission, but there we are, I never had a chance.

I must say it was a most interesting lunch conversation, but this is all local colour. When we were having our coffee this fellow, Max Denton was his name, I remember, the conversation turned inevitably to *Pandora*. Max Denton asked me how James Bellingham was getting on, he had heard he was back from the Far East. He said to me, "you were a friend of his, weren't you?"

As soon as he asked me, I thought to myself, well, how do I answer this? Indeed, I asked myself, how is James Bellingham getting on? Is he doing well, having completed what was becoming increasingly clear as one of the most successful small ship commissions in recent years, to put it that way, or was he just about to fall from grace, never to get another decent job as long as he was in, and all for letting the side down and doing a dirty deed, to put it that way? I wondered how this young man from the other end of the country whom to my best knowledge I had never met before, how did he too know that James Bellingham was my friend? It was all rather eerie, all these complete strangers knowing so much about you.

So, first, I asked him how he came to know James. Apparently he had served with him for eighteen months. He had been a sub, getting his watch-keeping ticket in a frigate where James had been the First Lieutenant. It was, in a hair-prickling sort of way, a kind of mirror image, or forecast of the future in *Pandora*. I wouldn't say that Max Denton's face exactly lit up when he mentioned James, that would be too much, but he definitely beamed, his whole face showed that he was remembering something very pleasant. I thought it was so odd that I, for instance, had not been able to put across a good impression of James to Fiery, whereas this young man had no difficulty with me.

Then I asked him how he had come to know that James was my friend? He said James had often mentioned me. I had mixed feelings at that. I was pleased and yet suspicious, because I could not believe that they would say something nice about me. He said that "whenever they had a particularly hectic run ashore in that ship, James always used to say it was just like one of Freddie's haircut runs."

Haircut run. I must say that was a magic phrase from the past. It brought up all sorts of memories. When James and I were doing our small-ship time, we were both serving in destroyers in the same flotilla in Malta. So we used to see a lot of each other. I remember it all in a golden haze of nostalgia. That Maltese yellow stone, the hot sunshine, Maltese vino, the dghaisamen that used to row us out to our ship, it was all straight out of a travel brochure. Of course it smelled and you were likely to get Malta dog and it really was a little too hot in the summer. But all the same, we loved it, and the words haircut run brought it all back. I used to ring up James, ship to ship, when we were back alongside in Sliema or send a message across, and say, come ashore for a haircut, and then a swim on Tigne beach. We'd go ashore in Sliema at four in the afternoon, honestly and genuinely intending to have a haircut. But somehow the main objective would get lost on the way and we used to roll back on board our respective ships at four the next morning, having neither of us been anywhere near a barber. Max told me that in that ship Freddie's haircut runs had "become legendary." "Anything unusually enjoyable, or strenuous, or unexpected, or just enjoyable," he said, "was like one of Freddie's haircut runs."

He was a thoroughly nice young man, that Max Denton. I don't think I ever met him again, never came across him, but I still think of him occasionally. He was a very nice young man, and good at his job, too. The Navy has always been very fortunate to have dozens of his type of thoroughly nice, competent, healthy, well-balanced young men, with enough common sense to be able to run things on their own, and enough sense of duty to be trusted. Thankfully, the Navy is still getting them. I could see the shape of the future in that young man. He was somehow the right shape for the Navy. I wouldn't have said he was very bright, intellectually. About average. But he would do. It said something for James' personal qualities that he had apparently succeeded in impressing such a liking and respect for himself upon two young characters so different as Max Denton and Simon Fiddich. Not for the first time, I realised that James must have something.

When I got back to my office, there was James again. He was sitting in my chair and reading my newspaper.

He looked just as angry as before, in a very dangerous sort of way, but this time he did not look as if he would fling off one parting shot and then go. He looked in fact rather alarmingly permanent. He was there at least for the afternoon. I have to introduce this note of flippancy because it's exactly how I felt. I was afraid, but just about to giggle, too, any moment. I knew this was going to be important, crucial for us both, but I could hardly keep a straight face, all the same.

That must have been one of the most astounding conversations I ever had with anyone. James threw off all restraints. He was all over me. Attacking me, flattering me, brow-beating me, sometimes ignoring me, as he sometimes tried it out, like trying it on the dog, using me as a trial horse or an anvil, as he had so often done in the past. I don't know how much of what he said that day was true and how much was said for effect. Even if all the words were not strictly to be taken at their face value, I think that the person behind them was. It was James all right, vintage James, one of those cases where one can believe the whole person behind what he is actually saying.

He said, "I've been very conscious of you, Freddie," he said, "very aware of you since we came back. You pop up unexpectedly and uninvited on the day we got back and you've been lurking about like a bad rumour in the background ever since, like a bed smell," he said. "You seem to have interviewed most of my officers and my ship's company, dropping hints and innuendoes that none of them could understand. Just what is it you want," he said. "What are you getting at?"

But then before I could answer, or before I even wanted to answer, he said, "you've been hatching something with Fiery, that I do know. That does worry me slightly," he said, "because I know you are fairly harmless most of the time, but I know Fiery is extremely dangerous all the time. The two of you don't quite seem to go together. It needs a longer spoon to sup with Fiery than I think you've got," he said. "I should watch out, or he'll gobble you up, not that I really give a damn what happens to you," he said. "Not now."

That was the way that conversation was to go, an extraordinary combination of sneering and concern on his part. Sometimes I thought he still liked me and I was still his friend. A moment later he would say something that cut me right open.

Most of it was way over my head. The gist of it all was that here was a very able naval officer, one of the best of his day and age, in spite of everything that had happened, here was a very talented man talking as though he wanted to leave the Service. It was all very puzzling. If I had had half James' talent, I would have been only too glad to stay in and be promoted. It seemed to me nothing short of blasphemy. James was blaspheming against his own ability. That parable of the talents has always seemed to me to be one of the most psychologically accurate stories in the New Testament. That is how life happens. To him that hath shall be given, from him that hath not shall be taken away, even that which he hath. There is a rightness about that. Even the very words have a kind of rhetorical symmetry on the page. And it describes the relative positions of James and I absolutely to a T. Yes, here was James seemingly about to fly in the face of all this. It seemed to me he was wrong, wrong logically, professionally, even wrong biblically.

Looking back on it now, I see of course that he was a very much more mixed up and complicated character than even I knew or guessed. The better he was at his job, the less it satisfied him. And yet, even putting it like that makes it seem far too simple.

He said so much, in brilliant flashes. I can only remember the flashes now, the headlines, so to speak. "A good commission," he said, "was an almost mystical thing. It was a tremendous celebration of fellowship and professional skill and dedication. It was a satisfying reward for work well done, with a slice of luck thrown in. *Pandora's* had been an excellent commission. And yet," James said, "it was not enough. It did not even begin to be enough. It was not on the same planet" as what he really wanted to do. "It was in a world which had ceased to be his world." He said that "commanding a ship, having the ordering of her people and the governing of her ways, was a tremendous thing." But he said it was "such an obvious, theatrical source of satisfaction" that he "felt it had to be suspect." He said he was "horrified to find how satisfied and pleased" he had been "at doing well." But, he said, he was also "still, deep down, rebelliously delighted that he was doing well." He said he never thought he could be "seduced like that," he of all people.

I myself thought privately that James, of all people, was just the person to be seduced like that, as he put it. But I let it pass. He said that "commanding a ship was dramatic and thrilling and important. But life, real life, was not dramatic or thrilling or important in that way." So what he had been doing in *Pandora* "had no meaning, it had no bearing, it did not relate to the life of service" that he wanted to lead. It was service, but not his service any more.

I said that perhaps in that case he ought to become a monk.

That for some reason made him absolutely furious, although I certainly had not meant it as a joke in any way. He said it was exactly the sort of cliché he expected from me. He said that nearly everybody in the Navy had this extraordinary tunnel vision about their notions of service. If it's not the naval kind of service, then they immediately sprang to ideas about becoming a monk. The two were not even remotely comparable.

Again, while I was privately thinking how odd that the phrase 'tunnel vision' should come up again, in two utterly different contexts, I still could not let him get away with anything as sweeping as that. Oh come on, I said, there are all manner of physical, mental and emotional comparisons between life in a ship and life in a monastery, in fact, I would say it was one of the most obvious and apt comparisons one could make.

James agreed with me, but he looked rather resentful, as though I was spoiling a good story or messing up a train of argument with an awkward fact, which I was, of course. He had a sort of I've made up my mind, don't confuse me with facts, look on his face.

James always did have a quite diabolical power to conjure up the past for me. He could do it with a phrase or a word, or even just a look as he said a word. He had the knack of bringing back all the times when I had not behaved well or had been embarrassed or ashamed or hurt. I am sure he didn't mean to do it, but that is how it nearly always happened. I am not a particularly sentimental man, but he could nearly always cripple me with nostalgic memories.

"Do you remember our haircut runs," he suddenly said to me. How curious it was, that I had not heard the phrase haircut run for years and years, and there I was, hearing it twice within a few minutes on the same afternoon.

"Do you remember Cathy who fell out of the dghaisa," he said. Of course I remembered. I had forgotten the girl's name actually, but I remembered the incident at once. We were in the middle of one of our haircut runs, both more than somewhat tight, and we were crossing for some reason from Sliema to Manoel Island. Somewhere on the way we had picked up this girl Cathy. Now that was very unusual, because there were precious few spare women about in Malta, then, in the late nineteen-forties, or any other time, come to that. One simply did not expect to acquire a woman halfway through a run ashore. I believe she said she was a nurse. She may even have been an enthusiastic amateur whore. She rather fancied James, and he rather fancied her. I expect he was casting about in his mind to decide where he could go to bed with her. We were getting into this dghaisa, when she caught her heel on the gunwale and with no more ado, tipped bingo right overboard into Sliema Creek. Without giving it a thought I jumped over the side to rescue her. But, it turned out that the water was very shallow and in any case she proved to be an excellent swimmer. But, you never know about these things. There could have been an accident. Alcohol and late night swims don't go together. We lost a member of our term at Dartmouth through just that sort of thing — trying to swim across the Hamoaze from ship to ship after a mess-dinner. James had stood on the jetty the whole time doing nothing, except, if anything, laughing like a drain about it all. This got me a bit nettled and I said to him, I didn't think much of his just standing doing nothing. He said it was much better, and much braver, he said, to see that no action was needed and take no action and run the risk of being called a coward afterwards. I think that was the nearest James ever got to expressing his own philosophy of life.

"Shall I tell you why you were passed over, Freddie," he said to me.

I said no, I didn't want to hear it. I mean, really, it was too painful.

But he went on all the same. It was just like old days, when James treated me like a bloody carpet. "You were passed over," he said, "because you're the type who does go leaping in regardless. And then," he said, "being Freddie, you talk about it *ad nauseam* afterwards. Your trouble," he said, "is that you're an anachronism these days, Freddie," he said to me. "Just like me. Somehow we've got out of joint with our times. Without being too solemn about it, we're not really needed any more. I've only just come to realise it. The better the Navy is to me, the more I want to leave it," he said. "There is a bleak, puritan streak in all our generation that doesn't fit any more. We all joined at the wrong time, and we're all going to leave at the wrong time. We are paid more nowadays," he said, "we are looked after better, they try to look after wives and families better than they ever did, more married quarters being built, the Navy's got more buildings," he said, "more gadgets, more gear of every kind, there may be fewer ships but they have all the latest tackle, the opportunities are greater, people come from far and wide, from foreign navies all over the world, to get their training and buy expertise off us. This would be an absolutely marvellous time to join the Navy. You couldn't go wrong. So," he said, "you can see this is not the old, old griping that used to go on, about why people wanted to leave the Navy. This is a new discontent. There is no reason to leave now, none at all. And perhaps that is why I want to go. They need more of the genial committee men type now, I think," he said. "It would be positively disastrous for the Navy if I ever became an admiral, feeling the way I do," he said. "The Navy is just about to have a change out of all sight and recognition and people like me are not the ones to carry out that change."

"It is a very odd thing," James said, "but the Navy has such a very subtle way of doing its selection. When you think about it, they hardly ever chuck anybody out. They would never be as crude as that. They just somehow get it across to the person concerned that it is time he went. They somehow manage to get people to persuade themselves that their time has come. So there is a process of selection going on, from the moment a term joins at Dartmouth, with those who are not going to make it shredding away like leaves all the time."

And you think it is now time for you to shred away like a leaf, I said.

"Possibly," he said. He said he knew "everyone wanted to read a wider significance into his own circumstances. Everyone wants to be able to say, look, it's not just little me, but something much wider and greater than just any case. You ought to be able to appreciate what I am saying, Freddie," he said. "The Navy found you out long ago, and now you are just beginning to find yourself out. You know enough now," he said, "to know what I'm talking about."

I said I was not at all sure what he was talking about. I said he was certainly more maudlin and self-pitying than when I remembered him last.

But he was off again, on another tack. He said he could "remember reading somewhere a marvellous description of how to sharpen a scythe." James had never done it himself, and nor had I unfortunately, but he said "there was this marvellous description of how the sharpening stone grated very roughly over the blade at first, with a terrible hideous grinding and grating noise that set your teeth on edge. But as the sharpening went on," he said, "so the sound began to soften, so it became smoother and quieter and everybody was much calmer. Until eventually the stone slid over the metal with a lovely silky purring note. That meant the scythe was sharp, and ready for use." He said "it was just the same with *Pandora*. They had all sorts of alarms and excursions at first. Everything only worked with the most frightful grating and jangling. They were all nerves and jumpiness and sharp edges and ragged ends. But as they went on they got better. It came good. They all came good."

Except for occasionally firing on unarmed small shipping offshore, I said.

"I don't know what you mean exactly," he said. "You keep hinting about things like this. Simon was saying that you were breathing heavily over him the other day about some sampan or other. Do you mean one of those operational incidents, where we fired an offshore shipping?"

I said, yes, that was what I meant.

This seemed to exasperate him. "Why are you pressing this," he said. "Why are you chasing this up? What's in it for you? What incident is this that's bothering you?"

I said, one particular operation when you gave covering fire for a landing force of Royal Marines who rescued some people who were hostages up river. You opened fire on a very small native craft while disengaging. Your helicopter pilot, at least, thought it was unarmed.

"That one," he said, noncommittally. "Well," he said, "there really was not much to interest anyone in that."

It interests me, I said.

"Yes," he said, "I can see it does, but why?"

I decided it would be my turn now to tell him a thing or two. I said it interested me because it concerned him and because I knew him so well anything that concerned him concerned me, just as it had done for years and years. I said that until I was able to clear it up in my mind, I would not be able to rest easy about it.

I refrained from mentioning Olivia, although she had a great deal to do with my feelings on the subject. In fact it would not have been too much to say that she had everything to do with it.

The Captain of a ship, I said, like any top man, like the editor of a newspaper, like the managing director of his own firm, any top man with extra responsibility often has an extra sharpness. He has an extra sixth sense of perception. The responsibility adds an extra sharpness. It happens too often, for instance, for it to be coincidence that the captain on the bridge sights a ship on the horizon before anybody else, even before the lookouts who are supposed to be doing nothing else but look for ships on the horizon. The top man can see and knows when something is real or bogus, whether it's harmless or dangerous, phony or genuine. He can do it when his subordinates might often make mistakes. It goes with the job. In this case, I told him, I believe you did have an extra sense about it. I believe you did know there was no harm in that little sampan, whatever intelligence might tell you and whatever appearances might have been. And yet you went on. You had that little bit of flash of insight or experience and you betrayed it. You betrayed yourself, I said. That's what I think happened, if you ask me.

At last, I think, I really reached him.

"You're a devil, Freddie," he said, "a real devil. You keep on pointing at something I don't want to look at. But betrayal is far too strong and melodramatic a word. All our intelligence guff suggested that all offshore shipping in those sectors was hostile. I couldn't fire at them all, so I fired at the nearest, to encourage les autres, so to speak. Intelligence kept on suggesting we had done the right thing afterwards and in fact all the time. Mind you, there were in my opinion," he said, "other incidents just as bad, much worse in fact. Once we nearly lost one of my petty officers. We did lose him, as far as *Pandora* was concerned. He got shot up and very badly wounded. We had to send him ashore. He'll never be the same again. That was through not taking proper precautions beforehand. But on the other hand" he said, "we mustn't over-condemn ourselves. You can't win them all, that's a cliché nowadays. Everybody is bound to make some mistakes. Bound to, and that little sampan, I concede, was probably, probably I said, a mistake. As you say, I had a hunch it was harmless. You ask me then, why didn't I stop firing at it? Why did I fire at it at all? I can't answer that," he said. "I had a moment of mental helplessness. I failed to react. It was psychologically easier to let things run on than to step in and prevent them at the very last nick of time. Mind you, it could still be pretty convincingly argued that I was wrong to hesitate about that sampan and quite right to go on, that it would have been inexcusable for me not to have fired, in those circumstances. But it's true, I give you your point, Freddie," he said, "I did at the last moment think there was a chance there was nothing wrong with that little widger. But it ends there. Don't think you can make anything of it now. Nobody's ever suggested to me officially that we did anything wrong, and they never will. There were one or two mild enquiries a day or so after we got back. But everybody is quite satisfied that everything was in order. Everybody but you, Freddie," he said "it seems. And my chopper pilot. I am afraid I had to bawl him out pretty fiercely afterwards. Poor lad, he thought he was quite justified in saying what he did and I had to treat him rather roughly. I have a feeling he never got over it, properly. It certainly affected his performance in his work, I'm sorry to say."

I then asked James what were the feelings of his ship's company in general when they came home. He said he "wouldn't like to be dogmatic" but he "thought they were very much what one would have expected." He said he "expected they were in a very funny mood. Half delighted. Half sad. In a small ship where everybody knew each other well and when people had been hurt, when there had been excitements and successes and failures and losses and general emotional upheaval, there were bound to be scars," he said. "Nobody was going to be quite the same again. There would be those who would be pleased with themselves and those who were going to regret chances missed and would think bitterly to themselves that they would never have such a good chance again, maybe."

I asked him who did he think the people were, who might be bitter about opportunities lost? He laughed and said "I wasn't going to catch him out like that. I would have to find out for myself." And he "expected I probably would," he said. He went on like this all the time, first appearing to confide in me and then turning round and pricking me with a small nasty remark. To keep me in my place.

I said, let's be quite clear now what you've said. You knew in your heart of hearts that you were wrong to fire that day and yet you went on. Do you realise, I said to him, that some people would call that a war crime?

He laughed and laughed and laughed. "Rubbish," he said. "Piffle and poppycock." "Look," he said, "we'd had ships and craft operating off that coast for months and months. All the local shipping knew what the score was. They knew very well there were certain places and certain times where and when they had to be careful. They knew very well the signs when there was likely to be excitement and unpleasantness. Besides which, a number of warnings were given in the equivalent of notices to mariners out there and even if they couldn't read those there were two minesweepers and any number of choppers from the commando carrier further out to sea, warning people they were in a zone where there were likely to be loud bangs and lumps of metal flying about. No," he said, "nobody had any business to be where they were. Certainly not hanging about like that, and certainly not flashing."

I said, flashing? It was the first I had heard of it.

He said "yes, flashing. Hickey said they were flashing as he flew over them."

Hickey hadn't told me that. I said I didn't know that.

James said, "well, that shows you don't know everything, in spite of all your researches. Hickey said he saw them flashing.

It could have been glass or a mirror or they could have been flashing to someone on shore or it could have been anything. But at the time, in the heat of the moment, these things happen. Operationally," James said, "it is often wiser to shoot first and examine the other side of the label afterwards."

I said that was all very well and no doubt he was right but still, he knew that there was nothing wrong with that sampan. He said "yes, but what did I want," him "to admit having committed a war crime?" I said yes. He said, "you've got a bloody hope."

Of course, it didn't really matter what I hoped or what anybody else hoped, or what anybody else thought or said about it, the only person who mattered was James himself. In the last resort it was what he thought that counted, nobody else. And I told him so. It was a cunningly insidious thing to say, because it was both unanswerable and flattering. Nobody can resist the suggestion that their own opinions are of paramount importance. We are all self-centred. All egomaniacs, everyone. James was a bigger ego-maniac than most.

"All right," said James, "I'll tell you what happened, as I saw it, once and for all. Anything to get you off my back," he said, "although I don't suppose I'll ever manage to achieve that. But it's what I came here for this afternoon, I suppose."

Now, James, I should say, was always a very good storyteller. Very good mimic, tremendous sense of timing. He could tell a tale marvellously well, and I must say that his account of *Pandora's* adventures really did give me a clear picture of what it meant, what it felt and sounded and looked like, to be there. He said "it was a shaky sort of operation from the very start. It had to be hastily planned and mounted, because of the circumstances. It meant messing about in a narrow tidal river opening, at night, with darkened ships, and the gooks ashore getting more and more sophisticated weaponry. It was rumoured that they had infantry surface-to-surface missiles, although nobody had ever actually seen one." It was not James' idea to approach up the estuary. He would "sooner have stayed to seaward of the peninsula," he said, "to give himself more freedom, more sea-room, more room for manoeuvre in every way." So much for one of the tricks that I thought and Hickey thought James had missed. But it was decided that "the nearer *Pandora* lay to the scene, the sooner they could all get away. They had to do it that night, in spite of the weather or anything else, because they had heard that two of the hostages were going to be executed, murdered one should say, first thing in the morning." James reckoned the Royal Marines "went about it all in the most cack-handed way. If they had slapped it about a bit they could have been gone before dawn, and left everybody in the opposition wondering how they had managed to spirit their people away. As it was, the whole thing was done in an absolute blaze of lights and a running fusillade of shooting. They all stood on board *Pandora* listening to it all and wondering whether World War Three had broken out. The upshot was that when the sun came up, burning everybody's eyes out, there was *Pandora* still in the river, bold as brass and twice as natural. Every gook for miles around could see her. By the time they heard all the firing ashore and suffered all the delays, and dawn coming up in the middle, their nerves were in a pretty bad state."

"And yet," James said, he could recall himself being "in a strange state of elevated confidence." He felt "in the best of spirits." He had trained his ship's company and he "felt himself being buoyed up by them." *Pandora* was a most complicated weapon, but he felt that he had "perfect, finger-tip control over every bit of her." He said he wondered "why anyone should ever be forced to feel ashamed of such a feeling. There is nothing wrong in commanding one of our warships. There was no reason why we should always be put in the position of having to justify ourselves. The State licenses a certain amount of applied violence on its behalf. They were applying that violence on behalf of the State." It was as simple as that.

"However," James said they were "all fully rewarded for everything when they saw the faces of the people they had rescued." He said "the sheer relief, the joy, the sheer pleasure and delight of being amongst friends and safe amongst fellow countrymen again, that made everything worthwhile. The people had been shamefully buggered about with almost no protection or even interest from the Government at home who were far more interested at that time in trying to safeguard black people from the outrages of other black people in Africa than in the personal safety and property of our own people who were far from home. If it hadn't been for the Navy and the Royal Marines those people ashore would have been massacred and for all the interest the politicians at home took in it they might as well have been living on the moon, in fact they would have been a damned sight more concerned if they had been on the moon. Those people had been abused and shouted at and insulted by a load of ill-mannered thugs who had the nerve to call themselves a provisional government. The children were crying. The women looked exhausted, with their clothes in rags and their hair all filthy. The men looked as though they had been through some ghastly trial, which they had, of course. Apparently their gaolers had refused to allow them to keep themselves clean, and kept them in a tiny room with no washing or sanitary facilities, they had spat on them and urinated on the women's skirts." James said that "if these people in the sampan had any connection with the people ashore" then he "was damned glad he fired on them." He was sorry he couldn't "shoot up a few more of the savages."

I said, did all this weigh on you when you gave the order to fire? Was it a means of getting your own back? Was that it? James said he "didn't think so." I said, perhaps all that talk about commanding ships and the State's license for violence and all that, perhaps all it boiled down to was clobbering those who had clobbered us. Getting our own back.

James thought about that for a while. Then he said "that would have been a highly satisfactory, near solution. But it was far too neat, far too cut and dried."

Can you rule it out completely, though, I said.

He said, "not completely," he couldn't. "Not absolutely and utterly." But he was "ninety-nine point nine nine nine recurring sure," as sure as anyone can ever really be of their own motives.

"After all" he said, he had "only seen the people, some of them, briefly when they first came on board. They looked in a pretty terrible state but that was rather to be expected. They hadn't been staying at the Savoy." He didn't hear about "all the abuse poured on them until much later. Most of them had changed their clothes by then, had baths and generally looked different people." He "didn't hear their stories in detail until much later." Most of them he didn't hear at all, from them, but "read about them in the intelligence summaries." So their stories did not affect his decision at the time.

"Besides," he said, "there's another way of looking at this. Most people in those circumstances would have fired on the sampan without giving it a second thought, then or later. Or, alternatively, they might never give it a thought either way. I was good enough to do both," James said. "It's because I'm good at my job," he said, "that I changed my mind. A less good at it bloke would never have guessed. It's a bit like cricket," he said. "There are some balls bowled that are so good it takes a very good batsman to even touch them and get out to them. A mediocre batsman would get nowhere near them. I was good enough to suspect that sampan, and then good enough," he said "to dismiss the suspicion."

But not good enough to stop firing, I said.

"You're a devil, Freddie," he said again. "This is a new role for you, isn't it," he said, "acting as the still small voice of conscience? As for talking about war crimes," he said, "that's a pretty fierce accusation. That strikes at the root of our whole concept of duty in the armed services."

I think the words 'war crime' had really stung James. He came back to them several times. Not surprisingly, he fiercely denied anything he had done came anywhere near a war crime. He said that "presupposed a level of personal involvement, or personal responsibility, it suggested a kind of knowingness," that he simply did not have. "If there was any suspicion of a war crime then we should all pack up and leave the Service. The two could not go together. Once we started talking like that, we would get lost in the world of semantics, splitting ever finer and finer hairs of meaning."

James defended himself very well, but the conversation worked its purpose as far as I was concerned. Anything that weakened James' self-confidence was to my advantage as far as Olivia was involved. But James was magnificently defiant to the point of being pompous. "I am employed by the Queen," he said "to command one of our warships, one of hers I should say. That gives me a certain place, a particular authority. The decisions I came to and the actions I took were proper to my status."

I wanted to change the subject a little, so I said, why didn't the press mention you or *Pandora* by name after that? He said, rather indignantly, that they had. I said I had not seen any mention. He said I "couldn't have been looking at the right papers." He said "there was some sort of silly time block on the publication of names, for fear of reprisals, but they were given as much mention as anybody else at the time."

So there was another of my theories about James and *Pandora*, that their part had been quietly suppressed, gone for a burton. With all these revelations and explanations James was coming out of it all better and better every minute. Frankly I did not know whether to be glad or sorry.

Mind you, I think there was a deeper point here, which both James and I and everybody else who gave it thought at all must have realised. That the forces out there did not get anything like the newspaper coverage they deserved. James himself said they had "done their best for press relations, they had reporters and photographers on board at every chance they got and gave them every possible help and encouragement. But it was no use." James had actually worked out some figures. He said that he reckoned, that "between a fifth and a quarter of all our armed forces were in some way involved in that Confrontation," as it was called. "There was a major war going on out there, which was going to have the most tremendous effect politically on the Far East and on our position in the Far East, and yet to read the newspapers from home you would have thought nothing was happening at all. The sailors were very disappointed. They love to read about themselves, whatever they may say about newspapers. There they were, on the other side of the world, digging out and working as hard as they could and yet the papers from home were full of nothing but pop groups and discotheques and bloody fashion designers."

It never seemed to occur to James that this indifference of the press might have saved him some embarrassment. He could argue that sampan business any way he liked, he could rationalise it to his heart's content, but the fact still remains that a mischievously minded reporter could easily have worked it up into something really damaging. He still could, because the lapse of time does not make any difference to that sort of story. You could say that scandal, like game, is all the better for being well hung. Anyway, it never happened, and James never realised what an escape he had had.

There had been a note of resignation, literally as it turned out, in James' voice throughout our conversation. There had been a general air of *nunc dimittis* about it all. When I commented on it, James said I was "quite right," he was going to retire. He had decided that it was time to go. He had been discussing things up in the Ministry of Defence these last few days he had been away. He said he felt so strongly about it he had had to do something about it right away. That was why he had asked Simon Fiddich to look out for him. Fiddich had been showing his face in all the right places and making polite noises to all the right people. Meanwhile, James said he was very grateful to the Navy. He owed it a lot, almost everything in fact. It had taught him, he said, a whole wide world of experience. He was leaving, but that was not the fault of the Navy. It was his. He said he had tried to explain to me why he felt he had to go and if he had failed, then it was too bad.

He suddenly stood up, behind my desk. Our conversation, and what has since turned out to be our last meeting, was over. I knew we were both thinking of Olivia and, to be honest, she was the only part of the whole business that I really cared about. *Pandora* had only retaught me something I had always known, that there are always at least two ways of looking at anything. What is honourable to one is dishonourable to another, what is excusable to somebody is absolutely unforgivable to somebody else and every single thing that had happened in *Pandora* was capable of being construed in two different ways. There simply was no solution. And, to be honest now, I had been in some ironical way forced into the position of being some kind of prosecuting counsel in an affair that I didn't give a damn about. I didn't in my heart of hearts give a brass monkey's for that sampan or for anybody in it. I was like somebody who just happened to be passing by the court-room when it was all going on and noticed that somebody I knew well was involved. But really, deep down, I didn't give a tinker's cuss.

James was looking at his watch, and then at me. "She's at North Road Station, if you're interested," he said. "Simon Fiddich took her to catch the Southampton train this afternoon. I forget when it goes. You might just catch her. You never know."

CHAPTER 11

I forget now what else I was supposed to do that afternoon, Freddie said, if anything. Friday afternoons were never very energetic times for the staff unless there was some kind of flap on. But in any case James had already thoroughly disrupted my afternoon. I ditched everything. Olivia was far more important. There might be a little hope, if I hurried. Laughable now, when I look back. I mean, I knew there was no chance, but I just had to go all the same.

I can remember distinctly, bloody near running out to the car park. I can remember driving to North Road Station like a madman, overtaking everything, hooting my horn furiously, generally behaving like a lunatic. I had no idea when the train went or how much time I had or even if the train had already gone. For all I knew it could have gone an hour before, or any time. Olivia might not even be there. James could well have knowingly done that. I remember not being able to find anywhere to park my car and I drove round furiously all over the place looking for somewhere, and then eventually I just left it and rushed into the station.

I couldn't think, I hadn't a clue where to go. It was the oddest thing, because Plymouth North Road must be the station that has played the most tremendous part in my life. I know it's a cliché but that gloomy railway dump has been part of my life. I've arrived there to join ships or go on courses, gone there to go on leave after being abroad, but for all the times I had been there I couldn't remember where the waiting room was or the booking office or what platform for trains to London and Southampton. I couldn't see any signs so I just milled about frantically for a time inside the entrance, trying to find out what was happening. You know those moments of complete panic. I thought I could hear a train leaving and I thought that might be the one. When I tried to get through the barrier the chap there naturally asked me for my ticket. I must have been to that station a thousand times and yet I didn't seem to know how to behave. More delay, while I had to go and get myself a platform ticket. By this time I was absolutely desperate and I think if that ticket inspector had obstructed me any more I would have knocked him down. I said to him, has the Southampton train gone yet? He looked at me as if he had never heard the word train or the name Southampton before in his life. He took about a century and a half to look at my bloody platform ticket, turning it over and over until I began to wonder whether the silly bugger thought I had forged it or something. He mumbled platform three, or some number and I took off like a rocket and reached the platform in one mighty bound.

To my absolute amazement, there was nobody there. Not a soul. Absolutely deserted from end to end. I thought to myself I must be going mad. I couldn't believe my eyes. I stopped, turned back to the stairs again, and back to the platform again. I walked along, quicker and quicker until I was damned near running, sweating with panic and rage that the train must have gone already.

Then I saw her, just like a shot from one of those films. Standing inside the waiting room door, looking out at me. She seemed not in the least bit surprised, as if she had been expecting me. When I said I was surprised to see her and where was everybody, she said where did I expect everybody to be? The train didn't go for another forty minutes. Again, I was amazed. Forty minutes. I said, didn't Fiddich stay? She said no, he had just taken her to the station and then dropped her. I remember being surprised, although there really was no earthly reason why he should stay. It was James who should have come and seen her off himself.

So I had forty minutes to make my point, less if the train happened to be early. But now that I was there and she was there, I hadn't a clue how to start. I said we ought to have a word together. She said why? Meaning, of course, what have you to tell me that is new? I said because there were some things we ought to discuss together. I had not had time to prepare what I was going to say. Perhaps that was a good thing, but what I had to do, in short, was to convince a woman, I had to entice her to leave one man and come and live with me.

That's the long and short of it. The tide had started to flow in my direction. Pretty sluggishly, true, but I thought that all I had to do was to begin to paddle like hell and it would start to flow a bit stronger. Of course, I quite realise now what a task I was setting myself. I was trying to convince Olivia of something I had never got near convincing her of in the past, that I was a better man for her than James. I had a history of second bests, going right back to the time when we were children. My track record was all against me. But this was definitely my last chance. I was well aware of that. She was bound to be in a state of mental and emotional flux and upset. If ever there was a time, this was it.

She said, "all right, let's walk up and down the platform." Anything to pass the time, she meant. I remember asking her about her suitcase. It was inside the waiting room door. She said that if anyone wanted to pinch it, they could, they were welcome to it. So we started to walk up and down this platform. It was drizzling with rain, I'm sure. I have a memory of it raining, as it nearly always did the whole of that damned miserable summer. Olivia had one of those transparent macs. I had nothing. Not even a cap, though I was still in uniform. Luckily nobody saw me.

I can recommend it, as an emotional test, and as an intellectual exercise of the most difficult kind, to try and convince a woman of what I was trying to convince Olivia, in forty minutes or less, while walking up and down a station platform in the rain. Of course, if things are really going for you, one minute will do, and it won't matter where it is. I tried. I really tried. By God I tried. I am not a stupid or insensitive man. I know how to appeal to people. I know what to put in and what to leave out. The one advantage I had, I thought, was that James was going to leave the Service. I sensed, I knew, that Olivia was the kind of woman who in some strange way needed her husband to be in the Navy or in some recognised profession, or some easily definable way of life. It gave her married life a shape, a framework, if you like. Whatever she might have said about it herself, I think she needed the reassurance of that. My point was that I could offer her that framework, I could keep that same pattern going, but with all the things that James was not, all the things that she had said she didn't want any more. It would be a really new start, a new go at things. Yet it wouldn't be like starting off again with somebody totally new.

I suppose it was always a hopeless task. It was never really on. I was trying to convince a woman who had known me nearly all my life and yet she was somebody who knew almost nothing about me. There was nothing new I could tell her and yet there was everything I could tell her. Perhaps I made a mistake in making a sort of emotional confrontation out of that platform scene. Perhaps I should have played it cooler.

After all, life goes on a long time and there might be other occasions. That day on the platform need not have been the final end. I suppose I could have lain low for a bit and then tried again. It just seemed so final at the time. Anybody looking at us must have stared at Olivia looking so cool and polished and svelte, if that's the word, and a rather breathless, red-faced, stroppy-looking naval officer without a cap, pacing up and down beside her, obviously trying to convince her of something.

As the time for the train came nearer so more people began to gather on the platform and it was more awkward to walk up and down without having to dodge, she on one side of a barrow of luggage or people, me on the other. Always there was this terrifying train approaching. The clock never seemed to move when I looked at it but every time I looked back it seemed to have jumped a whole five minutes. Talk about time's winged chariot hurrying near. This was the four-fifteen or whatever it was to Bournemouth and Southampton. The trouble was there was no peace, no privacy. There were people everywhere. I never had a proper chance. I couldn't get my thoughts properly together. I couldn't get my case forward. Given a better chance, more conducive circumstances, I am convinced I could do better.

The trouble was I had nothing to argue with except my own convictions, my own longings, and for those I needed someone with the same longing and convictions themselves. As far as that was concerned, Olivia might have been on another planet. There was no new reason why she should go with me. It was different ten years before. That would have been the time to chance my arm. Only I never did. I told her, it is embarrassing to recall it now, and it was not easy then, I told her how I felt about her and said I thought I had always thought about her ever since the first time I ever clapped eyes on her. She said she knew that, although she said she "thought I had changed recently." I said in what way? She said that night at Mickey and Dawn's had "rather shocked" her.

I must say I thought that rather a low blow below the belt. I thought she had enjoyed herself, in fact I didn't just think I knew damned well she had enjoyed herself and for her to talk about being shocked was pure malarkey. However, I didn't press the point. I said I was very sorry if I had shocked or embarrassed her. I said I was just as sorry as she was that our only experience together had been in a sort of parlour game. I said I agreed that it cheapened the whole thing. But for someone like me, I said, there was not a great deal of alternative. Beggars couldn't be seducers, I said. She said, "don't talk in epigrams, you must have talked yourself out of several good marriages by saying something too witty at the critical time," she said "it would be like being married to a poor man's Oscar Wilde." I said even that would be better than being bored stiff. She said, "no," she said, "I must say you're not a bore. But it's no good," she said, "it's no good you pressing me, with those big eyes like a hungry dog," she said. "You're not going to get anywhere. I'm very sorry," she said, "I can't tell you why, it's just reasons, heart reasons. It is just not you. I can't tell you any more than that," she said.

I said, but you did give me some reason to be hopeful. "Oh yes," she said, "that was when I was all mixed up and not sure of myself." I said, does that mean you're sure of yourself now? She said "certainly not," but it had nothing to do with me. "It's nothing to do with you Freddie," she said. "That I do know," she said. "You're not in it," she said.

There was always a callous, brutal streak in Olivia. Sometimes she could have a cutting edge to her, like a jagged dagger. Just like James, in fact. Talking and thinking of James, I said to her, are you going back to him? She said, "I don't know," she said, "I must think about it."

It struck me then that James must have been pretty sure of himself and pretty sure of how Olivia would react. Whatever his own feelings about her, he was not particularly bothered if I saw her and spoke to her. He knew I would get precious little joy from her. It takes a diamond to cut another diamond.

The train was absolutely on time, I remember. Early, if anything. It would be, of course. I picked up her suitcase, found her a seat, put the case up on the rack, kissed her goodbye and walked off the platform and out of the station and drove away. I have never seen her since, from that day to this.

Freddie's voice broke off so gruffly, bringing his narrative to so abrupt an end, that the listeners felt an almost physical sense of shock. They could see that Freddie had quite clearly underestimated the force of the feelings he had repressed for so long. His tormented face showed his pain and bewilderment that such old and carefully tended scar tissue should still have such power to hurt if it were roughly handled.

To crown it all, he said, I later found a stupid little chit on my windscreen for parking in the wrong place.

The engine notes changed once again, and the aircraft frame jolted slightly several times, as though bumping down a shallow flight of steps. Once more, the attitude and atmosphere of the aircraft took on the expectancy of landing. The starboard wing dipped suddenly and through clearing cloud they saw the olive green and straight white patterns of Rome set in a tawny-yellow background of hazy hills. The sun flashed on the surface of the river and when they crossed it they could see it, brown and knotted like Freddie's description of that river Hickey had flown over. In the brilliant light they could see the traffic in the streets but from that height it had no appearance of speed. Small, knitted lines of vehicles moved along almost imperceptibly, split up, and joined again.

The stay in Rome was the shortest of any of the journey but it unexpectedly brought the biggest changes inside the aircraft. There was the greatest changeover of passengers. It seemed to Freddie and his listeners that they were almost the only survivors from Singapore. The strange silhouettes and altered profiles they could see in every seat made Freddie's party feel like the oldest members of a club. The dominant language on board changed from English to Italian. The crew also changed, a fresh crew taking over for the last lap home. These newcomers were unmistakably English. Their faces and voices brought England nearer. The captain, when he spoke over the loudspeaker after take-off, had an unmistakably cockney accent, endearing and refreshing after the mid-Atlantic, nationless twang English of his predecessor.

There were English newspapers on board, too. Their suddenly familiar appearance was all the more welcome contrasted with the papers the passengers still had from Singapore, which now, in their type-faces, column spacings, the very colour of the paper, looked doubly strange and oriental.

Now that English papers were available, Freddie perversely began to read the newspaper he had brought with him in Singapore, although he had not looked at it before. The others eventually noticed that he returned again and again to the same story, folding and refolding the sheets to the front page.

The others were sure that Freddie's story was over and, now that he no longer had the place of central narrator he had filled so long, they no longer looked in his direction and returned to talking amongst themselves. They were surprised to find him apparently ready to resume, as though there were still more to say.

I've been reading this thing about Mickey Gibb and *Pandora*, Freddie said, at last. I've been putting off reading it ever since we left Singapore. Jealous, I suppose. Although really why should I be jealous of Mickey Gibb? It's not often one of our warships gets the front page. But it is a good story. Thrilling, actually. Like something out of the *Boy's Own Paper* again, as I've said before. Tramp steamer aground on a reef in the South China Sea. Typhoon coming on, mountainous waves, fire on board, truly apocalyptic weather, it says. I like that. Truly apocalyptic. That sounds very much rougher than force ten or eleven on the Beaufort Scale. Here we go, the crew giving themselves up for lost, firing distress rockets without much hope. Skipper had his wife and his little daughter with him, to keep him company. Just as they are all preparing themselves for a watery grave, who should arrive but one of the Queen's ships, commanded by Commander M. R. J. Gibb, RN. Boys in blue to the rescue. Everybody saved, tearful thanks of survivors, plucked from death's yawning door. I don't want to sound cynical. I am just paraphrasing what the paper says. *Pandora* is properly in the news at last.

Freddie put his Singapore paper down and reached for one of the English papers. I wonder if it's in here, he said. It should be, by now. He ran his eye down the columns of the front page, turned over the other pages one by one, and then folded them back. Here we are. Five lines. Crew of Javanese ship picked up by HMS *Pandora*, it says, after typhoon in South China Sea. That's all. Three columns on the front page in Singapore, five lines on page seventeen in England. I think that shows a proper sense of perspective, don't you?

I suppose that Mickey Gibb was really the only one of *Pandora's* officers who came out of it at all well and who has thrived over the long term. I don't know about the Engineer Officer and the technical officers. I expect they have done all right. It's the executive officers that I have really had anything to do with. Nobody else seems to have done anything, not that I've come across, anyway. Actually, even Mickey Gibb has not been entirely the success story one might expect. He was late in his own first command. But actually, funnily enough, the only member of that ship's company I know who had a pure, uncomplicated real success which nobody could cavil at was Prichard. The javelin thrower. A year or two later I saw a signal which said he had won the Navy javelin throwing championship. It was the oddest thing. Reading that signal, and seeing Prichard's name, and the word javelin and all, it suddenly brought back that afternoon at the Sports very vividly.

But thinking about it, I suppose *Pandora's* was a very fair average. Take any commission in any ship and not everybody is going to do well out of it, by any manner of means. The success to failure ratio over the long term is very much the same. Everybody gets their deserts in the end, or rather, I should say, they carry on getting their deserts. I am quite sure that incident off the coast had nothing to do with it, in the end. It all seems a bit of an irrelevance now. I've been saying all along how important it was that you should hear James' story and how vital it was for anyone with prospects in the Service to read, mark, learn and inwardly digest what happened. I'm not so sure now. I don't think it matters a damn. I thought it was all so important when I began to tell it to you. Now I see that it isn't. I thought it would do me a power of good to get it all off my chest to strangers. The first time, by the way, I ever have told anybody. This is my last flight, that was my last exercise, last job, last everything. I'm going outside in six weeks' time. So I don't give a twopenny cuss what you think, of me or anybody else. But it has not been quite the release that I hoped for. I feel just as weighed down by it now as when I started. More so, if anything.

One thing, my own motives throughout the whole business are now a little clearer. I have achieved that, at least. I see now that it was Olivia I cared about, first, last and all the time. Nothing and nobody else. I can see myself more clearly now. I think I know now why I was passed over. It was the same reason that I didn't get Olivia. Just something mysterious, something vital, missing. It is not what I did wrong, it never is what you did wrong, it is what I didn't do right. Something lacking. It is nothing new. All that's new is that I know about it now.

Anyway, I have told you it as I saw it. I have not left out some things because they were discreditable to me, or showed me up in a bad or rather comical light. I've even been more cunning as a teller of a story than I ever thought I could be, by holding back some things now and then so that they could appear in the proper place to have the most effect. At the same time I must admit I had a somewhat selfish motive as well. I had the thought that the better I told the story, the more complete and full it was, the more good it would do me in telling it. But that hasn't happened. All I've done is set up a brand new set of tensions to add to the old. So much for the old psychiatrist's couch idea.

The really astounding thing was that James did carry out his promise, or threat, call it what you like, to leave the Service. It was a tragedy, but he did resign. Olivia thought about it all for a while and then she stayed with him. It's not so surprising really. As I said, she needed a husband like James. Where I went wrong was in thinking that James had to stay in the Navy for Olivia to stay with him. The last I heard was that they were running an old people's home in the Lake District. If it weren't so true it would be howlingly funny. But it's sheer fantasy, of course. I have not been to see it. The mind simply boggles at what it must be like. The idea of James running a hotel for Darbys and Joans, and Olivia as a sort of geriatric matron, it's unbelievable. Perhaps he runs it like a ship? Simply unbelievable. As I said, I have known James for years and years and years and nothing he ever did or said would ever have given me cause to think he would run off and do a thing like that. Possibly it is the same impulse that makes some naval officers become parsons at quite a mature age. He could have been an admiral. He should have been an admiral. There are any number of people who can run old people's homes. Not so many who are fitted to be admirals. It was a gross waste of the talent God gave him. Not that I could care less now whether the Navy gets its due or not, at this stage. It's no skin off my nose, what happens to them. Anyway, it's all over now. In six weeks' time I shall be a free man, with a gratuity and nothing much to keep me in one place or another. I may go up there for sheer devilment, and see how they are getting on. For old times' sake. They may clap me inside the place and never let me go. I'll finish up stoking the boilers and pruning roses and drooling over Olivia from afar.

And that finally, said Freddie, is that. He returned to his newspaper.

The others were left to ponder for a time upon what he had said. They could see at once many ironies and contradictions. They conceded that it had been a tragedy, as Freddie had claimed it was, but was not a tragedy in the way he intended.

His story had been worth telling and important, as he said at the beginning, but for reasons he thought not worth telling and unimportant. It has been an attempt at self-vindication in which Freddie believed that he was revealing something of himself in order to make his point. He had indeed revealed far more of himself than he ever suspected. He had created for them all a world of peculiar power which they knew would haunt their memories. They had been given a special access to the thoughts of an unusual mind and had had recreated for them, in a specially intimate way, events which they had heard before at second-hand and personalities they knew only slightly or by repute. He had given them an insight into his own motives. They recognised his story as much as an appeal for help, which none of them could answer. As if aware of their helplessness, Freddie said no more to them.

The last meal of the journey was served somewhere over the Alps. It was roast beef and Yorkshire pudding served, incredibly, in an Italian bolognese sauce. They ate it, looking down on a blindingly white layer of clouds, like the cottonwool clouds of nursery rhyme pictures.

Over the English Channel the quality of the light changed as they had hoped and expected it would. The sun vanished in a watery haze. Swirling mists moved across the windows. The sky contracted in an aqueous blue vapour. The aircraft began to slip and lurch downwards again. Until then the listeners had had one common destination in mind, but now that they were almost there, their thoughts travelled on to their next journeys from the airport, to London, to Portsmouth, to the Clyde. From one company they had reverted to single passengers. After so long on the way, the end came so suddenly it took them by surprise. They found themselves close above the interminable rows of London suburb roofs, in rain. They crossed a broad road, so close they could make out the colours and the manufacturers of the individual motor-cars.

When they were ready to go, his listeners hoped to say something to Freddie, to reassure him, perhaps oddly, to thank him. But he had forced himself first up to the doorway and was first through it when it opened. He walked up the long gangway to the main terminal, a lonely, enigmatic figure.

A NOTE TO THE READER

If you have enjoyed this novel enough to leave a review on **Amazon** and **Goodreads**, then we would be truly grateful.

Sapere Books

Sapere Books is an exciting new publisher of brilliant fiction and popular history.

To find out more about our latest releases and our monthly bargain books visit our website: **saperebooks.com**

Printed in Great Britain
by Amazon